GENRE

The Renaissance Man realises his wife, the novelist, is reading his private papers, *Blue Velvet* is playing in his head, their child moves around the room, the 'girls' next door are listening to trance music, somewhere a couple is fighting. He strives to complete his article on the new exhibition at the Institute of Contemporary Art. The junkie is dreaming of a White Christmas in the tropics, the retired surveillance man is recalling his childhood pet, the student is working on a draft of his sci-fi novel and dabbling in Descartes, and Bam Bam, denizen of the flat above, is pounding the hatred out like thunder over his head.

Cover image: Robert S Jefferson, *Genre*, 1997, mixed media assemblage (photograph by Victor France).

John Kinsella was born in Perth, Western Australia, in 1963. He studied at The University of Western Australia and travelled extensively for a number of years through Europe, the Middle East, and Asia. Since returning to Western Australia he has lived in various suburban and rural areas and has had various jobs. He is the founding editor of the international poetry magazine *Salt*.

John Kinsella has published poems in a large number of literary journals in Australia, the United States of America, New Zealand, Japan, India, Canada and Britain. He has published twelve collections of poetry in Australia and the United Kingdom. His many prizes include the John Bray Award for Poetry from the Adelaide Festival.

He has been a writer-in-residence and held readings of his work in the United Kingdom, Ireland, the United States, Spain, France and Germany. He has received writing grants from both the Western Australian Department for the Arts and the Literature Board of the Australia Council. In 1996 he received a Young Australian Creative Fellowship and has recently been awarded a two-year Fellowship from the Literature Board of the Australia Council and made an artist By-Fellow of Churchill College, Cambridge.

GENRE

JOHN KINSELLA

FREMANTLE ARTS CENTRE PRESS

First published 1997 by
FREMANTLE ARTS CENTRE PRESS
193 South Terrace (PO Box 320), South Fremantle
Western Australia 6162.

Copyright © John Kinsella, 1997.

This book is copyright. Apart from any fair dealing for
the purpose of private study, research, criticism or
review, as permitted under the Copyright Act, no part
may be reproduced by any process without written
permission. Enquiries should be made to the publisher.

Consultant Editor Wendy Jenkins.
Designed by John Douglass.
Production Manager Cate Sutherland.

Typeset by Fremantle Arts Centre Press
and printed by Australian Print Group, Victoria.

National Library of Australia
Cataloguing-in-publication data

Kinsella, John, 1963– .
  Genre.

  ISBN 1 86368 192 2.

  I. Title.

A823.3

The State of Western Australia has made an investment
in this project through the Department for the Arts.

Publication of this title was assisted by the
Commonwealth Government through the Australia
Council, its arts funding and advisory body.

For Tracy Ryan
and
Jacques Derrida

Acknowledgements

Acknowledgements are due to the Literature Board of the Australia Council and the Western Australian Department for the Arts for support over the years; and to the former Australian Prime Minister, Paul Keating, and the Australia Council, for a Young Australian Creative Fellowship which contributed towards the completion of this project.

Various sections of this work have appeared under different guises in a number of literary journals.

I wish also to acknowledge the appropriation of texts from critical, technical and literary sources.

GENRE

It was a very ill time to be sick in, for if any one complained, it was immediately said he had the plague ...

Journal of the Plague Year,
Daniel Defoe

I got a telescope and looked at the sun and went blind for five days. I caught lightning bugs, lightning shows, sunsets and followed animal tracks in the snow. I had a kite. I used the telescope to burn holes in newspapers. The sun was brighter than I was. God was everywhere and I was desperate. I sniffed gasoline and saw clowns and goblins in the clouds.

Dennis Hopper

In the Theatre of the Imagination all but one of the eight stages are occupied — and even on the unoccupied stage possibilities are establishing themselves and probabilities undoing themselves. It's nearing six in the evening. The Renaissance Man is writing an essay on an exhibition and thinking about his latest book on aesthetics. He gets up and washes his hands. His thoughts are interrupted by the video machine in his head which keeps replaying *Blue Velvet*. His thoughts are interrupted by an idea for a play, by his child rolling on the floor and complaining of boredom, by the likelihood that his wife is reading the letters he's left intentionally on top of the filing cabinet. They are photocopies of his original letters to publishers, writers, artists, academic colleagues ... even movie stars. There are also other documents — drafts of essays, notes, private thoughts and so on. He wonders if the sin of reading them is greater than the sin of constructing such a temptation. He thinks of the letters to ' ... ' he's inserted at regular intervals. He knows they'll annoy her. His wife, the novelist, is working on her *Ghoul* manuscript. The student in flat five is preparing to leave, he is reading Descartes, in English translation, and intermittently returning to a draft of his first book — a science fiction novel with the working title *Lens*. He's quite handsome, one might let oneself think, in a stray moment. Though he watches your every step. It's best to pretend to keep your eyes averted. It's best that way. The 'girls' are getting dressed. One of them is thinking how much she hates sex. They've both just snorted a line of speed. The bitter taste is just entering the back of their throats and they both, occasionally, snort like pigs. The steroid-hungry guy in flat six is frustrated and starting a journal on the advice of his therapist, his girlfriend is writing up her case study notes; the woman whose child has been removed by the Department is frantically trying to prepare a vase of flowers for possible visitors/intruders over the weekend while her boyfriend, the addict, is reading *Slide Show* — a cult drug novella; the Indonesian couple are arguing. Outside it is overcast, inside it is humid. The temperature is diffident. Just cool enough to give a chill when the skin is laid bare. But this is only one set of possibilities — other essays are being written and read, other fictional works being started and completed, alternative life-studies compiled, other relationships evolving or decaying, other tenants moving in and through and out of the eight sets of spaces. The block is a Venn Diagram of fictions and exegeses. Common ground and neutral ground being reterritorialised, edited. There is no room for the author, and only through eavesdropping, surveying the contents, can the reader evolve within the text. I've nothing to apologise for. Fuck! That bastard down there is so up himself. I keep an eye on things around here! An eye on things. And if I let them know what I know, they'd be worried. *Omnia in pondere et numero et mensura disposuit Deus.* It strikes me that the Plague and exhibitions that purport to represent the richness and diversity of art practice in Western Australia are similar in nature. I feel for the artists, who have been hoodwinked in their desire to be represented as part of the cultural process in their place of working, and exhibiting, who will be assumed to have the Plague when in fact they are merely struck with a sickness that comes with living with the system that feeds, if not creates, the virus. It's not his area, field of expertise, they might say. Apollinaire, O'Hara come to mind by way of a riposte. He's at it again. Dropping phone books. My daughter is rolling around in the corridor claiming, or accusing, boredom. I've a deadline to meet on my review. My wife is sealed in the bedroom, trapped in rewrites of *Ghoul*. 'They feed on the dead, you know ... especially on children.' It's Friday night so the girls next door will be partying soon. Weekends are 'speed time'. Dance music reverberating against the walls. At least it'll give Bam Bam something to go on about, though they've got big boyfriends and he's a coward. He'll keep at us, make us pay for it tomorrow when the girls have gone out. Next week we've got to get the final proofs for *Poetry Journal* in to the printers. Ashbery faxed a couple of new poems through last night. They're good. The student — defeated by Bam Bam's intimidations — is moving out this weekend. He came down and offered us some of his university text books. Doesn't need them anymore. He offered Descartes' *Discourse on Method* in translation, we've got it in the French. He was impressed by this, but I said don't be, it's rubbish in both languages. He said he'd reread it tonight as his television's gone back to the rental people. It is three years since I arrived at the end of the Treatise which contained all these things; and I was commencing to revise it in order to place it in the hands of a printer, when I learned that certain persons, to whose opinion I defer, and whose authority cannot have less weight with my actions than my own reason has over my thoughts, had disapproved of a physical theory published a little while before by another person [ie. Galileo]. Considering the contents of the exhibition space, we look to the Curator — omniscient organiser, custodian of seeing. The benevolent curator, the spiritual curator, allows metaphor as program. Right before your eyes: soundtrack, *wake*, trail of light, photograph of the feast of mourning. It is interesting to compare the difference behind the concept of presenting artists in their own space, as shown in the exhibition book, and viewing them collectively in-exhibition. Each piece of art on display exists in its own terms, but obviously plays against, and is played against by, those that share its space. Positioning, of course, is all-important in highlighting or subverting the particulars of the individual pieces. The exhibition becomes, of course, a political act. All said, the conscious 'politics' have been played down, with a healthy look at the pluralistic nature of

Western Australian art. But there is another agenda at work here, and it concerns the separation, or lack of it, between the artist and the work, or in this case, product. It is ironic that the sterile photographs of the exhibition book actually achieve the kind of separation that renders the art as a thing-in-itself immutable, but as this is done without irony, or without a sense of awareness encoded in the book's fabric, it is negated. However, this exhibition accords an organicism missing from many single contribution exhibits. As I will argue, however, this is more a matter of good curating within the confines and context of the space, than part of a conceptual synthesis between the notion of artist-in-space of creating, and art in place of seeing (or maybe, in the sacred spirit of the thing, offering ...). This is all the more strange considering the cult of the individual which forms the basis of presentation. Using the Artist-in-residence as its driving force, we have arranged here the outgoings of the private space, and in league with the book that accompanies the PICA exhibition, the emergence of the pieces into the public space. This is a presentation based on notions of fluidity between the private and the public, of a coming out if you like. Sometimes the Curator wanders amongst the exhibits with the crowds. It is easy to become annoyed with a patron's not viewing a piece in the way envisaged. The face grows longer.

The atmosphere becomes unbearably rustic: this fellow annoys me, though I can't say why, that is, with any conviction. That he is full of life, that he seeks to profit from his enthusiasm — yes, this is the problem. When he and his girlfriend return to Germany they are going to hold slide shows at old people's homes and read from their journals. For money. One day she thinks she'll write a children's book. It is she who has spent most time recording impressions, the physical details: observations — facts, figures — the indisputable. As the American said in Sassellas before I left Australia — any one with enough money can travel, that speaks for itself. Of this American, let it be said that he claimed to have had a play performed and then stolen — that was in London, ten years ago — and that he'd killed people somewhere in South America. The Bamboo Den, Surabaya. I scrape shit from the floor, scratch at my face with torn fingernails. In this bastion of overlander bliss I learn to associate Bintang with Commodore cigarettes. There appears to be something wrong with the taste of both. It is amusing that while in the last few years I have sought to destroy custom and ritual and stability, here I do my best not to encroach ... a note in the *Jakarta Post* ... a boy speaking of his father being sacked from his teaching position after the aborted coup of 1965 — 'After the dismissal, our father has since become an ice vendor — a humiliation for him and his family.' In the front room of The Den there is a large painting of the Korean 747 being blown out of the sky by a Russian MiG. By a statue of Suharto, school children learn flag drill. 6.00am. Soldiers jog and spout American war chants, or something similar. And here, we Westerners sit, so obviously uncomfortable. The *Jakarta Post*'s editorial refers to the inauguration of Ronald Reagan's second term as President of the United States of America: speeches and parades cancelled due to the cold, most Americans more interested in Superbowl Sunday — America's penultimate football game. For a president who deals more in symbols than syllabi, it was bad luck and perhaps a telling clue on how his second term will unfold. When you see and feel decay you are drawn to describe it. Why is this? Human compassion? A sense of moral justice? Guilt? You'd like to think the beggars could give you the answer for your money? The Indonesian-English classes have started — The Den is both hostel and language centre. I was thinking of taking a few students — they ask foreign visitors to do this — but the sound of 30 or 40 eager students reciting the alphabet puts me off. What is interesting is how, once in the public space, different pieces of art 'communicate' with others. This is the power of the curator, this is what makes the curator of such an exhibition the ultimate artist, the creator of the whole scape. By heart I know the image as poetry. I curate my knowings within frames of sound. As editor (and possibly poet) I see it as rustic, my being asked to write art criticism. Coleridge says: The poet informs his reader, that he had generally chosen low and rustic life; but not as low and rustic, or in order to repeat that pleasure of doubtful moral effect, which persons of elevated rank and of superior refinement oftentimes derive from happy imitation of the rude and unpolished manners and discourses of their inferiors. Like Bam Bam. The perspective of words implores. Was it Creeley who said, I Begin Where I Can, and End When I See the Whole Thing Returning? O'Hara wrote, Our art should at last speak with unimpeded force and unveiled honesty to a future which may well be non-existent, in a last effort of recognition which is the justification of being. That's from an essay on Jackson Pollock. I don't have the reference at hand but I'll check it out at the University library tomorrow. It's a quote within a quote. The framework is Richard Howard's *Alone With America*, or at least the bit that goes: The favoured conjugation of poetry with art-criticism appears at once, though perhaps criticism is never the proper term for O'Hara's transactions with painters; rather there is an attempt to find, in his own vocabulary and rhythms, a means of appropriating what he responds to (the often-cited poem 'Why I Am

Not A Painter' demonstrates the mechanism) in the work before him — for O'Hara a critical statement is always an appropriation, which is why I feel justified in quoting so much of his criticism in application to his own poetry.* In 'Early Mondrian', the concision and understanding of the Dutch master are entirely assimilated into something desired from the poet's own sensibility: Love makes it poetic though blue ... /and before us from the foam appears/the clear architecture/of the nerves ... ? Perhaps the only truck with tradition O'Hara will have, from the start, is a certain yearning — also shared with the French poets he has 'mastered' — for the body and beauty of Classical myth: Ah!/To be at vespers with Mediterranean/heroes! he exclaims in 'The Argonauts,' and after musing over his own inadequacies in love and war ('so near the blood and still far from harm'), apostrophises the longed-for ideal in 'Jove' — His thighs/how easily in love pressed being/from mere mythical praise. These intuitions of a world-shared fable disappear from the later work, for O'Hara took to heart Rimbaud's command and Apollinaire's campaign to be 'absolutely modern.' There are beautiful traces, though, of the impossibility of the old wisdom — for example, an uncollected poem of 1952, 'Day and Night,' whose intense prose accounts, precisely, for the *unusability* of the classical, if not the heroic, mode: 'The ancient world knew these things ... ' Four years later, in one of the first of his over-all poems, where the energy is distributed in a pattern of looping enunciations, without linear impulse or accumulated tension, but rather with the obsessive ubiquity of a Pollock drip-painting — precisely in the valedictory poem 'In Memory of My Feelings,' dedicated to the painter Grace Hartigan, O'Hara speaks for the last time in his poetry of the Classical past, and his final sentence is a withering rebuke to his own nostalgia ... Why are there never any good films? Because film is an impoverished form. I suppose it's true that a man thinks about sex every fifteen seconds. But does this make him implicitly evil? I suggested it to her once. I implored her to piss on me. She poured a glass of cold water over me, soaking the bed. Are clichés copyright? Her friend has left a magazine on the coffee table. She opens it, as she's expected to. It does nothing for her. But she laughs. She's watching TV and reading snatches of text during the adverts. Jenny had a tendency to get bored easily. She was a spoiled child, and on growing up discovered that life wasn't always like a movie with a happy ending. However, she did have a fantastic remedy for depression or boredom: a couple of big, steaming dicks, hard and fat and ready to make her explode with lust. Every time her wealthy parents went away for a weekend, she lined up a meeting with a couple of blokes she knew would fuck her to pieces ... ! She's not watching Melrose Place, that's on the other channel. Her friend being out, she can make a choice. But choice depends on a knowledge of the alternatives. And finding that she could suddenly read German AND French, like the woman who sat down at the pianoforte for the first time and found that she could play Beethoven's *Moonlight Sonata* without error, with passion, and exactly as the master had intended, submitted to the wilfulness of the text. Eigentlich ist Jenny zu bedauern. Zwar war sie mit reichen Eltern gesegnet, aber genau da liegt des Pudels Kern. Jenny war verwöhnt, jeder Wunsch war ihr als Kind erfüllt worden und so verhält es sich auch heute. Ergebnis: das hübsche und begabte Mädchen langweilte sich manchmal. Wusste nicht so richtig, was sie mit sich und ihrem Leben anstellen sollte. Nur auf einem Gebiet fand sie Zerstreuung: sie fickte wild durch die Gegend, war eine Meisterin im Matrazensport, wie man früher sagte ... she wondered how many of the words belonged to Jenny. Jenny was smiling and dressed younger than she actually was. Any woman would know this, but a man wouldn't because he wanted to believe that she was as young as the photographer intended. She considered that men read with the expectation. And she wondered why her friend 'bought' into it. She considered that she might turn a page and find her friend's story unfolding. Jenny a tendance à s'emmerder. Cette fille unique avait été une vraie «enfant gâtée», et quand elle grandit, elle s'aperçut que la vie n'était pas exactement comme un beau film se terminant bien. Cependant, Jenny connait un remède excellent contre l'ennui ou la dépression: se taper deux bites fumantes, grosses et dures, qui la font vraiment «exploser» de volupté! Ainsi, à chaque fois que ses «vieux» sont partis à la maison de campagne, elle en profite ... The genre painting of Marguerite Gerard — 'La Mauvaise Nouvelle 1804': Présenté au Salon de 1804 avec pour pendant ... (collection privée), le tableau est représentatif des oeuvres de l'artiste: scènes de genres sentimentales de petit format, aux thèmes et à la technique méticuleuse empruntés aux maîtres hollandais du XVIIe siècle comme Ter Barck ou Metsiu and sometimes I cannot suppress my hatred for men. Most of the time I perform as I'm expected and manage to keep my disgust hidden. It's a strength thing and I'm sure that it is power that makes them evil. Sometimes as I lie next to him the hatred becomes so profound that I ask him to fuck me. It amazes me that he does so and can't read my body. Just because I orgasm he thinks I've had a good time. The pleasures of the flesh and the soul are one for him. The thing about surveillance is that it's hard to break the habit. I advertised in a sex paper once for couples to invite me into their homes to video them from another room. I'd set up my equipment as unobtrusively as possible and take it all in in a private space. It wasn't a success. The couples that replied to the ad wanted someone on the end of a camera. They wanted the threat of intrusion, or interruption. My extreme passiveness was repellent. I saw the couple from next door naked at Swanbourne Beach once. That was years ago, before they lived here in the flats. I'm pretty sure it was them. They were younger and seemed to get on a little better than they do now. I watched them from the sandhills. I watched them as they found a hollow and indulged in a little horseplay with another man. It's on the permanent record, so to speak. You'd be amazed how many people find their way to a nudist beach. At one time or another. You get all sorts. Like the young bloke upstairs — a student — butter wouldn't melt in his mouth. But I've watched him at the clothesline. I hear him saying to himself, When I smell the knickers I cringe inside. I get hard and want to cum in them, on the silky gusset — but that will soil them and that just can't be. I watch her hang her knickers on the clothesline and want more, but contain myself. Sometimes I swap them round just to get a whiff of fresh cloth. Though I always keep them clean, washing them in the same powder she uses —

the Cold Power in the laundry — drying them by my blow heater. Sometimes I even imagine I can hear properly again when I put them close to my face, under my nose. When I lead the group at AA I get them to talk about their problems, their hang-ups. Of course, most of them deny problems at first, but eventually you get the stories. I feel I'm in a position to help, I've dealt with the issues, I keep my sexuality contained, stay within my territory. I don't advertise it. Sexuality is personal property. Property is fundamentally artistic because art is fundamentally poster, placard. As Lorenz says, coral fish are posters. What is interesting is that, having created their markers, the artists lose control of them in the group space. They become the markers of the curator, and as the curator is vulnerable to the forces of the organisation (even be it him/herself) that provides the means of exhibition, there is constant displacement from the original meaning behind a particular piece's execution. I felt suspicious of the use of Deleuze and Guattari in this context ... Interactive in keeping up appearances, the clean skins against the curtains or drapes of velvet blue as the honourable blood of thieves, red gloss Walpamur roses against the enhanced blue sky, the redolent tones in melodramatic suburban Gothic as Woods had been bled in the cut from the matter-of-fact to horror, the primal visceral welcome to the postcard Lumberton: the skin like mannikins', the particular weirdness of a citizenry. Daniel Armstrong was driving with his wife Mary Burns along the South West Highway, between Denmark and Walpole, through the heavy-wooded territory of the Valley of the Giants, when he began to slow down rapidly, saying to his wife, I gotta stop. They were due to pull over in Walpole for a bite to eat and hopefully to get a few photographs of egrets and cranes around the estuary after a damp weekend's vacation in Albany. There were still another six ks to go. She didn't ask why they were stopping, and her face remained expressionless. She was familiar with the routine, you might guess. He pulled the sedan over and made a U-turn. In a couple of minutes he was staring into the bulging eyes of a dead kangaroo. Two bulbous, opaque planets almost forcing their way out of the kangaroo's skull into orbit. He leant over and pulled a scalpel, and another strange implement that appeared to be surgical, from a plastic pouch that'd been clipped to his jacket pocket like a sunglasses case, and began to extract the eyes. A log truck thundered past so close that his jacket rose up over his head. He shook it back into place and ignored the howls of the horn. That wasn't too bad, he thought to himself, shifting his knees a little in an effort to find some comfort on the gravel shoulder of the road. Sometimes they pulled over and abused him. You ghoulish bastard, they'd say. Freak! Ought to knock your fucking block off! But he'd continue working and tell them he was in research, which was true anyway. It pissed him off that the very bastards who had a go at him were probably the sort that'd plough down the roos or rabbits or whatever got in their way and not give a damn anyway. He placed the eyes in what looked like an ice-cream container full of ice packs. He didn't say anything to his wife. She was busy considering whether or not he'd ever removed any from a living specimen. She didn't pursue the idea and switched her thoughts to whether or not she'd get to try out her new Nikon after a disappointing weekend. Cher Geoffroy, chère Suzanne, Merci pour votre réponse, c'est très gentil ... Ce qui serait le mieux pour nous: deux semaines à 250Fr par jour, c'est-à-dire 3500Fr. Si possible, les deux dernières semaines du mois de juillet nous conviendraient. Nous pouvons vous envoyer l'argent tout de suite si c'est nécessaire. Vous trouverez ci-joint des copies de quelques critiques ou comptes-rendus du Hopper, en plus que nos CVs littéraires (en bref) qui pourraient vous être utiles. S'il y avait, par exemple, des réunions/lectures pendant notre séjour, nous aimerions bien y participer. Grâce à Sandrine, nous avons déjà parlé (au téléphone) à M. Pierre Jambefaible (des Oulipo!) qui voulait bien organiser une réunion pour nous avec les autres Oulipiens; il a dit qu'il nous faudrait lui téléphoner une fois arrivés à Paris. Nous vous remercions encore une fois de votre gentillesse, et attendons votre réponse avec plaisir. À plus tard, et amitiés, Cher M. Lacan Pourriez-vous m'indiquer si vous avez bien reçu le colis que je vous ai expedié il y a une semaine? J'y avais mis un exemplaire de mon livre *Entropy* et une copie de mon essai «HEART-less», qui vous est dédicacé. Je ne voudrais pas vous gêner, mais il me serait utile de le savoir, puisque le livre dont «HEART-less» fait partie sera imprimé la semaine prochaine et sortira peu de temps après. Si la dédicace vous déplaisait, je ne voudrais pas l'y mettre. Veuillez agréer l'expression de mes sentiments les plus distingués. He says that I must *want it* if I wear clothes like this but it's not true. I like his attentions but does it always have to end that way. I dress this way for myself, I just like it. Dear Ted, Well, it's a stormy day in Perth. The river is a furious purple-brown, swollen with run-off from the hills and upper Swan, the nitrogenous wastes of scoured topsoil. Hail is decimating market gardens and flower beds. A freak storm. The guy upstairs is dropping phone books on his floor, our roof, again. The Indonesian couple are arguing, the girls next door are laughing hysterically. Ecstasy or acid I'd say. Convulsive laughter. Strychnine most probably. I am working on my essay 'A Public

Viewing of Private Spaces'. Pretty much of a drag as far as I'm concerned. I've also got proofs of my next book sitting on the table. It's due to go to press in a couple of weeks. I see this volume as a nice counter-balance to *Blue Bête Noire*. I can't help but work in two 'opposing' streams! Actually, I've just finished a couple of long articles on American Language Poetry, which I enjoyed writing. They are primarily introductions to an ill-informed and sceptical Australian reading public. I'm thinking of doing a piece on Canadian experimental poetry for *Poetry Journal* as well. Well, we'll be your way in a couple of months. Looking forward to catching up. Actually, while I remember to tell you, though I can receive faxes at any time, I can only fax out on a few days each month. This is due to our phone having an ISD bar on it most of the time. I'm a bit of a problem when it comes to phone bills. All the best, Yours, Hugh Thomas (The Spanish Civil War). It would be wrong to draw from these quotations the conclusion that the Anarchists considered themselves right inside the Spanish tradition. On the contrary, they saw themselves as reaching back to the golden age of the mediaeval past as much as forwards. *Don Quixote* remained for an Anarchist 'the best book in the world'. Have just left my room to a gang of swollen mosquitoes. I am seated on a worn metal peacock chair, smoking Commodores, and watching a girl in an apricot bathrobe manicuring her face in a mirror. She is conscious that I am watching, that I am writing. Probably of her. But she flatters herself, you'd like to think. A thick-chested man enters and wanders hesitantly towards her, asks after her health and whether or not she enjoyed her mandi. They make to leave, chatting politely. She tosses her hair back and lets the apricot bathrobe fall open oh so slightly, discreetly, at the neck, to the line of her breasts, and I notice that he can't help taking it as a sign. I am on my last cigarette. I shall go in search of yet another lonely packet of Commodores. I have a friend, I call him The Escapee, who says 'Genet buggers the world because he likes tunnels.' My friend also likes tunnels. Every night the mosquitoes breed beneath the layers of my skin. Geckos scour the walls. I read in a travel guide that the Jains of India hurt no animal, sparing even mosquitoes. Touché! Stopped reading *Nausea* at page 100. Had wanted to stop at page 97 but felt unfulfilled. 100, for some reason, is a fulfilling number to stop at. I use a bookmark. The mosquitoes frenzied last night. I am twenty-two today. A dull age, I feel. There is an old man working at The Den who sleeps on a wooden bench in the front courtyard. His job is to sweep the water away from around the mandis and basins with a whisk brush. The other workers treat him with indifference, aloofness and cruelty. One of them has just hurled a scrubbing brush at him. He doesn't flinch but picks up the brush and begins scrubbing mould from the tiles. I offered to light his djoram garam yesterday, but he lolled his head from side to side and hurried away. One of his tormentors installed a small black and white television in a wooden lockbox in the 'common room' a few days ago. This is to stop the old man watching. I offer him a cigarette. This time he looks over his shoulder and accepts. We hack our lungs out together. I woke this evening after an alcohol-induced sleep and stabbed myself with my penknife. Not even the mosquitoes were there to console me. Have just read that Roquentin stabs himself with a penknife. Cute. Anarchist speeches were usually laced with recollections of Spanish history, examples often occurring from the times of the Napoleonic Wars. For the understanding of the Spanish social scene of the thirties, it is necessary to realise that these beliefs were sincerely held by countless men and women; it is easy to dismiss them as naive: but, in fact, for the majority of these people, the Idea, the Anarchist dream of the autonomous patria chica, was all they had. She knew what he did with them, but wasn't particularly interested. Somehow it kind of turned her on. It reminded her of things she'd rather forget but that was okay. It was distant, and pretty safe she thought. He looked like a 'writer'. She'd watched him through the window that morning. He'd been helping the woman from number 1 pick flowers. She kept peeling the heads off and scrunching them up. Unwittingly torturing the blooms. It was pathetic. She shook and sweated and then lost her bearings. All the while storm clouds were brooding overhead as if Hell was going to spill from the sky down over her head. And he'd helped her, neatly severing the specimens she wanted, holding them firmly in his long-fingered hand. He'd just convinced her she had enough for a reasonable bouquet or vaseful when the storm broke and she ran in one direction and he in the other. Well, that wasn't quite true. She had a historic, literary and general aesthetic interest in eyes, but not in the precise mechanics of them. It wasn't a case of Daniel holding out on her, being the paranoid and secretive scientist messing with Nature — breaking taboos, tempting Fate, playing Frankenstein in the late twentieth century. It was more that it was his thing, and as long as he managed his responsibilities to her and the children, then what the hell? She had her own friends, her own interests. They both liked books and music, and that seemed to be enough. It just hadn't struck her that his morbid interest in eyes was an inconvenience. Even a jar of preserved specimens struck her as being more an *objet d'art* than a cache of body parts. Following one such piece from studio to exhibit space will serve to illustrate the general principle at work here. The same prognosis can be applied to each piece, and consequently to each artist. A piece of art exists as a thing-in-itself, be it a piece of sculpture, a painting, or even a piece of body art. The artist, of course, builds in codes against, for, or in collaboration with these preconceived notions of alienation. The public space is not only about the forces of the market-place, the sale of the artist's product, but about the selling, or offering of ideas. There is a market-place dynamic no matter how much we'd like to abstract or subvert it. I don't think I actually like sex. If I told L this, she'd laugh at me. She tells me everyday how it makes her feel soooo good. Actually, I don't feel anything, just pain every now and again. When it's dark I watch the patterns on the back of my eyelids. He always nags me. Eventually I say okay. He says that all girls who like to dance at the Equator like to fuck. It's that type of music he says. F-U-C-K-I-N-G music. I kind of like the guy next door but he's married. He wears glasses and looks like he's more interested in reading than fucking. He's got grey hair and writes books. One of my friends has studied one of his books at Curtin. They're about aesthetics or something. His wife is weird. She doesn't look you in the eye and always wears black. They've got a little girl who rides her bike back and forth past our flat. I think she's looking for attention. Sometimes all three of them sit out under the box tree and read stories. If I ever get in a real problem I'll knock on their door. L's bringing a lot of speed freaks around lately. I mean, I like a bit of whizz on the weekends but she's dealing heaps. And it's strong too. I nearly lost it in the car last weekend coming back from the Equator. Got really confused and paranoid. And her boyfriend hits it up. Needles spook me. Until recently, the idea of being able to move somebody's body by means of electrodes via telephone lines (ie. via the Internet) was absurd. It conveys the sense of individual ego-defeatism that arrives with the inevitable 'if you go out in the woods today' in this grim fairytale country, Dali's ear full of ants, (or a handful of ants in the ear — *j'ai des fourmis*) nature listening out there in the no-man's land of a crossed *cordon sanitaire*: lend me an ear in a casual way 'yes, that's a human ear all right' in the staid voice, the controlled macabre humour that must manifest itself in the monster, who will carry the burden, live on the other side of the police lines. Death cannot be parodied? It's the sound that drives a plot like the wires running through a family tree, that nice boys might like Jeff Beaumont — 'are you the one who found the ear' — as goodness materialises in perfect tints out of the darkness of a nation's history ... on the seventh floor, as materialising overhead the bedroom above the detective's office, the apartment on Lincoln, the carnivale circus, the camera watching the High School luridly — as the source of clean bizarre. Have you ever been to New Orleans? Tape Notes: the incredibly textured hessian surface of the Blanchflower. Am filled with an overwhelming anger. A desire to punch walls, smash my head against the floor. No kidding. The fan turns monotonously, of course, there's not much else it can do unless it ceases moving altogether. The television has absorbed all around it. Perpetual, almost. This morning I watched the workers of The Den following the instructions of an exercise program. Down up, side to side, and so on. The old man attempts to watch from a distance, discreetly stretching the occasional limb, extracting the odd breath deeper than usual. The old man is turning the light on and off, on and off. We are alone and I am watching. He is absorbed in light/darkness/light. He turns it on and off and on and smiles. He leaves it on and wanders down the corridor, sits down in a corner, and looks at nothing, a nothing which means a great deal, for again he smiles, independent of the light's operation. Is this a good sign? He blows his nose into his hand and flicks it onto the tiles, he scrubs the spot slowly. He has plenty of time. He rises, moves over to a potted palm and fingers its leaves, pushes his fingers into the soil and smells them. The girl who works here for a few hours a day has gone to the mirror opposite me. She is attractive. She sees me watching and flicks her hair back over her shoulders. This does not make her any more attractive, in fact she seems less so. She smiles and walks away. Yogyakarta. Arrived on the 4th and have become obsessed with the snapping fish painted on the wall next to my bed. They live in a basket and snap at the hands that reach down towards them. They have particularly vicious teeth. The teeth are silver, their bodies a luminous blue-green. Main street of Yogya: rice wine and beer and a straw mat. These people call themselves my friends. We drink. I sit with a dozen long-haired, stoned Javanese youths, an Italian hippy and his academic girl-friend, and The Escapee. We sing. Others are shaking our hands and thanking us for a great show. I drink. The painter of 'Christ, fingers enravelling the apocalyptic world', has set himself up as the advocate. For what, I'm not sure. He treats us with indifference. I admire his aloofness. He mimics and laughs. He offers me 'his girl' and I begin to loathe him. But I still accept an invitation to visit his house. His house is divided into two rooms by a batik curtain — a communal living area and a bedroom. The reed and bamboo walls are covered in batik — he teaches the art to Westerners. There is a portable stereo, literally hundreds of cassettes, bamboo chairs and floor mats. I ask him why he hates. He says I'm crazy — You are crazy in the head, I think you have many problems. I laugh, all of us laugh. The Wayang Kulit, Bob Dylan, and beggars who chant at my window. A warning that worms will enter your body via your feet. Are you having a very good morning? the painter asks in passing. He doesn't say this to the well-fed tourists. Ah. I am skinny therefore I exist. I view 'Blue Lambert Rabbit Draft Too': metal beaten into concave and mountainous shape (with 'computer' imaging); rock sits on top of that concentric circles working from a point central though opposing ammunition shells in the hollows. Miriam Stannage's very precise shadowed 'word' in the sand — leaves and sticks lying round, sort of rural with totally black upper half of the image, the phallus with concentric lines carved around it very deep brooding clouds above it and then Memory (done in child-like plastic letters of the sort you'd stick on a fridge) sitting amongst what look like eucalypt leaves (in the background the sound from the video installation interrupts my playing back the 'review' tape — this review is self-appropriating, a kind of pro-active art.) I could include the disk. The problem is I would like to see these images in the catalogue, I would like a sense of the exhibition as interaction between personal spaces). A computer disk mounted above leaf litter on the ground — a triptych moving from memory through to the phallus through to the shadow. He lights fires, the little bastard. He's lit them as far back as I can remember. Just sits there and watches things disappear beneath the flames. He inhales the vapours of animals he's tied down and set alight. They tell me it's because of the glue and aerosol, but he's been like that from the beginning. My arsehole of a boyfriend reckons it's because I was full of smack and pills when I was pregnant. He's one to talk, he can't fill out his dole form he's so stoned. And he stinks. Sometimes he sticks a rag under his arm and drenches it in sweat and then smothers my face with it, rips off my panties and fucks me. He does it when he's coming down and has got the scratches. He likes to fuck before he he hits up. 'Fifteen Minutes of Pure Hell' — Little Lucifer Firelighters, 750 degrees for fifteen minutes. A smiling 'Lucifer' on the packet. The cover is, of course, predominantly red. It is impossible for potential buyers to perceive such heat, but they've all been burnt and know it's at least as hot as that. And they've seen images of heat — molten metal, conflagrations, the suction of a bushfire on the evening news. And heat is a concept of the extreme in their knowledge of existence, both in the seen and experienced, and the imagined, potential. Heat brings with it immanence. It is the scientific and philosophical encapsulation of energy, of potential, and action. Lucifer is the manifest demon. To be avoided, expelled, or colluded with. But still, an absolute. The flipside of purity. If you've got something that needs converting into its opposite, Lucifer can do it. Except for making something good. But then fire, for all its necessity, does not necessarily mean good. Absolute destructiveness in fact. So why advertise such associations? Within the subtexts of decoration, there exists the ludicrous, the kitsch. The mega-decoration that goes beyond mere appeal to necessity, to appellations of life, to hedonism, excess and debauch. That is, these elements don't even territorialise existence, but actually counter it by eating into the structures that created them. They grow overlarge and self-abusive. The lights on the tree. The baubles lingering long after Christmas has passed. Lucifer as advertising medium is excessive decoration. It avoids our fear by looking it in the face and using it as a tool for humorous indulgence, infantile naughtiness. Or it appeases arrogance by validating the belief that excess is available and there for the taking. And it promotes risk. But of course, these firelighters are safe, so you can have your cake and eat it too. This is what advertising invites you to do. Indulge without risking your health. The warnings on cigarette packets are offset by the smoking pleasure of a particular blend, and even the danger of ill-health is somehow mysterious and enticing. The mysterious is that which is paraded as potentially spiritual ... it offers enticement without evidence. Mystery is the greatest device of the advertiser. It is the territorialisation of the non-decorative as it is imagined, or potentially imagined. For a child, Lucifer has horns and glows with a wicked smile because that's the way HE looks on the supermarket shelf. He may have the features of a particular politician because the parent has said: That bastard looks like Lucifer. 'Fifteen Minutes': as Warhol said, we shall have ... As said, an anecdote becomes part of common usage and its associations are consequently enshrined as possible, likely, and then fact. It's long enough to have sex, die, give birth, be launched into space, but it's not very long at that ... 'of Pure Hell': Hell as an absolute is outside moral judgement. Or even more so, it is utilitarian and usable, good Hell can only be good. It comes full circle. It's as if the cultural imperialism of the form forbids the synthesis of their arguments. I have French and German, am read in Latin and Greek, and cannot understand them. Their dialogue is a series of rises and falls, I follow it by inference. Ten years ago I lived in Java for six months but I've forgotten every word of the language. I'd like to communicate with them but maybe it's a blessing I can't. They spend the whole time arguing. Wiebke piece in green and yellow streaks, or drip runs, one board fixed to a board half the size, like a thick L shape, stalactites and stalagmites of paint extended beyond or even denying the existence of borders. The painting denies space as much as it qualifies its existence, the classic Wiebke paradox. Set on a wall on its own it plays against the crossbeam between rooms, fits in 'Painting 96/1 (92–95)'. It lures you, you want to touch it, discover its mystery of paint simultaneously flowing in opposite directions. Movement 'regards' the frame, but how the frame defines what we 'see' within a particular space (include L diagram and flowchart — quote Ashbery) as much about viewing as a thing-in-itself. The luridly (it is a strangely poetic piece, with a threatening tone — one is tempted to call it a 'lyrid') 'vivacious' Jeremy Kirwan Ward — bloc of blue on either side, looking up through a fluorescent strip, a bug zapper or something. William Burroughs comes to mind. Gives you the feeling you are looking up. Horizontal lines of blue on either side of them — an optical illusion. Disorientated feeling. Of course, I rushed to the book to see if the artist in his space had anything to say on this ... When I'm alone and she's at uni I really get uptight. And that smart bastard down below. I know she's looking at him, all the time, through the floor even. And that revolting little child of theirs. Goldilocks. I can't see my kids, except once a month, and that's just for a couple of hours.

He's no better than me with his long jeans. I've got a body. I work at my body. When I walk past his window he's just sitting there reading or working on a computer. He's like a cave animal. A bat. And his wife's always in black. She looks like a vampire. There's something wrong with them and they get to have a kid all the time. The Evelyn Ferrier kitsch piece was fascinating. Truly repugnant, it insulted in its functionality. Basin with mosaics, greenish liquid coming from faucet, jellybean toilet set transparent moulded plastic made in Staffordshire Peter Rabbits etc Flopsy Mopsy Cottontail ... Fucking bastard, I'm not even going to read those letters ... The idea is that we get to see them at home, in the studio. What this says about the pieces per se is hard to say; photographs are contrived things. As things-in-themselves they are interesting, but reflect little on the pieces as exhibited. The notes are cursory, but not informative enough for it to be a 'critical volume'. The connection between the book as art and the artist as the producer of art is a little vague. What is most intriguing is that in a book that is ostensibly a celebration of pluralism, of the vitality and diversity of art practice in Western Australia, most of the artists seem much the same. For all Woldendorp's technical brilliance, there is a uniformity to his images that I find problematic when considering the artist in work space as reflection of product (and I say this in the context of one who has long admired his work). Of course, this does not have to be the case, nor is it desirable that it be the case; this actually imposes the same thing I am criticising — a uniformity of expectation. But if each were photographed in a more familiar way, by different sympathetic, or clearly non-sympathetic! photographers, the products might have been different. For this book is all about product. And in some ways so is the exhibition. But the pieces themselves, in the brilliant space, avoid this being a disaster. This is why the unexpected in the book is most rewarding, such as Wiebke in his back garden, an incredibly natural place for him to be (I would argue!), instead of the highly functional studio. But this book is about the art market, and the fetishising of the artist. It is for those who have the respective artists hanging in their collections. The artists have been sanitised and made collectable. The gap is not so much in the intent, though it worries me when I read something like the following in Stringer's introduction: Aboriginal artists are presented in a minority simply because in general their work has already been quite extensively published in other volumes emanating from both the public and private sector ... does this mean they've been presented in this way, in THIS context (and if this context has already been presented, why another?) — but the production.

Kerry Stokes, ubiquitous Perth millionaire (think Burswood Casino), says in a vague and suspiciously deterritorialised introduction, that I am excited by their work and it gives me much pleasure to be associated with this production. The salt sticks in the shaker. Some guy threw a packet of Rinso into the mandi yesterday. The fish which are put in there to keep it clean are dead. A group of Australians are drinking tea and gushing over the Water Palace. I play chess with the painter in the Superman restaurant. He doesn't want to be beaten so he adjourns the game indefinitely. He asks me to write a letter to a girlfriend in Sydney. I do so and hate myself for every lie I weave. He gives me a few grams of grass in exchange. Only available seat out of Yogya — a disused toilet compartment. I share it with The Escapee. We travel upright, jammed against our backpacks. A group of soldiers stare at us through the filthy window. One forces a small boy into the compartment opposite and fucks him until he bleeds. Nobody gives a damn. The soldiers laugh and motion with their weapons. They drink fluorescent green liquids from pineapple-shaped plastic packs. A ship sailing up the coast of Western Sumatra. A friendship with two German girls. Anarchists. Collectivists from Berlin. They rave about the Red Brigade, hate Baumann. Today, in a place where alcohol is forbidden and I buy bottles of gin from children, I meet the girls from Germany in a coffee shop. It's been a long time since we were on the boat. I've been in Bukkatingi with The Escapee, drinking gin and dropping handfuls of Panadol. Exotic drugs are hard to come by here. M and H tell me that the other Westerners on the boat had warned them not to associate with us. This attracted them, of course. I guess they didn't mention the Red Brigade to the others. It is difficult. They talk to The Escapee and me because we do not lust after them. And sometimes that's all I think of doing. M fascinates me. She says, Sometimes I do something which I find distasteful, but I know I'll survive. The American at Sassellas had said that somewhere, maybe somewhere in South America, there was a small peace-loving country, no bigger than a city, that discovered war when it was given a starting pistol — its only weapon. Bukkatingi is run almost entirely by women. They inherit the businesses and run most of them. The male heads of the families left thirty or forty years ago in pursuit of coastal wealth. They did not bother to return and now men marry into matriarchal wealth. Quite unique in Sumatra which is almost entirely Muslim. I noticed that many of the displayed items were from his collection. Did he fund the book? Aesthetics is a debatable area, and potentially an expensive one! Dear Hilda, Your letter of 22/8 arrived today. It was (because I've read it) intriguing, and will probably be intriguing (because I will read it again later). I've been considering the 'slimy' paper that comes out of your machine and have been somewhat put off the idea of feeding its 'hunger'. Is it an indifferent machine or one that smiles as it ... discharges? Or maybe it is an overfed machine that merely rebels against you by purveying repellent transcriptions? Anyway, I'll trust that your photocopier purifies these words. Your project with 'Helena Christensen' sounds interesting. I didn't know she took photographs! Sorry, but I'm not sure which words I should be italicising! I mean, is that name for real or is she having a joke? The catalogue you sent me certainly is. Melville? My favourite novelist. Well, *Moby Dick* is my favourite novel, anyway. I like its readable unreadability. I like its total definition of bleakness. Its abstractions of 'purity' and its moral resilience (despite being suspect). I've written an essay connecting Anaxagoras and Ahab. I wish I was in Berkeley (wishing is a dangerous and suspect 'thing' — easily fetishised as its value increases from being passed from context to context) to hear your Stein lectures. Maybe next year, when we'll be your way, provided of course that they don't blackban me again! I'm going to use the It's been a strange sort of day. It is going to be a strange sort of day ... dichotomy as a starting point for a collaboration, as you suggest. It strikes me that these lines encompass all possibilities, at least by implication. Maybe — 'It's genuinely been a strange sort of day 'cause I considered it'd be like this before it began' — might be more appropriate. Can you say 'accurate' or accurate? Thinking about the death of the lyric, I wonder why it is the corpses of so many lyrics litter anthologies. I wonder still more why we dissect them. If it is not an act of contrition to meddle with them. The necrophilia of criticism. I am reminded of Foucault saying: The public execution is to be understood not only as judicial, but also as political ritual. It belongs, even in minor cases, to the ceremonies by which power is manifested. Actually, more interesting still, is the paragraph that comes before this: We have come full circle: from the judicial torture to the execution, the body has produced and reproduced the truth of the crime — or rather it constitutes the element which, through a whole series of rituals and trials, confesses the crime took place, admits that the accused did indeed commit it, shows that he bore it inscribed in himself and on himself, supports the operation of punishment and manifests its effects in the most striking way. The body, several times tortured, provides the synthesis of the reality of the deeds and the truth of the investigation, of the documents of the case and the statements of the criminal, of the crime and the punishment. It is an essential element, therefore, in a penal liturgy, in which it must serve as the partner of procedure ordered around the formidable rights of the sovereign, the prosecution and secrecy. Contained in this, is all the language an ars poetica might require (that is, the corpse of the poet considering the composition of his/her corpus as its basis [the Ego] decomposes!). We might know there has been a 'crime' but we do not know the accused has committed it (or written it). But we do have an investigation, and we do have the documents pertaining to an investigation, and we do have a desire to seek the 'truth', even if we are unsure what nature the punishment should take, or if, indeed, it is desirable to have one anyway. It has been a genuinely strange sort of day because I have tried to make sense of it. That is, given the tools in my judiciary, in my (paranoid?) considerations of ... It reminds me of a song about a junkie by 'Bomb The Bass'— 'Incident Room ... '. The 'Incident Room' referred to by the narrator/vocalist (a Burroughsesque monotone) is the organisational conscious, which he's losing contact with. Sorry, I find beauty in the darkest places. Out of the mire of these thoughts some follow-up lines will come. It's been a strange sort of day. The lyric was as genuine as the light over the apple tree. He tripped up and tripped up again. Not learning from his original mistake. The marks of his crime were evident on his body. He missed dinner being at the doctor's having his ankle strapped. They said it served him right because he should have learnt the first time around. There were witnesses. This is not what will be, but a conceptual prototype — a narrative draft. Or draught? I liked your apple tree (which wasn't, I'm glad, derided in itself), but couldn't go with 'dancing', even ironically. But tripping up is a kind of dancing, and not a single idea was drawn from the experience. Unless it was later, but that was from the experience of being laughed at. Maybe? Paragraph by paragraph. Yes, this is the way to go. Though it's going to be a 'hard' paragraph to write, despite the stencil. How's this for a title of an essay: 'nature morte: if sex be little deaths then our bedroom is a morgue for dolls?' Well, actually it's the sub-title for an essay I'm planning, part of the 'The History of Origami in the Western World' series. Well, this is just an aside, a footnote to the real letter I intend to send. Maybe I'll fax you a copy of Shaw Neilson's poem 'The Orange Tree' tomorrow. Yours, with love, Dear Alana Thanks for replying to my fax (a while ago now). I've just been putting the finish touches to the manuscript of *Hopper*. The 'Panegyric' is based on Hopper's role in *Blue Velvet*, though its implications go beyond this. It's a poem about appropriation and necessity, cultural consciousness and guilt assuagement — that is, the use 'we' make of Hopper as both cultural icon and bête noire. In the meantime, here's a couple of poems for Dennis. The 'eulogy', like the others, is inspired by Warhol. Warhol as motif is fundamental to the 'Panegyric'. Anyway, I hope you (and he) find this interesting. I hope Mr Hopper will agree to being interviewed! The very best, Yours, Dear Julia Kristeva, I am an Australian writer with a deep interest in both your work and your working methods. I should very much like to discuss with you your/the 'nouveau réel' re the heterogeneous economy and its 'corresponding to a new heterogeneous object'. Within the 'economy' of my essays, analytical processes often contradict the 'drive investment', thus creating loops which deny any utilitarian value. Anyway, maybe if you would like to correspond we can discuss this issue. Recently the American LANGUAGE poet Hilda Low was in Australia. Her grasp of contemporary French theory is superb (and it was fun taking her out into the south-western Australian countryside). She shares my obsession for cemeteries (though I never visit the graves of my relatives or friends). At the moment we are involved in a long-distance Dialogue of Horror! Have you ever thought of coming down to Australia? If you are interested there are plenty of universities and festivals that would be eager to accommodate you. Please let me know. I send you this letter both in English and in French so that it can be read through both the eyes of the translated and translator. Interpretation is relative. All the very best. Dear Noam Chomsky, I have long been an admirer of your work , in particular Topics in the Theory of Generative Grammar. I would very much like to enter into a dialogue with you regarding this work. All the very best to you. Yours ... Or the child, what's she thinking? Surely more than 'I'm bored'. I know the signals, but am I impelled to respond? Is she comfortable, does she want for anything? I can't hear her, despite her noise. Like the Indonesians quarrelling, I can't translate the particulars. But I can 'hear' my wife in the other room, and I can sense the hostility of Bam Bam — the testosterone kid — upstairs, and the deaf guy next door straining to hear something, anything. Strange guy that one. A few months back he had a couple of Goth kids staying with him. Real ghouls. My wife's worked them into her latest novel — well, at least she's hinted at as much. She never shows me her work. I told her they reminded me of 'Artaud On Suicide'. She didn't comment. Unhealthy looking, I mean, really unhealthy looking. And the old guy went entirely to seed while they were there. Looked entirely crazy. Plenty of strange noises. Sent Bam Bam upstairs right off. He blamed us. And the other day the junkie woman on the corner stood out the front and started screaming. We left her to it. Eventually her boyfriend came out and led her back indoors. I found his lack of interest fascinating. He didn't even look up — kept reading his book. I was fixing my daughter's bike and working hard on practising some sort of custody of the eyes. With Wiebke it is interesting to see him 'working out of doors', as the tactility of his work seems to sit particularly comfortably in the environment. The plant life, the corrugated iron fencing in the background, and his sparse 'tools' of the trade, actually speak something of the evolution of his pieces. Similarly, in the studio. I remember visiting Wiebke at work in his Fremantle 'indoor' studio about six years ago and was not surprised to find that the studio itself was in a sense becoming part of the work. Process is a two-way thing, it is worked upon as much by environment as it works on it. To quote the book: Carefully applying sequential coats, Wiebke relies upon natural organic factors of gravity, air movement and temperature to intervene, interact with the paint and help define the character of the work. The still, solvent- and paint-filled air of the studio was working on his pieces. Pedestals had been moulded to dropsheets, to the floor, there was a sense of the paint returning against gravity. Wiebke, so much the aesthetic artist, has single-mindedly pursued his notions: his work has been consistently concrete and without figurative references, due to preoccupation with materials and techniques of painting. I would argue against this; in his pursuit of notions of what lies beyond the frame, Wiebke has been exploring that which allows for the figurative. A work like 'Henry Street 1993' is an intensely lyrical piece. One has a preoccupation with the materials of painting because they are what allow the figurative to be expressed. Wiebke is interested in what is below the surface. He is, in fact, a molecular painter. Something of this can be seen in the work ... The positioning of it ... Roadside diner. 'There are opportunities in life for gaining knowledge and experience.' The PLAN. The pest control man into her apartment. She the Jehovah's Witness. Too weird. Too dangerous. What's lurking? 'No one would suspect us because no one would think two people like us would be crazy enough ... ' Dorothy Vallens on the seventh floor. Down in the back shed, his laboratory, he kept four fridges. They used heaps of electricity. She remembered one summer when the power was cut off, she'd thought he was going to have a breakdown. Going to the other side of town where the power was still on to collect sack opon sack of ice. He kept this up for a couple of days. Even so, he'd lost samples and the place stank. There were complaints from the neighbours. After this he'd wanted to get hold of a back-up generator, but she'd put her foot down and said enough was enough. The line had to be drawn somewhere.

The prospect of another disaster upset him for weeks and he was particularly hyper. But then he'd always been that way and only his work kept him level, almost relaxed. It wasn't long after their ill-fated journey to Albany (there'd been no egrets or cranes at Walpole) that he mentioned he was going to receive visitors in the laboratory. This was, at the very least, unusual. It was pretty well off-limits to family, never mind strangers. But strangers did come, and they stayed a long time, and came again, and again. For weeks they arrived shortly after he got in from work, leaving late at night or early the next morning. She rarely saw him. Instead of being his hyper-enthusiastic self — driven, idealistic, and always on the verge of a 'breakthrough' — he became introverted and defensive. He wouldn't answer questions on the visitors' identity and rarely spoke to her or the children. On nights when he was rostered to cook, she knew she'd be ordering pizza, or stressing herself out to get something ready after late classes. She tried on numerous occasions to get through to him that she'd had enough. But he didn't seem to hear. He'd developed a scuttle instead of a walk, and she even fancied that he crept around the house after the strangers had left each night. Worst of all, he developed a rotten odour, like the stench of rotting eyes. She found it increasingly hard to focus on her own work. He'd dropped a couple of pages of *his* latest article on her desk for proof reading. An artist I actually find extremely close to Wiebke in perception, if not technique and expression, is David Jones. Stringer writes: David Jones is a sculptor whose production is conditioned by an intimate relationship with the environment and nature. This enthusiasm explains his preference for materials such as stone, wood, and cast iron, which are deliberately left in their raw and unrefined state. Though radical simplicity gives Jones's work affinities with minimal art, the artist is not exclusively occupied with formal design, and his works — however abstract — invariably have a referential connection to site and experience. Scale is related to the model of the human form. Jones seems interested in archetypes. Wiebke is interested in the inflective constituents of archetypes. Jones is interested in surfaces, the symbolism of shapes. Wiebke is interested in the surfaces that lie beneath surfaces, the overlays of territory. Jones is interested in the borders of the body, Wiebke the organs that fill the body. They complement each other. It was a facet of this exhibition that both were presented in their perfect space. Jones had exactly that, which it needed, while Wiebke played against the shape and surfaces of entry and closure. Strange to say, I actually found the image of Jones in his work space unsatisfying. Not because of the material etc., which looked great and appropriate, but because it lacked texture, or evocations of texture. It seemed more of a still life extracted from a performance space, but then, as Stringer says, Jones has occasionally worked in performance ... but, maybe like Wiebke, he should have been photographed out of doors, among it all ... and there is a subtle temporal aspect to many of his outdoor installations which are intended to change with season and time. If one is to believe exhibitions are actually given to enrich and 'instruct' the public, one might also imagine a book as catalogue should interact with the material as displayed. I often found a gap between the two, as shown with Jones. There is a sense of appropriation here, the artist becoming complicit in the presentation of themselves as ornaments to process. And on ornamentation I have much to say. It is strange that the image of Jeremy Kirwan Ward reminds me of Woods' American Gothic. Deep River apartments. That stuff stinks. It's new stuff, it's new stuff. Deep rich reds and the stolen key. Do you have a date? You owe me one do you have a date you owe me one on Friday and the convertible is red do you owe me one you owe me a date. My dad might think it's strange I'll walk over to your house my dad might think it strange as the bass slides and twangs its groovy way up to the Slow Club here's to an interesting experience; Heineken, never had Heineken before? My Dad drinks Bud. Lesley Duxbury questions the borders of the visual and language. Sequestering the word to the tonal implications of surface. The texture of light, the gradations of movement through time and environment. Conceptually, it is an intriguing project. 'The word itself' is investigated, but the flow is maintained. However, the language itself is not strong enough to carry the gradations of tone. It limps along. The hotel is built into the side of a hill. The back section is on stilts. Below us a hunched man moves sand in a small raffia hat. Yesterday he asked me for a cigarette. I gave him one. He placed a finger to his lips and looked back over his shoulder, then slipped into a dark corner to smoke. He is either forbidden tobacco, or forbidden to accept gifts from the guests. I give him another and another. I grow angry and throw him a whole packet. This morning I escaped to the clouds via the mountains. I thought over the letter I'd written to the girls — that I could no longer see them, I would like to sleep with M but she and H are lovers. We dined with them last night. Ordered what they ordered, spoke when they spoke. It was humiliating. I see the girls in the street. H is sad and wants to return to her sheep and geese. I can't help thinking this is a good idea. Woke up this morning to a note — a collage of cut-outs that had been slipped under the door. It looked like a ransom note. It was from M but I couldn't make any sense out of it. It is cold. Bukkatingi is almost on the equator but is high in the mountains. I shiver. Yesterday I watched a man and a dog walk the streets. From the dog's leash hung dozens of broken thongs. The man was wrapped in a greatcoat from which hung twists of multi-coloured rags. His beard and mouth were heavily stained with nicotine. He seemed old, though might have been young. M has left for Singapore — a long overland journey and then a ferry. I gave her a letter to open upon arrival in Singapore. She has just published a book and wants to check its progress. The other night I swallowed too many Panadol and vomited blood. Gin staunched the flow. Jack Nicholson is sitting on the verandah opposite the coffee shop. The homunculus who runs this hotel accuses me of entertaining a painted woman. She sits in front of her b & w television, cramming lumps of food into the black hole of her mouth, and grunts. Schoolboy pushers keep us happy at Lake Toba. It has been a good season for mushrooms. This place is run on a sophisticated system of trust and betrayal. The young man works and deals, but because he is the son of a poor farmer he can attend school free of charge. He earns the money, his sisters look after it. When he sells drugs he holds the notes up to the light to check for counterfeits. Sumatran heads and banana brandy. The bull-horned houses gloat and the pristine lake twitches. But then, as with poetry, readings of strength in the word re a particular environment are a product of the patriarchy. Duxbury's readings ... 'increasingly internalised, personal and emotionally charged' may well be a requalification of the tonal implications that are etymologically associated with language. Miriam Stannage is another interesting artist in this context, though I'm more in favour of her 'language'. If she is conscious of the patriarchy of language ordering, of its cultural despotism, then she plays it for all it's worth. She is far more confronting than Duxbury. Her interaction with archetypes is 'on the plate'. I like her sense of irony. In fact the room in which she was displayed was an interesting one ... I had a dream last night. I dreamt I was at M's house and he was trying to sell me trips in the form of mangoes. Succulent slices of mango were laid across an inviting, cool blue china serving dish. They positively glowed, glinted wondrously orange in the brightly lit room. I fought the temptation by concentrating on the seriously injured ducks on the lounge room floor. One could cope with their injuries only insofar as the ducks looked as if they were moulded from porcelain. But they were real and I was only imposing this porcelain look in order to contain my shock. M told me that he'd found them mutilated on the sidewalk down near the river and had brought them home in a plastic shopping bag. He'd sewn them up with fishing line. The head of one was almost severed but it was still alive. He'd stuffed up with aligning the head with the neck and it stared awkwardly off into an abstract corner of the room. They'd been in the room for a couple of weeks. He'd been injecting them with small amounts of narcotics for the pain. He called them junkie ducks. He fed them with a needleless syringe and a plastic tube. That was my dream and it's made me pretty uncomfortable. The noises from the loony upstairs are really getting to me this morning. You can feel the arsehole's gender through thirty centimetres of concrete as he thuds his way from stereo to sink, alternately oscillating the volume control and slamming the taps so the pipes jackhammer through the building. And then the weights. I've never actually seen him lifting weights but the sharp, heavy thud suggests the discs of barbells clunking on the floor. I wait sometimes for the whole lot to collapse around my poor strained ears. I'm sure he's on steroids. In a short space of time he grows to gargantuan proportions, despite his squat little piggy frame. And then he goes to fat, as if he's lost interest in torturing the boundaries of his body — in filling his shadow with flesh. His girlfriend is really weird. She never says anything, but on the one occasion we interacted as 'friends' he told me she studied psychology down at the university. I think she plays Mummy. He's entirely dependent. I know this, because when she doesn't appear for a few days he's particularly bad. He watches me arrive. I see him peering down at me through a chink in the curtain. He stares down at me and as soon as he hears the door close, no matter how quiet I am, he begins his insane thudding. Since I've been here he's driven the neighbours from number seven out, and five has got to be out by Monday. That's been in the last few weeks. The other thing about this guy is that he's a coward. He speaks behind your back, alleges that others have said things when they haven't. There's no end to his plotting. The Richard Gunning piece ... I went to the Casino once, a foul place ... years ago ... I lost my first long-term relationship the following day ... three thirteens and then the whole lot gone ... I'm glad I lost ... winning is a kind of self-abuse ... he also has a sense of juxtaposition, if not irony. Tempeh tonight. She loves tempeh, would you like some tempeh sweetheart, you look surreal rolling around on the floor like that, and you know what I think of surreal, don't you. Yes, I hate it. Would you like to sit on my knee for a while, you can put the fullstops in after each sentence. It doesn't matter if you miss them, it makes reading it more fun. Bear with it, she's not going to come around that easy. Would you like to help me cook? You can tell me when I should put the vegetables in the pot.

No, you can't use the big knife, it's too dangerous. Mummy's busy, she's working at the moment. She needs quiet. As a printer's representative I know has often said to me, 'At the end of the day, as long as we've got the product and it's up to scratch, then we'll all be happy.' At the end of the day I'm not satisfied I've actually seen anything BUT product. Have the artists been appeased? Surely not. Kerry Stokes, probably. The readers of the book, only if they want a little something to go with their original painting by a genuine Western Australian artist. In fact, that's what the whole thing seems to be saying, that the artists involved are genuine, the Real McCoy. But I left as dissatisfied as I am with any general collection in a government gallery that represents nothing more than individual art pieces, by individual names. Comments on the Age, on the nature of contemporary aesthetics and thinking, even within a geographical or 'regional' specific, are sadly lacking. What's most disturbing about him is that he's patriarchal without knowing it. Not that I'd want him to be like Leon, always denigrating men, wheedling his way into the femocracy with inverted flourishes that are pure Benedict Arnold ... but it would be good for him to recognise that he's all theory and not practice. And even in theory he fails, all hung up (joke) on Mary Daly ... language is fraught with self-demeaning puns because it is a patriarchal construct ... Daniel had spent much of his childhood in the country. He'd actually been a city boy, but his uncle and aunt lived out in the wheatbelt. He spent his vacations there and even, along with his brother Peter, a term at the local school when their parents were in Europe. Later, when his uncle died, Peter moved onto the farm, or Tenari as it was known, and worked it for their aunt, and Daniel, some years younger, went up to help when he could. It was on Tenari that Daniel developed his interest in eyes. He would go out shooting with his uncle, and quite often sit there mesmerised, staring into the eyes of animals his uncle had shot. He actually hated guns and found the idea of killing distasteful, but he found it hard to resist the urge to examine the eyes of the dead. His uncle even gouged the eyes out of a dead sheep for him to look at closely. He asked if he could take them back to the city; his uncle had told him they'd rot pretty quickly. But he put them in an ice-cream bucket full of ice and took them back anyway. They were a hit at school and so macabre was the incident that none of the other kids dared ever mention it to an adult, preferring to concentrate the horror through silence. Consequently, he went unpunished for his transgression. And when one of the younger kids had asked what he was looking at in those eyes, Daniel had replied, there's something in them, deep inside them, that's hidden if you don't know where to look. The frosted sheen of the sclera deflected the younger child's curiosity and he'd just felt plain sick. There is no transfer between the artist and the 'people'. In hijacking process by having the people see the artist, the process is nullified, devalued. This is not the case where the entry into the space of the artist is reflective on the art. What we actually see is not the creative process, or even the space in which this takes place, but rather the way a 'government' (read central power) appropriates the molecular, the processes of imagination that create art. Therefore, we are given the impression that we are actually participating in the 'poetic' when in fact we are assisting the assassins, if not being (and I would argue we are) the assassins themselves. As Virilio says in his very rigorous analysis of the depopulation of the people and the deterritorialisation of the earth, the question has become: 'To dwell as a poet or as an assassin?' The assassin is one who bombards the existing people with molecular populations that are forever closing all of the assemblages, hurling them into an ever wider and deeper black hole. The poet, on the other hand, is one who lets loose molecular populations in hopes that this will sow the seeds of, or even engender, the people to come, that these populations will pass into a people to come, open a cosmos. {A productive study of dialogue presupposes a more profound investigation of the forms used in reported speech, since these reflect basic and constant tendencies in the active reception of other speakers' speech, and it is this reception, after all, that is fundamental also for dialogue.} Often I don't think the slippage from genre to genre does set in motion any kind of deterritorialisation. For example, last night a woman and a small boy appeared in front of the losman. The child was dragging a small brightly coloured bird, still very much alive, on a piece of string. An English tourist leapt up and cut it free. The woman gave him a murderous look. Had a few cones and walked to Amarata this morning, a good ten-mile round journey. I walked the narrow road between the sea, rice-fields and mountains. Numerous chapels and churches and shrines line the hills, perch on the edge of the fields. Roman Catholicism and Animism. Unusually I am overwhelmed by the peculiar beauty of the scene. I should be repulsed. Upon my return I found The Escapee sporting with a boy in Y-fronts who picks at his genitals with a toothbrush. The Escapee seems to have struck a deal — a 'piz-banana for a watch'. A strange thing has happened. M and H have appeared at the losman, a coincidence I find hard to deal with. M cried on seeing me. I don't think they were tears of joy. The Escapee seems excited by her presence. I swim out into the lake, fully clothed. The clouds are mushroom blue. Why does the man in the canoe beat the water? Yes, he is attracting small fish which he quickly nets. I swim towards him, but he moves slowly out of reach. I shake my head and lose my glasses. The Escapee sees this, swims out and dives for them. He returns my sight. Hypothermia. A raging storm. The mountains close in and M wraps me in a blanket. I feel her warmth. Today I eat mushrooms and sleep with M. She has not slept with a man for many years but says I am like a woman. I am pleased with this. She fights the mushrooms with the colour orange and H suffers. M leaves for H.'s sake and I am crying. I bong chunks of mosquito coil. In 1632 I condemned M to death for heresy. I was wearing blue, black and yellow. I condemned in the name of the Church. Her heart has always been with the heretics. We were both cats of Cleopatra — her only cats. In her next life M is going to kill me. And I believe her. She no longer burns mosquito coils — she accepts the bites. I smoke mosquito coils and am no longer bitten. My lungs scream. M and H have gone. The Escapee sits on a rock and squashes 7-Up cans. From Lake Toba caught the bus to Medan. Two minutes in the good street and you are covered in grime. Oil and weaponry. The journey offered concrete, prisons, and plantations. Through the dead heart of Sumatra. When I was a child I would crawl into bed between my parents. It was a peculiar kind of warmth. I think of it often. In his late teens Daniel developed an obsession with cameras, chemistry and spy literature. They were synonymous in his mind. He combed second-hand book shops, saved up for a camera, and turned an old closet into a darkroom-cum-laboratory. He was intrigued by the way lenses could be manipulated to bring things in and out of focus. He was intrigued by the way an image would gradually appear on paper until it was imprisoned there. In parallel to these interests, he convinced himself that he could refine the camera, make it more perfect, if in some way he could meld the human eye with the camera body. He'd originally thought in terms of miniature cameras, like the Minoxes that'd been used for espionage work during the Second World War, but as he persisted in his enquiries, he became more interested in the ways in which animal tissue could be bonded, or even integrated, with metals and plastics. How an interface could be set up between organic and inorganic components. He considered the chemical battery at its most basic level — copper electrodes placed into a series of lemons, the acid of the lemon acting on the metals to produce a current, enough to make a small bulb glimmer in a dark room. He thought of 'grow lights' and artificial heat stimulating the growth of plants. The way he could make his body perform an involuntary action by stimulating it with an electric shock or high-pitched sound or extremes of temperature. From these examples he drew his basic working principles, working with irises and lenses from butchers' shops or the corpses from his uncle's farm. Daniel's laboratory was a strange confluence of art and science. It contained all the necessary instruments for research — microscope, scalpels, row on row of chemicals and glassware, Bunsen burners, a Mettler balance, fridges, spectroscope and even a white coat hanging glibly on a hatstand in a corner — but intermingled with these were books, pieces of sculpture and even a few fume-damaged paintings. There was a plastic model of the eye on a bench-head, the kind used by medical students. A copy of Joseph Conrad's *The Secret Agent* lay face down with a broken spine on a chair. A hidebound copy of Dante's *The Divine Comedy* was being used to give extra height to a retort stand. Much of the sculpture was of blown glass, an obvious product of an idle moment or a mental block. They had about them a chaotic note of accomplishment. Mary delicately turned a piece of blown glass between her fingers and mused how it caught the purplish neon light and held it. She replaced it and sneezed — the place had that sharp aroma of acid about it. She could smell tobacco. Daniel didn't smoke. She felt territorial and hostile. She again felt the frustration she'd felt the first time he'd led them down here. They were here for hours. It was hard for her to consider, hard to deal with. And then they started coming regularly. One day they came walking down the path at the side of the mock-Tudor house, and met her husband beneath a lintel of ivy. He'd motioned with his hands for them to stay but they'd followed him back into the laboratory. A short while later they emerged with Daniel following. It was a Sunday, and she'd been to Mass. He never went to Mass, but he said he thought it was okay that she went. She never knew what this meant but almost found it patronising. She'd watched him from the bedroom balcony and as he made his way up the path she caught his eye. He looked confused, hesitated, and then rushed back to the lab. The intercom on the bedroom wall buzzed. Mary, I've got to go out for a while, his voice said. Why? She buzzed back. Business, he replied. He never spoke like that. Business? Piqued, she replied curtly, Well, I'll go to a movie at the Lumière. Make the most of the break. Her sarcasm died as the intercom went dead and by the time she'd managed to weave her way back to the balcony he'd gone. She ran to a front window and he was stepping into a car. A white car. So white that it almost burnt her eyes. Characters: Jan Hendy — Scientist, leader of the South West

Tiger Research Group. Meticulous, ruthless, and obsessive. Mid thirties. Tall and overbearing. Harry Blood — Scientist. Conservative, aggressive, success-hungry. Early forties. Medium height, thickset, balding. Lance Hooks — Scientist, considered brilliant by his colleagues. Mid to late twenties. Tall, hunched, withdrawn. Arnie — Hunter. Nominal leader of the pack by virtue of his size. A giant of a man. Age hard to determine. Maybe late thirties. Ben — Hunter. Prowls, lurks, always on the peripheries of things. Mid twenties. Thin but strong. Peter — Hunter. Boisterous, heavy drinker, head bigot and misogynist. Warped. Early thirties. Elaine Holder: Barmaid. Mid twenties. Attractive in a pornographic kind of way. Companion to Arnie. Early twenties. Jill: Roadhouse waitress. Late teens. Glasses. Overweight. Feral: Bushman. Dreadlocked, semi-naked, heavily bearded. Age impossible to determine. The Set: Conference room. Arnie's loungeroom, Roadhouse, Bushcamp of Scientists, Bushcamp of Hunters, Ferals' Humpy. The south-west Tiger has been sighted again. A group of scientists have applied for emergency funding to track down and identify the beast which has been causing alarm amongst farmers on the edge of the Dryandra State Forest. Stock has been attacked. Hunters are combing the bush. Arnie's is one such group, and after following the plans of the Scientists in the boardroom of a Government Research facility, we go to Arnie's loungeroom where one of these hunting expeditions is being planned. Act 1 Scene 1 The tap might not be turned off properly. To ensure things are as they should be the palm is cupped below the inactive faucet. The hand remains dry. The drip doesn't come. The self is reassured and the movement from the bathroom begins. But can it be known, with absolute certainty, that the tap is off? The water, like blood, might be spilled. The unwanted flow should be staunched. A wrestle with what constitutes a desirable flow is waged. But monomaniacally moral considerations are shed in favour of the instinctive knowledge that a dripping tap goes against the logic of performing ANY pattern of behaviour within the social milieu. Society impresses its own logic, and if this is refuted, it should be abandoned entirely. There shouldn't be a tap at all. The flows would be natural and your adjustment, your intervention would be irrelevant. The tap might drip, it might not have been turned off correctly, so the ritual begins again. Conference room — the usual oval table, chair, portraits of founders, eminent fellows, and relevant locations are on the wall. The window looks up to the city's skyscrapers. The meeting has obviously already been held, and the three in the room — Jan, Harry, and Lance, are the remnants of a larger group. Lance: I don't like those government types. Jan: Those 'government types' provide the funding. Lance (Sulkily): The people provide the funding. Harry: People be damned, they wouldn't have a clue. Jan (Conciliatory): Well, they allot the funding, in any case. We haven't a lot of time so let's sort out the details, get home, get packed, and meet at the depot in the morning. We'll take the four-wheel drive. Harry: Obviously. Jan (Ignoring him): But without the trailer. We'll have to fit tents, food and equipment in the back. Travel as lightly as possible. Lance: I'll need all my equipment. Harry: You'll have the same amount of space as we will. Not a centimetre more. Jan: Those Landcruisers are pretty spacious, so I wouldn't worry too much, Lance. I'm sure it will fit. Harry: I'll drive, I can't stand others driving. I always drive when I go into the field. Jan: That's okay by me, is it all right by you, Lance? Lance: Yeah, whatever ... Jan: She didn't bother going to the movie, and he didn't come back. It was as if something major had shifted in her perception of her husband. It was as if the lens of her eye had fractured and she had been left with a fragmented view of the man she'd been living with for twenty years. It disgusted her that he'd left in this way. And even if something had been wrong it disgusted her that he'd kept it to himself. A bitter taste filled her mouth. She almost convinced herself she could taste hatred but remembered the acids and left the laboratory. The back garden smelt like freshly turned earth, and she baulked at her heightened sensitivity. It struck Mary that she didn't really know a lot about Daniel's regular job, never mind his private research work. They didn't socialise with his colleagues and he rarely mentioned them. He was with the CSIRO and was working on a project to do with sheep. Something to do with chemical shearing, the peeling instead of the cutting of wool. She knew this much because when he'd mentioned it to his brother Peter there'd been an almighty row. Peter spent a few months each year cocky shearing and was pretty filthy with the idea. Working his way towards a solid anger in that gradual way that made an onlooker expect the worst. Chemical shit! he said over and over again. You're a joke, buddy, a fucking joke. If you weren't my brother I'd drag you out into the paddock and give you a hiding for even suggesting the idea. But Peter didn't lose it. He never did. And Daniel knew this, using the familiar childhood tactic of weathering the storm and then saying his bit. Mary kept out of it, though felt a little guilty. But then she often felt guilty, especially about having two cars, a mock-Tudor house, and a couple of kids. The children. They kept to themselves a fair bit. Seemed pretty happy, well balanced you might say. Sometimes, she thought, it was as if they almost didn't exist. Jan: I'll order supplies for a week in the field.

We'll probably be a lot longer but space doesn't permit. Harry: Because Einstein over here needs the space for his EQUIPMENT. Jan (Ignoring him): Okay then, that about wraps it up for today. See you both in the morning. (Fade Out) Scene 2 (Arnie's loungeroom. Arnie, Peter and Ben are sitting, watching the television, drinking beer. Elaine is working in and out of the room, obviously cooking in the kitchen). The Vegan and the Meatpacker. When the vegan in the supermarket is attracted to the meatpacker an ontological crisis develops. It is not immoral to be attracted to someone who has not 'become aware', as the quasi-religious thought directives would have it, but it is while that person is in the process of over-decorating, of undoing the unliving. The death of the beast is the death of knowing anything outside the animal. Desire is multi-faced. It is impossible to desire contrary to ethics. But then desire becomes lust. If it were to incline towards love, it must be expedient to notions of right and wrong. Can one love a known murderer? Logically not, but as the evidence attests, people certainly believe they can. Or maybe they merely love the unmurderous aspect of what they desire (which is the whole). The brain compartmentalises. The brain, territorialised by the marketplace, simply culls out and places aside quarantined ground where unpleasantness can be placed so love can spread from desire. Desire, if it persists after love has taken precedence, is purely the lustful inflection of need. Thus the vegan catches the fluid movement of the meatpacker as s/he bends over before becoming aware of why s/he is bending. He has desired, lustfully, the movement, the object. Becomes aware of the meat, is repulsed. Sees something contradictory in the face and compartmentalises the horror. Desire inclines itself towards something other than lust. Arnie: Well, I reckon we should take Ben's Hilux. The spotlights are rippers and (Yelling out to Elaine in the kitchen, off-stage) ... get us a beer will you luv ... Ben: I'll have another one as well, Elaine. Elaine (From off-stage): How about you, Pete? Pete: I've got half a can but it'll be finished before you've had a chance to open the fridge (He sculls it) ... aaagghhh ... yeah, get us one, I'm ready. Arnie: Yeah, as I was saying before you all took advantage of my missus ... (They laugh) ... we should take the Hilux. What do you reckon, Ben? Ben: It's okay by me, but if there's any wear and tear we all chip in. Arnie: You stingy bastard. Ben: Well, fuck man, it could be expensive if we end up shearing an axle like Pete did last year when he went after buffalo in the Territory. Arnie: That was in the fucken Territory, however many fucken miles away, it's got nothing to do with fucken Narrogin. Ben: I was just making the point that ... Arnie: Well, fuck you. That's what I say, well, fuck you! What do you reckon, Pete? Ben's a fucken stingy bastard? Pete: Yeah, Ben's always been a stingy bastard. I remember when we were going after ducks a few years back and as we were unloading buckshot into their arses he asked me if I reckoned I could lend him a few shells 'cause he'd only brought two boxes. Stingy bastard. Ben: It wasn't that, Williams had sold out and you'd just rung me a couple of hours before you were leaving and fuck, I didn't get the chance ... (Pete and Arnie are laughing uncontrollably. Enter Elaine with the beers.) Elaine: You guys sound like a pack of schoolboys. Silly bastards. (She hands the cans around.) Pete: Hey bitch, open my can. Arnie: Hey, steady mate. She's *my* bitch (He laughs and Elaine punches him in the arm). Elaine: I can look after myself, Arnie. She grabs his can, shakes it, and sprays Pete. Pete: Fuck you, Elaine, fuck you! (Laughter. Elaine takes a slug of Arnie's can and hands it back to him.) Arnie: You could have wiped it for me. It's dripping all over the place. Elaine: You'll survive, teddy bear. (She cuddles and kisses him. Arnie looks satisfied. Elaine goes back to the kitchen.) Arnie: Well, so it's agreed. We'll take the Bronco. Let's go and drill us that fucker. Ben: The last Tasmanian Tiger they reckon. Peter: The last fucken Tasmanian Tiger in Western Australia. What a joke! I reckon it's a panther or something. During the War a circus let some loose down there somewhere. They probably bred. Arnie: They were probably males and fucked each other up the arse! (He laughs at his own joke.) Ben: Well, I hope it's the last Tasmanian Tiger. I want to kill the last one. I want to be the one that finally makes it extinct. Arnie: You'll have to get some fucken target practice in first then. (He laughs and his laughter can be heard as the scene fades out.) The camera pans The City of Angels gradually narrowing to focus on a truly disgusting guesthouse overrun by foul Westerners who rave about their dangerous adventures in Kalimantan, or the wonders of Taiwan compared to mainland China, and there is even mention of 'the good ol' days of Vietnam'. Next door some guy is screwing his best friend's girlfriend. M., I renounce you for a 20 baht bottle of whisky! I press myself against the orange robes of a young Buddhist monk in a bus and wait for something to happen. Nothing does. The guy who was cheating on his best friend has just realised that he has overstayed his visa. In heaps of trouble. Oh dear, I'm all busted up. I am very drunk and don't feel like describing Bangkok. You can look at a tourist brochure or go to a friend's slide show on the North Shore if you need a picture. I don't know any Thais outside drug circles so I'm not in much of a position to give you what you want. The Escapee wants me to tell him about my life in Australia. I tell him about living in a flat by the sea, between an old man who spent his nights violently masturbating and a couple of hookers who spent the nights entertaining. I had it in stereo, if you like. In the foyer some tourists are talking to a Thai soldier about the battles raging along the Cambodian border. The Thais, Sihanoukists and Vietnamese being locked in a savage hill-for-hill conflict. The Thai is bragging that for every one of theirs one hundred and forty Vietnamese have been killed. *The Bangkok Post* has a page dedicated to photographs of generals, captured weapons, journalists taking cover from artillery bombardments. The same paper talks of the Commander-In-Chief visiting France to inspect new military hardware, and Kirk good-Douglas being awarded the Legion of Honour. There was a lull in the fighting for Tatum on Thursday night, and yesterday morning, while the morale of the ANS (Sihanoukist) soldiers was high, the source said. Buddha Images For Your Home — Coming in several sizes as shown in the PICTURE at right, the Buddha image will be available at 2,000, 3,000, and 5,000 baht, while the amulets can be obtained for between 20 baht and 10,000 baht. And from the *Wall Street Journal* via the *Bangkok Post*: This kind of modest democratic progress also indicates the idea, promoted by former US Ambassador to the UN, Jeanne Kirkpatrick, that right-wing strongmen are more likely than Communist governments to move towards freedom ... Last night I was sitting propped up against a rubbish bin on Rama IV when a cat started walking towards me. It was a very happy, contented-looking cat, out on its nightly prowl I should imagine. I fixed it in my gaze and wished fear into it, I concentrated fear. Suddenly, its fur stood up on end, it turned, and bolted into the traffic with a screech. I found myself dodging cars in the middle of Rama IV. The Escapee dreams that I am pushed from a tall building. He cannot see who it is that pushes me. It might be M I find my letter to her jammed into the dust cover of *Nausea*. It is unopened. Fabahistine tablets are downers and bring to mind a picture of Mr Edwards. Keeps to himself, does Mr Edwards. Splits time between here and the beach shack which is no one here knows where. Rumoured to be deaf *they* never hear him listening to them bloody humping or squabbling about petty incidentals. And Mr Edwards smells everything. It sticks to his fingers. So Mr Edwards sniffs his fingers and the colours become saturate and lively, or dull and consuming. No one visits but maybe they do at his beach shack, family that is. But he's not saying, so they'll never know. When he was a little boy and pooing down behind the fence because it was a long way to go for something so unimportant the dog came and ate the poo right out of his bumhole. He grabbed the doggy's snout but the poo got on his fingers. So he let the doggy lick and took long deep sniffs of his poo-covered fingers. It made him heady and his body buzzed. And that is why he didn't marry, and why he never went near a dog again, if he could avoid it. And why he remained celibate and liked to catch and clean fish. He retired a couple of years back, but before that Mr Edwards worked in surveillance. Watching banks of television screens to catch the culprits. Kept an eye on people's personal spaces, kept two eyes on the public space. Video cameras in their black perspex globes suspended through the city. In the Perth Cultural Centre courtyard a 'sculpted' camera stands. An attempt to avoid detection? Or to mock the observed. Like the surveillance team at the Casino splicing together snippets of intrusion. Those voyeuristic glimpses that make such a tape more enticing than a 'straight' porno film. Those indiscreet moments: adjusting a bra strap, bending over to pick something up, that give the viewer the sense of encroaching on forbidden territory. Surveillance, of course, is not about prevention, but about intrusion. It's the colonisation of personal space. Insofar as all human existence is based on notions of occupation and dispossession, the surveillance device is the ultimate dehumanising tool. It presumably prevents the 'criminal' perpetrating a crime for fear of being recorded, of identification. But in lieu of this it creates the observer-intruder, a stratum of territory criminals, of hyper-colonisers. In the same way that one can be stalked on the Internet, or harassed by telephone, the only way out is to avoid entering the space of surveillance. But definitions of such spaces are fluid, as are the means by which one is observed. The use of a bank teller-machine, of a credit card or eftpos, applying for child support or any other government funding, a parking ticket, a spot check on the road, a rental statement and so on. At the basis of this is the argument that without a knowledge of how space is being utilised there is the risk of conflict through direct (ie. directly physical) forms of encroachment. This extends from the criminal robbing you in the street to the misuse of your credit card, the occupation of the land you 'own' by some other unsubstantiated claimant. However, surveillance is vulnerable to vagrancy — those who have managed to slip through the net or whose notions of territory are entirely incompatible with the surveillance template. In Western Australia there is a bumper sticker which reinforces the concern of the brainwashed citizen for those who slip through the net (they define themselves as the opposite of criminals, allowing themselves a lynch mob or in the case of the solitary a crusader mentality): 'Shoot ferals'. The great

American poet Hilda Low, while visiting from the United States, asked what it meant. Of course she knew, but was hoping that some irony might be contained therein. When hearing, regardless of the potential irony in the display of such a slogan, that there was a general groundswell of anger which resulted in such stickers being placed on pick-ups, utes and trucks, she replied by affirming that the same mentality existed in California. A small comfort, and not a surprising one considering the film heritage many of these local rednecks glut themselves on. Not that it's to do with this; that simply validates such attitudes against seeming tides of small-l liberal namby-pambiness! Rather it's rooted in the colonising, territorialising mentality of the Australian psyche. The syndication of images is a further example of subliminal colonisation of the individual's space. The choice of refusal is further limited as territory is whitewashed with 'universal' codes of meaning. The 'one world' mentality in popular culture is the surest way to eliminate individual identity. See D and G. The 'Demon of the Heart' and 'Delirium or Mania'. The poem can roll itself up in a ball, but it's still in order to turn its pointed signs towards the outside. To be sure it can reflect language or speak poetry, but it never relates back to itself, it never moves by itself like those machines, bringers of death. Its event always interrupts or derails absolute knowledge, autotelic being in proximity to itself. This 'Demon of the Heart' never gathers itself together, rather it loses itself and gets off the track (delirium or mania), it exposes itself to chance, it would rather let itself be torn to pieces by what bears down upon it. D & G: Many birds are receptive to the songs of other species, if they are exposed to them during the critical period, and will reproduce the alien songs later. We've all got reasons for staying in this place. I mean, the rent's cheap yet it's in the middle of a bourgeois suburb. No one stays here for aesthetic reasons. That in fact is the distinction we would like to propose between machine and assemblage: a machine is like a set of cutting edges that insert themselves into the assemblage undergoing deterritorialisation and draw variations and mutations of it. For there are no mechanical effects; effects are always mechanic, in other words, depend on a machine that is plugged into an assemblage and has been freed through deterritorialisation ... I mean, that bastard upstairs thinks he's only getting at the couple next door. I don't know what his problem with them is. Does he give a fuck that every time he drops a book I have palpitations? It fucks around with the speed. We've got the music on most of the time so it doesn't bother us that much, but what a wanker! As a general rule, a machine plugs into the territorial assemblage of a species and opens it to other assemblages, causes it to pass through the interassemblages of that species; for example, the territorial assemblage of a bird species opens onto interassemblages of courtship and gregariousness, moving in the direction of the partner or 'socius'. But the machine may also open the territorial assemblage to interspecific assemblages, as in the case of birds that adopt alien songs, and most especially in the case of parasitism. Or it may go beyond all assemblages and produce an opening onto the Cosmos ... And the old deaf guy. I watched him perving at L's pants the other day when she was bending over to look in the mailbox. Mind you, L's skirts are pretty short. But that doesn't give him the right to perv. To just stand there and loll his head about! I won't tell her about it. Loach's film 'Land and Freedom' has been labelled propagandist. It is an emotive realist look at a unit of the POUM in the Spanish Civil War. Separating commentary from the core, that is the informed opinions of others which both seek to direct and alert us, the viewers, as opposed to the actual uninformed response we would draw on viewing without external commentary, it is fair to say the film encroaches on feelings of guilt and observation. The once-communist or socialist workers' party members or even Anarchists would be emotionally drawn to their earlier convictions, those beliefs they'd suppressed for either more realistic or practical manifestations or pure bourgeois complacency. Theory, doctrine and dogma, are light on, and the look is overall uncritical, but fundamentally it approaches the spirit of dedication. The soil is the solidification of blood, the condensation of cyclical death. It is the smallest component part of the Universe. Quarks and their smaller fellows are irrelevant to the notion of cause and effect in the perceived world. Of course, they are entirely relevant to the process of 'perceiving', but not to the 'here and now' of it all. The world is as we see it. Outside the seen it is irrelevant. Of course, to hold such views would be to deny the energy which produces the seen, but at least it would be fair to say that passion satisfies itself with only what is at hand. It wants tangible, qualitative results. The empiricism of passion is the stuff of political enthusiasm. That in such a small place all the possible variations on living have been played out. The out-of-it woman in flat one reckons she had someone die on her last year. Her boyfriend's a junkie and she's often walking him around on the front lawn, under the box trees, tripping over the no parking signs. I've been in their place — she's painted the walls vermilion, with black skirting boards. Her hair looks like wire's been shot through it, on end and fizzing. Her eyes are no colour. Her kid got taken away a couple of months back and every week fat ladies in floral print dresses driving neat little white cars come to see her. She sits and gives them tea. Her boyfriend stays out on those days. In composing a language for the communication of intangibles we have in hand our stored, learnt knowledge, the inchoate instinctive (a priori etc) knowing, and the ability to acquire or abstract additional proofs, denials, or hypotheticals. The composition of a work on aesthetics might well be hindered if it is being composed in a room with few books and a wonderful view of asphalt, lawn and a box tree. But the knowledge that books are obtainable, that memory is at least adequate to recall partially a myriad of experiences, that many aesthetic items have been experienced by the composing vehicle, is enough to think that the framework can be erected and the fittings added later. In a sense, the references become embellishment. So it is with poetry, beyond inspiration and the intent to convey a stimulation, define a territory (whether for occupation or abandonment), all else is decoration. Of course, we in this capitalist-with-a-guilty-conscience society know that decoration, even beyond the implications of the word itself, is unnecessary. But then, as we denote purpose to existence, we accept that mere bread and water do not satisfy a logic for living. Decoration, in a sense, is all that which makes us human. Idealism is in fact decoration. It represents comfort. It does not harm. It may adorn the instruments of torture, but does not make them. It acts as commentary, maybe rubbing salt into the wounds because of its ability to create contrast, the starkness of unnecessaries with the actuality of the machine inducing pain. Learning is decoration. Poems about themselves are supreme forms of decoration. Moral concern as decoration. A Beardsley picture. Scene 3 Daniel Armstrong had often considered that capitalism was the root of all evil. He insisted that it had always been there, though had only been made a 'science' in the last couple of centuries. He read society through post-Marxist eyes. All services as well as goods had been fetishised. Prisons, instead of reforming, were designed to make a profit. Mentally ill patients were consumed by a self-advocating and self-perpetuating industry. Ideas were items in the market-place. Great inventions or concepts, developed for the well-being of humanity, were only recognised as such if they had a value — that is, could be sold. And if he swapped his 'invention' for a sack of potatoes because he was in need of food and could not go on inventing without it, he could be sure that those who produced the potatoes would only swap the invention for something equivalent to a field of potatoes. Value-added, fetishised. But Daniel was determined to be different. His research would be of universal benefit, and would be done without the motive of profit. Sometimes he found himself thinking that it would be nice to be comfortable, but he quickly suppressed these thoughts in favour of his utopian vision. Of course, he also realised that utopian visions were what drove ideas-people. For, looked at realistically, profit could be more reliably assured by following certain tried and true procedures. Only occasionally did the inventor come up with a 'winner'. 'Sunshine Is Not Weather': Bluff &/or Anxiety — An extract from a response to the poetry of John Forbes. Most studies or commentaries on the work of John Forbes have been of a socio-critical nature rather than textually based. Forbes has been examined as a kind of phenomenon as much as the author of a particular oeuvre. People 'recognise a Forbes poem straight away' — this is a common statement. And there has been a preconception, maybe because of this, that he writes in the same way every time. I would argue that Forbes as the poet of *Humidity* etc, is a very different poet from the Forbes of 'Four Heads & how to do them', or 'Stalin's Holidays'. There has been a shift not only in world-view, but also in technique. While on the surface there are familiar verse structures, and a familiar outer tone, there have been fundamental changes within the line itself. For example, a Forbes poem such as 'Stalin's Holidays' is quick, sharp, and soon over with. It leaves a pointed impression.

His later work, however, has more breath in it. You can actually hesitate mid-poem and have a think. There is much more than tone to it. He has developed a sense of the volta and caesura, and there are undulations in his rhythm. I suggest this breath has come hand in hand with Forbes' increased anxiety about his work, his place in the world, and the nature of the Art itself. I'd also, consequently, argue that his earlier work, though assured and witty, was often built on bluff — a kind of resistance against the possibility of self-doubt. And self-doubt, or at least explorations of self-doubt and its deceptive cousin, confidence — in one's position in the artifice of the social milieu — is what his poetry is all about. If the maxim 'once a Catholic, always a Catholic' has any meaning, then it assuredly applies to the guilt of John Forbes. A couple of 'reservations' to begin with. One is that, whether conscious of it or not, Forbes reads society through Cold War glasses. Not as a warrior, but as a product. This is not to say his concepts, themes, or the expression of these are a product of Cold War values, but rather that he shows a consciousness that this has been the way of it through the bulk of his life. It's much the same as those who have directly experienced the shock of war and forever ground their metaphors in its turbulence. This Cold War is as much about relationships between people as it is about relationships between threatening and threatened Global Powers. Intrinsic links between people and the State can be and are made. And the component parts of a State — its legislature, its judiciary, its people and inherent cultural baggage — interact with each other in much the same way as different States interact with each other. In other words, all forms of relationships run on common principles. Appropriation is the hallmark of contemporary culture. The reinventing of old forms, the repositioning of said things. That existence is the extension of perception is no longer a valid debate. The imperative nature of the market economy dictates that perception is constantly changing, being reinvented. The forces that drive the equation derive from the need to increase Pleasure, to add more baubles to the decorative tree. Ontology is linked directly to comfort, to relaxation. Time, as a verb, is luxury. Reflection, introspection, investigation, are for vacations, or out-of-work hours. And luxury has a price. In a sense, the market allows for ontology, or at least the time for its 'existence'. Pure self-investigation is the window through the ocean of plagiarism. The hydraulics of modern society are interfused, one substance mixes with another, new trends flow at every juncture. The sources are no longer recognisable. God, if it resides here, does so in the vacant flat. Soon the student will be gone and it will be able to spread itself around. Sometimes a priest visits number three. I've heard them speaking outside, the woman and the priest that is. I can hear them because my senses are sharp from the speed. She speaks in short, breathless undertones. He is bold and loud. He asks if she would like to attend their group for abandoned wives. She tells him her husband came back from the 'Islands' a year ago. He asks why they live in such a small flat, the flat he'd found for her when she'd been 'left on the street.' She tells him it suits them and he goes away. *Pulp Fiction* plays games with genre, with the items of popular culture. It sanitises the criminal because the criminal is part of our day-to-day dialogue. The market has plagiarised the criminal. It is, of course, immutable, because it is only a device, a finely tuned device that reacts to quantification and qualification in the environment in which it operates. If something surfaces it adjusts. It's the subterranean, the underground that collectively locates the windows. Self-investigation is the only other route. But in its appropriation of genre and popular perceptions of social discourse *Pulp Fiction* becomes a victim of itself. It makes reference to other films, as seen in the background of the Bruce Willis taxi scene, the *film noir* consciousness in general, and musically it 'refers' to the earlier *Reservoir Dogs*, which itself was accused of plagiarism from the Hong Kong gangster films. But then

Tarantino has recognised his debt to video, in fact has used it as a 'device' in his process. Self-referentiality is the plagiaristic articulatory loop that contradicts and even resists investigation. The poems of John Ashbery ... As a kind of inverted plagiarism, here's a delicious quote from Donald Thomas' *The Marquis de Sade*: Three days later Sade wrote to the Journal de Paris complaining of the 'insult', and adding, 'It is false, absolutely false to say that I am the author of the book entitled *Justine, or the Misfortunes of Virtue*.' Electric fans, nasal inhalers, Enesco, Bizet, and a Biman Airways flight to Dhaka. My chest aches. A procession of luggage trolleys stacked high with electrical goods. Lady and man, presumably husband and wife, sit talking to each other with nasal inhalers stuck up their noses. Dhaka. Two packets of Dunhill for ten grams of smoke! S., the man who accosted us at the airport, is *making good own business* as a guide to Iraqi delegates staying at the Sheraton. He takes us down town. Cheap. He is going to buy his own hotel. He and his friends make themselves comfortable in the room he has 'found' for us. Anything we want he can get. S is in his early twenties and can speak twelve languages. B., the ringleader and S.'s older brother, quickly asserts himself. He takes over from S. He is friends with the police, for a fee. He loves capitalism, he loves socialism, he loves anarchy. He says equality does not necessarily mean freedom. B says to take no notice of the dead on the streets. Take no notice of them, Bangladesh is a beautiful country that drinks snow water from the Himalayas. B reads books on left-wing prisoners in India. And he reads Graham Greene. He gave me a copy of *A Gun For Sale*. And he tells me how his village was burnt to the ground by West Pakistanis. That he welcomed the Indian incursion, despite everything. That he paid for his own education and is proud of being a Muslim. B kicks the chair from under the table and collapses into it. Karin glances from the reception desk and shoots a look of disapproval. He returns to filling out his ledger. A few minutes pass. He looks up again. Sakid has been smoking, it's obvious — red eyes, soggy lips. Smoking in the front room. Probably English cigarettes given to him by the Australians. Things are bad. The only Westerners in weeks and he can't stand them. They don't clean their room and rickshaw men are always yelling up to their window from the street. Nobody else at the airport? he asks sulkily. No. B produces a cigarette and lights it in front of his boss. Karin winces. Put that filthy thing out now! he shrieks. B blows smoke rings and laughs and tells him to shut his face or he'll have to find himself another man who is friends with the police, who can talk with the Westerners. Karin retreats to his ledger. Karin eats his rice and swallows phenol to clean the gut. Every day the same meal. He does not consider his diet. He can afford better, unlike his neighbours. It is enough to know this. He neither likes nor dislikes his food. He eats alone, though his wife will occasionally glance into the room and laugh. She feels she can afford to laugh, not being devout and observing only one prayer time a day. Relics from Afghanistan are being flown into Dhaka, repackaged, and transported to France. B will sell shares in the operation 'if we are interested.' We decline. The hash that B has brought is good. I shall buy a large quantity. I recite Keats to B and he feigns tears. I ask him about the fight in the foyer early that morning. He says it was over the telephone and that he ran away. Though not onto the street because there is a curfew from midnight to dawn and the soldiers shoot on sight. B orders a younger man to fetch him food. He says that he is the boss. I protest but he says that poor people — really poor people — have their own concept of humility. B is clever. I give B a loan of 100 takas so he can 'make a profit' to feed his family or whatever. And now he's telling me about friendship. Apparently we were not friends before I gave him the money and he lets me know that the blue lady IS Mrs Dorothy Vallens! She wore blue velvet bluer than velvet was the night softer than satin was the light from the stars she wore blue velvet, the eyes have it, red drape background, blue blue blue blue stars silhouette blood drapes into impending music, shouldn't do this because it's crazy and dangerous because it's crazy and dangerous a detective or pervert for me to know and you to find out. It occurred to Daniel that the most efficient devices or concepts were the most practical. Visiting Peter at Tenari he would marvel at the beguiling simplicity of the 'bushman's' tools. One that had particularly impressed him a few years back was a home-made fence-post digger. It had been designed to solve an immediate problem, with no thoughts to patenting or profit. When finished with, it was stuck in the toolshed, only resurfacing when a neighbour had a similar problem to overcome, and the device was just what was required. A couple of years later and most of the farms around the place had one sitting in a toolshed somewhere. Whipped up out of scrap metal and stuck together with an arc welder. Australian farmers had a long history of innovation. The landscape was about innovation. Daniel was just waiting for the day when he walked into a hardware store, or saw a photograph in a Father's Day lift-out, for the very same tool. Expensive, cheaply made and patented. It wouldn't be long before the vitality of the device was destroyed and it became just one more element in the commercialisation and destruction of the land. When someone cleared a patch of land with an axe, and hacked the stumps out by hand, you could at least show them some respect. As they said, their blood had paid for their destructiveness. They were giving back something of what they'd taken. But it was pretty hard to respect a tractor, ball and chain, and a plan of attack that would lay waste to all in sight. It appalled him. He considered these things when working on his sheep project. He thought these things when he was arguing with Peter, not that he'd admit it. But he appeased his conscience by convincing himself that the research would fail. That they were barking up the wrong tree. What the hell, a few sheep would suffer but plenty wouldn't. And then, and this had been the problem at the core of his research, he would hit the kill-switch on guilt and stop thinking about it. Turning his attention to a technical rather than moral problem, or creating art out of lengths of glass tubing and a Bunsen burner flame. T. likes his sex 'dangerous'. He tells me he'd like to tie me up. To strangle me. He says it makes you cum with a bang. You almost burst, he says. He's done it with A., because she's told me. I don't want to be here really, but at the moment it's what I'm doing. That was what Daniel was like. He was like that when he picked the eyes out of dead animals. They were always dead, though they were often pretty warm. He had this way of turning a thought off mid-flow or shifting moral fine points around in his head. Placing notes of conscience in some musty file in a back room, occasionally coming across it and reconsidering the contents before misplacing it again. It wasn't a case of being absent-minded, but rather a kind of mental damage control. If it was too hot, drop it. And if he needed to access one part of his conscience but ignore another, he could comfortably set up a direct line of communication. Interference-free. Yeah, anyway — Capitalism stank — that's what he thought. So when these people came and offered him big bucks, it was against his principles to say, Yeah, that's what I've been doing this for, but it was also characteristic of his tolerance and pragmatism to say, I'm listening. This betrayal of his principles, or rather this refusal to make them clear, had often got him into trouble. He was the kid at school who disagreed with setting fire to the wastepaper basket but would watch anyway. He should have asked them how they'd heard about his project because he had kept it pretty much to himself. He hadn't published any papers in journals or spoken in detail with colleagues at the CSIRO about it. But his curiosity steered him around the obvious questions and he more or less went along for the ride. Maybe they would be useful in disseminating the information. He had to play the system to beat it. He had the key, but needed a lock to open.

Anyway, the fact was they were with him in his laboratory. And they were offering research facilities and capital. He considered that if he hesitated they'd think he was angling for more — money, benefits, fame. He didn't want to create this impression. He said, Yes. He'd play capitalism against itself. When they announced it was time to leave he said that he'd need to tell his wife and get a few things ready. They suggested that it would be a bad move as she'd only protest and that would affect his ability to work. He accepted this and went with the promise that all would be provided and he could contact Mary from the research facility. He didn't even bother asking where this research facility was located. He gathered his essential papers into a portfolio and followed them out. But Mary had been on the bedroom balcony and he couldn't avoid her eye. She looked disturbed. He raced back and lied to her over the intercom and then left as quickly as he could. He carried with him the trappings of a man who had sheltered behind an obscure hobby and satisfied himself that he wasn't like one of the boys who hid from their families in the pub, downing beers and listening to the races. In a personal relationship one must remember that love is one factor (the most intended if not the most desired, the most longed-for if not the most wanted) while negotiations of individual territories and rights are others. Thus we are constantly at the bargaining table of conscience and desire; always one step behind our wishes are realities. Forbes, the metaphysical who'll never pull off that party trick of logic that will convince *his* coy mistress, instead tries to convince himself that his ability to reason makes up for his loss — on paper that is, not in the heart. Forbes does NOT accept his failure to love or be loved entirely; if he did, he couldn't write poetry. For Forbes being smart is making do, the best way he knows how. He could be stylish, but then he's probably got more chance finding love hanging out down the beach and feeling guilty for forgetting the white zinc. Secondly, while there *is* interesting variety in his work, it is within a certain tonal scale. This is why he has been accused of little 'poetic development'. However, Forbes is more metaphysical than Drydenesque and has made astute use of conceit (often layered). And this is not only referential conceit but tonal conceit (ie. his apparent tone is not necessarily the tone he intends). It is not as simple as calling this technique 'irony', for although it exists in abundance in his poems, it carries with it a moral implication that is not always present. Forbes the lapsed Catholic sometimes forgets himself. Instead of loading irony with guilt he becomes dedicational — love as a pure if unrealisable notion. His apparently assured tone is in fact a mask for frustration. The outer tone preserves him, the inner tone conveys the true poem. Three poems with love in their titles are worth looking at: 'Love Poem' and 'Love's Body' from *Stalin's Holidays*, and 'Love Poem' from the *New And Selected Poems*. The most recent poem I'll quote in full, using it as an axis for the others to turn around. In a sense, though post-Cold War, it is the definitive Cold War poem — both in its social and emotional concerns: Love Poem/Spent tracer flecks Baghdad's/bright video game sky/as I curl up with the war/in lieu of you, whose letter/lets me know my poems show/how unhappy I can be. Perhaps./But what they don't show, until/now, is how at ease I can be/with military technology: e.g./matching their feu d'esprit I classify/the sounds of the Iraqi AA — the/thump of the 85 mil, the throaty/chatter of the quad ZSU 23./Our precision guided weapons/make the horizon flash & glow/but nothing I can do makes you/want me. Instead I watch the west/do what the west does best/& know, obscurely, as I go to bed/all this is being staged for me. In Iraq we find the trappings of a decayed Soviet Imperialism. The weaponry is familiar cold war stuff, the idea of watching it on television, American via Vietnam. It's not so much a case of draft dodging as of jumping into bed with the enemy. The particulars of the weaponry have a slightly sexual overtone, a bit like vital statistics. In the 'throaty chatter' of failed love there is a kind of scientific detachment that allows the persona to take it all. 'Perhaps'. Herein the key — of course he can't but he's got to feign that he can. That to the writer of the letter his 'unhappiness' is much like the military knowledge he owns — distant from the real suffering, removed like television, as the culture in which he resides allows and insists: 'Instead I watch the west/do what the west does best'. In a sense, the poem is a case of the best form of defence being attack ... 'Love's Body' is a very different poem. For all its attempt to reason it falls victim to its bodily, animal urge. The idealised, the fantastic, is a foil for the real. It works in reverse to the more recent 'Love Poem'. In a sense, one can never rationalise away desire. The poem ends with a more relaxed, 'occasional' language, but it's here, in this recognisable obiter dictum that we confront the real notion of the poem. Something like the case that people who live in glass houses shouldn't throw stones. That in the end, it's all as simple as: But for the moment rather, relax, watch/the inflight movie or the way the tiny nylon/squares on the hostess' stocking stretch to/rhomboids, or squash up as she moves past you/along the plane. Ask her for a drink or/think of going to bed with her in Teheran or/London, as past experiences fall away like/the memory of their superb engineering and/the gleaming world of eighteenth-century metaphysics/opens to your smile and naked body. There's also the irony of using the more assured, less superstitious nature of 'eighteenth-century metaphysics', as opposed to the more easily overwhelmed (and religious) Renaissance science and seventeenth-century metaphysics. It's as if the surprise has gone, that it's all too 'gleaming' for one to be part of. Even the 'smile and naked body' seem clothed in doubt. But not a dark, dismissive doubt, more of a 'go on, tell me I'm wrong' kind of doubt. Many of Forbes' techniques are taken directly from Donne and Marvell. Forbes would not object to the term 'stolen'. A different world-view, but the same methods. David Norbrook, in his introduction to *The Penguin Book of Renaissance Verse* says much that we might, in a roundabout way, apply to Forbes. Of course the difference is that Forbes lacks Donne's certainty. His convictions are tenuous. Norbrook says: Donne may draw attention to the argumentative structures of his poems, as in 'Loves growth': 'I scarce beleeve', 'But if', 'And yet', 'If'. The case the poem makes is not a rigorously logical one, however: the speaker is working with enthymemes, the merely approximate arguments of rhetorical proof, rather than logicians' syllogisms. He begins, after all, by blithely assuring us that he has 'lyed all winter', so we are hardly prepared to take his words at face value. The poem works by assertion and counter assertion: he insists that his love has changed but is also keen to deny that change may entail decay and death, so that by line 15 he is protesting that it only seems subjectively to have changed, and his final declaration that the winter will not change his love takes us back to the previous winter's lies. The argument is clinched by a series of analogies, which were considered by Renaissance logicians to represent a low level of proof. Critics have made much of Renaissance beliefs in natural analogies between the human body and the world at large, which meant that metaphor and simile might have a literal truth; but it should also be remembered that rhetorical training encouraged a profound scepticism about the literal truth of any analogy. In any case, literal truth, for the rhetorician, is not the point: analogies are significant because they involve the emotional nuances which are more significant for exploring concrete human relations than metaphysical categories. It is in the way he uses his far-fetched analogies or 'conceits', rather than the conceits themselves, that Donne stands out so sharply from his lesser imitators. If you don't have it, the best antidote is to write about it. In the case of Forbes, one couldn't refer to it as therapy — the concept would be so wholly unappealing to him that he would probably throw the whole lot in. For Forbes believes that he COULD have style if he wanted it. In his quasi-satirical manner (mannerisms?) he stands within the very society he jousts with. There is a kind of barter going on with culture. You allow me enough space and money and I'll immortalise you. But it's more than this; he's playing a kind of quasi-Shakespeare. Where Shakespeare writes to some unnamed love in his sonnets, so too Forbes writes to an unnamed love. This is not to say he doesn't dedicate poems of love to particular people, or is afraid of identifying them, but rather that his poems are dedicated to the concept of love, to its elusiveness. Style is what allows you to objectify love, to 'own' passion, to make consumerable desire. It is the signifier of the market-place, the fulcrum about which taste and its trappings revolve. Without style, there can be no identity. Without style. But what qualifies the social causes static in the inner self. Style is something you wish to have to make you consumerable, (and consumable) but it doesn't leave you with much after the fact: 'Everything you want/is actually happening/& a dumb model of it/knocks you out.' ('Poem On Style 1'). Deep River impends against the glossy lipstick the sounds of buildings stretched echoes (Eraserhead) room 71 opened with a stolen key blackout, interior glimpse of light candescent a glimpse of notes on a coned party hat object fetishised piss and

four honks lost to the flush of the cistern,
negated by chance and fate, the whites of her
eyes looking up; into the cupboard. Through
the slats she undresses to her black frillies ...
Franz, Ich möchte gern 'Wind' und 'Luft' (aus
Ferne) im nächsten *Poetry Journal* veröffentlichen. Das wird im Februar sein. Wenn
Du bis 1997 warten könntest, und wenn der
Text *Ferne* von keinem anderen schon
genommen wäre, würde ich das ganze Ding
gern veröffentlichen. Wie L. Dir schon am
Telefon gesagt hat, möchte ich gern das erste
Bild 'Sicher auf dem Weg' (Seite 30, *Bilder*) auf
den Umschlag *Poetry Journal* bringen.
Schi/Zaro (Seite 108) interessiert mich auch
sehr; es wäre schön, wenn ich es in diesem
Heft reproduzieren könnte. Aber ich würde
davon ein gutes Foto brauchen; könntest Du
mir eines in 10 Tagen oder so schicken? Ich
würde gern in Düsseldorf lesen; Mai (spät),
Juni oder Juli (früh) wären gut. Alles Gute
zum neuen Jahr (und auch von meiner Frau,
die diesen Brief übersetzt hat). Lieber Franz!
Dein Paket ist erst heute angekommen —
vielen Dank. Heute abend werde ich die
Gedichte gern lesen. Ich wußte nichts davon,
als ich Dir vor einigen Tagen faxte; sonst hätte
ich darüber etwas gesagt ... Ein Jahr in
Düsseldorf wäre toll; es ist sehr nett von Dir,
solche Gelegenheiten für mich zu suchen. Ich
faxe Dir jetzt meinen Lebenslauf (kurze
Version!), mit Überblick die letzten drei

Jahren. In einigen Tagen werde ich Dir *Entropy* schicken; das ist ein langes, experimentelles Gedicht (1993 veröffentlicht). Ich hoffe, mein Fax in Bezug auf *Poetry Journal* ist bei Dir gut angekommen. Herzliche Grüße von Dear Hals Thanks for the copy of *The Rhodes Review.* You should receive a copy of *Hopper* in a week or two. You mentioned you were interested in my writing for you. I can offer a comprehensive review of John Tranter's *At The Florida*, an article entitled 'Julia's Reply To Robert Herrick' (which looks at '90s readings of Metaphysical poetry, gender and the canon, and conceit as a means of cultural accessibility), and an article on Simon Schama's *Landscape and Memory* which reads the work from a post-colonial point of view (in a 'chatty' kind of way). I should point out, that regarding the latter, it was commissioned by the *Australian Book Review*, and is due for publication with them later this month (Australian rights only). You might also find of interest two interviews I will be preparing over the next twelve months. One will be with Harold Bloom (I'm recording it in New York next August) and one with Rita Dove I'll be starting shortly by mail and cassette. Looking forward to hearing from you. All the best, Yours, Dear Dennis Hopper, I hope all is well with you. Firstly, before outlining my proposal/s, I'd just like to say that I've been writing on and exploring your work for some seventeen years now. Yep, it all started with *Easy Rider* which I saw as a fifteen-year-old in a coastal town in the north of Western Australia at a 'film festival' organised by some local schoolteachers. It's been a strange and fascinating journey from that point. You, as cultural icon (and iconoclast!) have become central to my investigations. I've even applied Kant's 'Critique of Pure Reason' to your depiction and representation in critical interpretations of modern American culture. The wonderful contradictions and paradoxes of your characters add a depth to the classic bête noire creation of the psychological thriller. 'You' manage, unlike most other film stars, to exist outside film. In an article I'm writing at the moment I examine your characterisations through the statement, 'There is nothing to fear but fear itself.' Of course, Wim Wenders, in playing with the implicit contradictions and ironies of the American thriller (in *The American Friend*), exploited the duality of your 'image' superbly, but even there, you existed outside the film. The line seems yours, not the film's (or, in this case, anti-film's, if you like). Anyway, to the point. I am very much hoping I'll be able to interview you for *Poetry Journal*. This may be achieved either by fax, phone, or in person (I'll be in the States on a study tour next August). If the project interests you, please let me know which method would be most convenient. I also hope to use the interview, or 'dialogue', in a future book entitled *Hopper: A Book of Modern Aesthetics*, a 'creative' biography of your artistic work (a follow-up to *Hopper*). I'd like to have included a personal biography as well, but I understand that your 'official' biographers would probably have this sewn up. I categorically do not believe in writing on people's private lives if it is not their wish. Furthermore, unless such things are done with close attention to the work, they become artificial and ultimately worthless. I am interested in the creative aspect of my subject, not sensational details. Anyway, if you are interested in my proposition please contact me. Yours in admiration, He drools over the stuff. Popular culture is a big wet pussy, I heard one of his colleagues say. It makes me sick P.S. Your intro to *Out of the Sixties* is pure poetry. But then Style is a kind of joke in that upon inspection it becomes obvious that the prototype is always going to be better, that the inherent flaw in acceptability is the need to bluff the punters, convince them that it's something new they're getting. When all along things 'are', and only an awareness of this brings you to face the emptiness of pleasure in full awareness that you are craving for nothing: 'But now/elements of style begin to intrigue you/as they get rarer/& parody replaces the face of '82.' It's something like the knock-back irony of 'Speed, a pastoral' with its urban-scape logo-centrism and evocation of the sprites of an alternative reality, ('it's fun to take speed/& stay up all night') confronted with the bottom line of not only death but nothingness, a kind of 'you've slipped out before you've completed what you've set out to do' ('& he was the teacher's pet, who just put up his hand/& said quietly, 'Sir, sir'/& heroin let him leave the room.'). Like love — the intention is there but the mechanics don't quite come together, or are a load of bullshit anyway ... I remarked also respecting experiments, that they become so much the more necessary the more one is advanced in knowledge, for to begin with it's better to make use simply of those which present themselves spontaneously to our senses, and of which we could not be ignorant provided that we reflected ever so little, rather than to seek out those which are more rare and recondite; the reason for this is that those which are more rare often mislead us so long as we do not know the causes of the more common, and the fact that the circumstances on which they depend are almost always so particular and minute that it is very difficult to observe them. I wonder about the texture of the arm of this chair. It is varnished wood. I'm not sure what kind of wood, but it's a hard wood, old, well-seasoned wood. I bought it at a second-hand store down on the highway and carried it back. It is smooth. Is smooth really texture? Her skin is smooth, I can tell.

As it sits near the gusset it is smooth, I know this. It has not been corrupted by coarseness. My rooms are emptying. There is still a lot of stuff to load into my Uncle's ute tomorrow and on Sunday. I don't like the idea of working on Sunday, but I've got to be out on Monday, so there's nothing else for it. I hear myself saying that later I'll drop chain letters in each of the letterboxes. The onus will be on her to send more out. She will connect me with others. I have learned much, but must continue to experiment. I'll drop by quietly, keep my eye on her. The room is large when you look at it in its pure form. I have more than enough space, and yet I must leave. The guy next door has made life intolerable. I have first tried to discover generally the principles or first causes of everything that is or that can be in the world ... Though it is good the pictures and hangings are down from the walls, now I consider, in a clear light, they were merely adornments. They said nothing, just occupied space, crowded my thinking ... without considering anything that might accomplish this end but God Himself who has created the world, or deriving them from any source excepting from certain germs of truths which are naturally existent in our souls. I speculate that there is nothing surprising in living, and nor should there be. In the first few days of his absence, Mary felt as if things were focussing on her. She felt obliged to notify the cops of his absence, put it on the record. She didn't dramatise it but pointed out that he'd said he'd be back that evening. When asked why she hadn't reported him missing the next day, she said she kind of expected he'd be gone longer than he said. This, of course, buried the case in the eyes of the cops. A uniformed sergeant and a constable dropped around to interview her. They'd only pay lip service to it now — going through the routine inquiries in a low key sort of way. They came over and glanced at his laboratory, said that his colleagues had felt he was on the verge of quitting work anyway, and asked her a few questions. They told her not to worry, just to sit tight. That this kind of thing wasn't unusual. Fucking arseholes, she thought, how many guys leave their families and jump into cars with strangers, never to return? She put her point as politely as she could. The sergeant eased forward in the recliner chair he'd made a beeline for as soon as he arrived and ran his finger over the smoked glass coffee table, examining the dust residue closely under the floodlights. Mary shuffled and felt her neck prickle, resisting the urge to explain that she'd been so concerned over the last few days she hadn't had a chance to clean. Fuck him, she thought, remembering the cleaning woman was due that afternoon. What did they look like? he asked slowly. She looked at him, open mouthed. I mean, describe them. He hesitated and flicked his fingers pointedly. The people your husband left with. It struck Mary that she couldn't describe them. She'd watched them come and go time after time through her balcony window, under the backyard lighting, illuminated like a mise en scène in a film noir, but hadn't really formed an impression of what they looked like. She stopped herself saying Marcel Marceau. I never really saw them clearly, she offered. The sergeant cocked an eyebrow and sniffed his finger. What about the car then? You saw the car clearly? Yes, well, sort of. Sort of? It was white. It was a white sedan. Type, model, number plate? No, sorry, none of those. She was embarrassed. She wondered about her haziness. She was a particular person. She'd penalise a student for a spelling error. And yet. It was particularly white, she added quickly. Shiny white. The sergeant stared at her dumbly and the police constable stood up and stretched. She was pretty young, it struck Mary. She was staring at a Juniper on the wall. Like that? she asked the constable sarcastically. Yes, madam. The constable sat down, crossed and uncrossed her legs. The sergeant had switched his attention to her. He was staring at her legs. Mary felt sick. I'm heading to my brother-in-law's for a few days, taking the kids. Oh? said the sergeant. Yes, I think it will do them good. Defuse the situation. Oh? the sergeant said again. I'll give you his number so you can contact me if anything crops up. She scribbled it on a piece of paper and deliberately handed it to the constable. Her slight didn't seem to affect the sergeant who was now ogling her breasts. Well, anything else? she asked with obvious annoyance. She felt like gouging the sergeant's eyes out, and just managed to stop herself laughing when she considered they'd make poor specimens and were probably best left where they were. The policewoman annoyed her as well. Why was she there? She'd said practically nothing the whole time. Was she there to make her feel secure? Fat lot of good it was doing if that was the intention. Was this a kind of tokenism? In case she had an attack of hysteria and needed settling? She offered them a cup of tea and when they accepted she went into the kitchen, chose dirty cups, and selected a couple of bloated tea bags from the bin. Frank, please Frank, let me talk to you. Please Frank Sir, I like to sing *Blue Velvet* Don't don't it's all right don't worry ... Tom, what's the matter with him ... Mommy loves you, Frank, Sir ... How not to let responsibility for fairness take over: 'behind our belief in free speech e.g./these last words are only seconds away/and every second is a holiday.' One is prepared to drop awareness for sublimity but something always stands in the way. Vested interest commodifies love again. If you want someone's attention then someone else will assuredly want it as well:

The city is blessed. Yet just last week/its skyblue stupidity seemed tungsten/to me. I think those days mimed an accent/I've abandoned for the lovely weather/of you. I'll meet you at 1.30 outside/the museum's fabulous graffiti room, I/know you (plural) will be there. I know/the famous painting leads a double life. (From 'Love Poem'.) Forbes couldn't be so easily dismissive as Shakespeare in 'My mistress's eyes are nothing like the sun ... ' to validate his loves. He lacks that confidence. And irony requires confidence lest it degenerate into self-ridicule and bathos. It's an interesting condition, for the tone of Forbes would seem to dictate that 'Negative Capability' is paramount, but internally, this is not the case at all. Once again, it's the case of the apparent and the actual tone of his work. He's not aiming at a particular but at an ideal. If anything, Forbes' screening of his intention is often a case of the 'objective correlative' but only in so far as we come to read his poems in accordance with the Forbes index, or key. He has certain expressions, mannerisms or points of reference that evoke a certain mood, or imply a certain notion. But one must be careful, for this, if not read in the 'objective correlative', can easily become the Forbes that 'you'd recognise straight away'. It's not a case of Jekyll and Hyde, there's no sudden turning from one into another, but maybe on the psychological level there is an argument. Robert

Louis Stevenson shows Hyde is in all of us, that conscience is a tool with which to keep him in check. Things can only be 'better' if you possess the object of comparison in the first place. And even his negativity is a kind of anxiety about how his affections will be interpreted. Newtonian physics comes into play and the personalised imagery of emotion is just a guise, a misreading of the italics. Writing poetry is a substitute for wealth, and Forbes knows he'll only be able to break free of his anxiety if he stops bluffing. Maybe the beach isn't such a relaxing place? Moving inland. It was a beautiful drive through the southern wheatbelt at that time of year. She felt pretty good when they drove past the swollen corpse of a kangaroo and the kids didn't say a thing. Healthy, she thought. Peter's place was about a hundred and fifty ks south of Perth on the York-Williams Road. It was quite isolated and this suited her fine. She drove with the window slightly down, enjoying the sound of the tyres on the bitumen. They made an electric hum. Hitting gravel, the kids complained about the dust, so she sealed the artificial environment and turned the stereo on. The jarrah forest gave way to blackbutt and scrub. Granite outcrops nudged their way out of paddocks while creeks ran like mercury in the morning sun. Patches of sodden wasteland, shiny with salt, surrounded them. Sheep clustered around dams or grazed on green feed, indifferent to their passing. Willy wagtails moved from back to back, chasing insects. As the approached Tenari she saw a wedge-tailed eagle hovering over a hay stack. Mice, or rats. Snakes would be hibernating. The silver feed sheds dazzled her as she stared at them. The car swerved slightly and the kids looked up from their books. Nearly there, she said. Peter was at the gate when they arrived, collecting his mail. It was delivered on the third day of the week as Peter liked to say. That was counting Sunday. He saluted to them, opened the gate, and watched as they drove through. Closing the gate, he whistled to his red cloud and followed the car down the dirt driveway. Out of the dirt the crawling wig heads down the corridor walls light over tawny coach bathroom down corridor knickers slipped down towel around and into the cupboard he avoids her reaching hand she sits as he makes a noise and wanders from kitchen with knife and finds him Put your hands up on your head on your knees ... Jeffrey nothing ... cut ... give me your wallet what are you doing in my apartment Jeffrey Beaumont I wanted to see you who sent you here nobody see you what do you see see you what did you see and then and then ... GET UNDRESSED I want to see you GET UNDRESSED Dear Ms Lane, Well, a couple of years have passed since I last sent material to you for consideration. On this occasion I've enclosed two essays: 'Language Shift Census' and 'Abject Penetration'. Also find enclosed $18 Canadian for a subscription starting with your next issue. Yours, Dear Peter, Received *Bedside Lyr-I-Kill* this morning. It's bloody great! I'll definitely be reviewing it, and will make sure many others do as well. Your admiring friend, Dear Hilda, Thanks for the comments on *Tosa,* I ran them into the printers this morning and they'll be used as a preface to the book. It will be available in about four weeks so I'll send you copies along with those of *Poetry Journal.* I'm not sure if I mentioned in my last note that Charles Bernstein faxed some work through at the very last moment. It was fortunate that it was an 'interview' — it now makes up the 340th, 341st and 342nd page of *Poetry Journal* — as the last section of the book contains interviews with poets (including a full length version of Jill's interview with you). I also thank you for the 'domestic' comments in your fax. I've tried to visualise the demographic details of your area as well as the physical nature of the terrain in which you live. I picture a densely populated area with a mixture of cultures, a certain 'free & easy' aspect, with your house itself being a tall, thin two-storeyed building, with basement. In this laboratory of art and life, spells are woven and the 'music of the spouses' made. I hope this does not seem a romanticised notion, it's not intended to be.

I'm just one for detail, and sometimes given a lack of it, I construct a picture and then scrutinise it to see how 'likely' it IS. Please don't consider this as personally intrusive, it's actually part of my general 'worldview', and all (even the origins of a newspaper clipping — relevant today) come in for the same consideration. It was a storm-ridden night when your fax arrived. We are in for high winds and showers tonight. I'm sitting with my own words 'witnessing' their arrangements into forms that better suit themselves. Oh, did you ever receive that stuff (tapes and books) I sent seamail some months ago? Your mentioning Joe's CD reminded me. He has the voice of one who has come to terms with the mysterious inner workings of projected interior monologues. Maybe with the tautologies of jazz. But then, he is a bass player! Love, as always, Yours ... Chère Mme Kristeva, Pourriez-vous m'indiquer si vous avez bien reçu le colis que je vous ai expedié au mois de juin? J'y avais mis plusieurs exemplaires de mes livres d'essais, et des lettres en français et en anglais. J'espère que ma question ne vous gêne pas, mais je ne saurai pas autrement si ce paquet est arrivé. Veuillez agréer l'expression de mes sentiments les plus distingués. Dear ... I've just been 'enjoying' *Grand Street*'s 'Fetishes' issue. An amazingly grotesque cover! And Claude Royet-Journoud's 'La notion d'obstacle'. Which reminds me, I'll add an extract from a poem ('Muette') by Lucienne Durollet, a Québecoise poet, I've been 'interpreting' (with a little help from ...), to this letter. It's actually a huge work (some 200 or so pages) and eventually I hope to publish the translation. The extract I'm sending is that which I've included in *Poetry Journal*. *It's been a strange sort of day*. No kidding, it has. I use italics because it's always struck me that this line would be a great way to start the Appropriate poem. Anyway, I've been up to my neck in organising a letter of objection(?) to a particularly reactionary review in last weekend's *West Australian*. It's true that most of what the *West* publishes is reactionary, but this was one out of the barrel! The reviewer took two novels to task for being 'postmodern rubbish'. Armed with her prejudices she then reviewed the blurbs (she'd obviously not read a word of the text) and pronounced the death of all such literature. She of the cascading narrative fixation then wished doom upon the authors and publishing house and signed off. All too much for me, I'm afraid. Love, Dear ... , This is a letter faxed through a window of opportunity. Despite being able to receive faxes I can only send them at certain times, due to there being an ISD bar on outgoing calls on our phone. This is because I have an itchy dialling finger & have been known to fax whole books to people. Anyway, I can fax out for the next few days so I thought

I'd follow up this morning's morning phone call sent under indelibly leaden skies with a few printed words. Unlike the internet, which is open to the prying eyes of others, with the exception of stuff translated into a crypto-type language, we can 'correspond' without the prying eyes of officialdom tainting our words. The morphemes compile & there is no great necessity for continual use of glottal stops when speak-reading. I say all this because of a particularly savage ex of mine who is using old love letters in a semi-legal battle over the rights to 'truth'. That is, how 'truth' varies with the conditions (a fatuous & airy word) in which it is applied. All kind of silly really. By now I gather you will have received *Hopper*. What do you think? Well, it's 2.36pm and my daughter is asleep on the couch so I've got to wake her, while my wife is probably speaking German somewhere. I'd better get moving, though I intend to return to this letter. Actually, while I remember, I was meaning to ask if you'd heard of the yearly *Exact Change* and ask what you think of Michael Palmer's work and thought? I'm intrigued. Oh well, to waking the kid and then out into the narrow pocket of light between cloud & earth. It's about 3.30pm now. I've got to pick ... up in about half an hour. I think I'll go down to Booragoon Swamp this evening to watch the night herons wake. Strange primeval birds — shape changers. I'm quite obsessed with herons, egrets and bitterns actually. I've been going down to the swamp quite a lot lately. It's one of the major nesting grounds for cormorants, darters and ibises. Incredible place. Flanked by Leach Highway on one side, and the middle-class suburb of Booragoon on the other, it exists as something of an anomaly in the metro area. Few people know or care it's there. It's one of the few haunts of the night heron, or rufous night heron as it is often called. It would be wrong of me to describe the night heron as Gothic (as it is to describe it as 'primeval' though I'm sure it is a much more appropriate association) though I have no hesitation in describing the swamp as such. This is not so much because of its demeanour (since it can't actually, as a thing-in-itself, have one!) but because of the bizarre way humans have dropped notions of 'swamp' into this pocket of wetland. A wooden walkway has been built for photographers and bird lovers and photographs of the various species fade behind smeared glass. A kind of apology? Lately, I've been reading Simon Schama's book *Landscape and Memory* (interesting notions — at times — but with a coffee-table book approach to language usage), which I am also reviewing. I've also been looking at the Travitsky volume, *The Paradise of Women,* and re-reading *Finnegan's Wake.* It's funny re-reading a book which I once regarded as the 'ultimate'. It actually seems extremely 'amateurish', for want of a better word, to me now. Maybe this harks back to the 'truth' and 'context' issue I was hedging around. It's not that I mean it is intellectually trivial (far from it!) but rather that it works too much by files of association, via a pre-knowledge, almost an essentialist view of events and notions. It is a hybrid rather than something new. It's almost the manifesto for the death of modernism. I know this is taboo, but what the heck. Though I still love its 'music' and hear it when I say my 'prayers'. Oh, recall last year when I conjectured that L was visiting Swanbourne without me? Well, I'm pretty sure it's true. I've even been toying with a short story involving a German couple, a pervert and a psychopath ... Love and more ... I tell him I just go down for a dip. That I like the freedom. He rarely accompanies me but can't say much because we both walk around the house and back garden with nothing on. He says it feels great to be free. But doesn't like it in public. I say it doesn't bother me and he knows I like to swim and I like swimming nude best of all. So I go down to the beach and peel off my clothes and run down into the sea. I always run into the sea, though when I emerge I tend to take it slowly, almost loitering. I like to be looked at. I like looking at the other bodies. Sometimes I'm followed, sometimes I follow. I've been into the sandhills once and intend to go again. I didn't fuck that time but I might sometimes.

It was with a couple who were nothing special but seemed safe enough. I massaged her clitoris while he jacked off over my belly. I squeezed his balls while he did it. It was no big deal but it gave me a taste. That was a while ago and I don't remember that much. Just the basic details. They had German accents though not much was said. He had a small penis and she had a fat rump. Her tits were shaped like over-ripe pears. Maybe the ripeness had more to do with the colour than the shape. They were tanned but almost yellow, as if they resisted tanning no matter how hard their owner tried. There was something about them, and his penis as well, that suggested they weren't really part of their bodies. Afterward I ran down into the sea. People watch you. But lots do it. I know you have to be careful because sometimes the police go through on horses. There are signs. Young boys and not-so-young boys watch with binoculars. You see them glint in the sun. Sometimes I lie with my cunt facing the dunes and open my legs to let them zoom in. It's possible women are up there behind the glints but I doubt it. Women aren't that much into close-ups. Though I must admit to liking the ambience of bodies. A cock or a cunt just sidling past, breasts emerging lathered by the sea. The ritual that comes with the depleting ozone layer — the rubbing down of bodies with oil. There is something ancient in it.

Something orgiastic. *The beaches of Perth are renowned for their beauty. And cleanliness. No shit washed up from the sewers, no needles under the white sand. Drenched in sun with long lazy sunsets. Changing from yellow to magenta to red. Even the moon gives a tan. If you want gentle lapping waves of green water you can have them. Black reefs with surging swell, you can have them. Deep clear blue water, it's there as well. Once you've tasted it, once it has caressed your body, you'll be addicted. Even during the height of the summer season you'll always find a place to spread your towel. And the natives are friendly. If you want to walk your dog, there are places set aside. If you want to swim au naturel, no problem. There's regular pervert patrols so only those true-blue sun-lovers will occupy the piece of sand next to you and lap up the Mediterranean clime. And from Scarborough to Safety Bay there are first class facilities. Clean changerooms, places to grab a bite or cook your own meat, sink a cold beer, or let the kids loose. The beaches of Western Australia. One of the natural wonders of the world! Discover them for yourself!* Self. He asks if I believe there is anything beyond the Self. I answer: butterflies. He says that he is a poor man and does not understand these butterflies. He sarcastically asks me to explain. I tell him butterflies come in many shapes, sizes, and colours, but they are still butterflies. The dust on their wings is very sensitive. If disturbed, their flight is severely affected. B points out that if you lose a leg it is difficult to walk. B has made 300 taka from that 100 and will not return the loan. Okay. S says B will never change. B wants another 'loan'. I refuse. He looks for new friends and condemns me to damnation. Okay. Dusk. The sun, perfect golden disc, floats at the bottom of New Elephant Road. The rickshaws, multicoloured and polished and piloted by emaciated sari-clad riders, congregate at the base of the disc. The kaks screech over the flat concrete buildings — blank wrecks of a not-so-long-ago war. The stench settles. Girls make their way back from the factories — payday, 400 takas apiece. Had to renew my visa today. The Immigration Office — dusty rooms relying heavily on shafts of sunlight for atmosphere, wads of paper and files, printed safari suits, and officials with a penchant for bribes. S suggested I do The Beer Deal if I wanted an easy passage through the hideously corrupt process of visa renewal. Westerners are permitted to buy a few crates of beer each time they renew their visa. Then they flog it, via a middleman like S., to the black marketeers. In fact, you are almost impelled to buy crates of beer. The immigration people expect a few American dollars for the trouble of stamping your passport, for letting you stay and buy the beer. If you are not interested in buying beer, it's pretty hard to convince them to stamp your passport without a considerable hike in costs.

The Beer Deal is good for the economy they tell you. Have just visited a pharmacy and come back with a dozen mandrax, or 'mandies' as they are known in drug circles. Heard about their being available this morning from an American overlander who stayed in the hotel overnight. It would appear that Bangladesh is a dumping ground for pharmaceuticals banned from most other countries. Almost any chemical drug is sold without prescription over the counter. The pharmacist told me he prescribes mandrax for headaches. Got really scared last night. The shadows retreated into the walls and my chest felt like it was collapsing. Managed to get hold of ampoules of morphine. I've just shot one up. 25 takas apiece from the rickshaw men. Have been hacking up blood. Went to a doctor S recommended. It was an embassy doctor who refused to soil his hands dealing with poverty. He was educated in London. He told me this about five times. He told me I was wasting away to nothing. I asked him if he'd noticed anyone else in Dhaka having the same problem. Ate half-a-dozen mandies and set out for an X-ray. No protection, a line a mile long, a bombed-out building and some crazy dude zapping the hell out of his patients. I ran spinning and passed out. When I came to, a group of women were standing around me. I stood up and they quickly moved towards their houses. Women here rarely let you get close to them unless they are begging or hooking. Though it is different in the wealthier parts of the city. A few days ago I visited the English Language Library and talked comfortably with the woman behind the desk. There is a strange protocol to observe, stonings for social indiscretion are common. Dear Professor Schama, I am at present reviewing your volume *Landscape and Memory* for the *Australian Book Review*. This is something of an unusual project in that I approached the *ABR* to see if I could make 'use' of your observations in a discussion of the Australian landscape. The *ABR*'s mandate is limited to the publication of reviews of Australian books, or at least books by Australian authors. This is therefore something of an event. Now, to the point. I was wondering if over the next week or two you'd be interested in entering into a dialogue on these matters? That is, I could present you with an Australian model 'derived' from, or more accurately juxtaposed to, your lateral picaresque and you could respond, however you desire. From the point of view of the *ABR* review it is probably of little value in itself, but from a personal angle I am sure it would prove entirely fascinating. Furthermore, should the dialogue be successful I could easily find an Australian literary journal that would be willing to publish the results, should you be interested. Looking forward to your reply. Yours sincerely ... Cependant, je me sens moralement obligé de souligner pour vos lecteurs ma conviction, qui est aussi celle de la majorité de mes compatriotes, que la continuation des essais nucléaires est injuste. Bien sûr que les Australiens s'inquiètent à propos de la région Pacifique et de son environnement marin, mais il s'agit de beaucoup plus que cela. Il s'agit d'une vraie répulsion de ce qu'on considère comme un risque injustifié à propos de notre environnement mondial vulnérable. Bien qu'il y en ait ici-bas qui pensent que les Français devraient faire ces essais plutôt chez eux-mêmes, il y en a aussi comme moi qui préféreraient la simple cessation de tout essai nucléaire, quels qu'en soient l'endroit ou le pays responsable. Je vous serais obligé de bien vouloir publier ma lettre, car votre revue est très respectée parmi tous ceux qui aiment la littérature, soit en France ou ailleurs. Veuillez agréer l'expression de mes sentiments les plus distingués. Dear ... Have just got in after a long day. Have been working with my French translator, talking with people about an essay I've got coming up in *Westerly*, collecting my daughter and forgetting to go to the Fremantle Library to collect some information on something called 'The Time Ball' (I'm writing a piece on it). Tonight, ... and I are working on your book. Your very brilliant book. And this is what I'm contacting you about. We would like to convert to English/Australian spelling from the American, but what do you think? Please let me know asap. Oh, and that reminds me. Arnold has set his terms (re your book), and I have faxed him back with a couple of queries. It should be all sewn up shortly. He seems an interesting person, and I hope we will communicate often. Now, payment. I still owe you for *Poetry Journal*, which I haven't forgotten. And a contract will be posted next week with royalty details for the book. I excuse myself by saying that I've been waiting for my Fellowship money to arrive, and then you shall receive! This will be next week, so now, with confidence, I can assure you! We go to print on Monday. If you've got anything for the issue after this one, feel welcome to submit and I'll add payment to your cheque. If not, maybe you know of some brilliant student who's got a short piece on your work I could include. But no pressure, it's just that I'd like to include you in everything. Well, by way of signing off I thought I might include a paragraph of a letter I'm writing to a pantheist mate. He dwells on the East Coast and writes the night: I'm wondering if you'll be going out on the boat you mentioned tonight. Maybe you'll see that night heron on the old man mangrove tree again. It brings great joy to me that you also love and are mesmerised by this totemic and mysterious bird. It has haunted me from my childhood when my brother and I would explore Blue Gum Swamp and, late getting home, would chance upon one (sometimes even a group in a rookery) stirring with the waking evening. Now I watch them emerge from tea-tree roosting places on Booragoon lake, though it is always a subdued and hazy meeting. Though, in some ways this enriches the interaction, for me, if not for them! But then, they are incredibly 'aware' birds, and it probably has some deeply psychological effect on them as well. Maybe the experience I had recently down near the Swan River with the night heron that followed me in full daylight, displaying its wings, and swinging the tasselled feathers on the back of its neck, is proof of this? Well, looking forward to hearing from you. I'd like to post proofs to you next Monday by Xpress mail. I'll also include cover suggestions. If there is a colour image you particularly like please send it to me straight away. And then on to the next project! Lots of love, Pulped Factions 'I'm going through a transitional period ... ' Australian poetry in the last few decades has been notorious (at least in the minds of Australian critics and fiction writers) for being self-serving, fraught with factionalism, and plagued by a miasma of personality clashes. Furthermore, what actually constitutes an 'Australian poetry' has come into question. There are many fine writers here from various traditions, and writing in many languages other than English. These are as valid and as influential as those from the 'English Tradition'. It's interesting to consider how we as poets have been influenced by European, Chinese and other poetries in translation; or by American models. The poets of the '60s, '70s and '80s paved the way for the non-English tradition here. They've created a varied anthology to select from. It's almost valid now to write 'Language Poetry', or work as a concrete poet, or even incorporate other media, and, of course, 'performance poetry' has a strong following at reading venues across the country. Pi O's massive *24 Hours* will be a testament to years on the reading scene. I am sceptical about talking of movements in Australian poetry. So many divisions have been artificially applied, or retrospectively qualified. There is no equivalent to the Futurists, or the Surrealists, and so on, though all European (and American) movements have their followers and subgroups here. Recently I wrote a brief article on Language Poetry, stating that it was an American movement that could not really be equated with the work of those Australian poets who are influenced by, or use, its techniques. Some Australian avant-garde-identified poets wrote to me saying they'd been 'doing it' for years. His aim is not so much to colonise our space but to neutralise it. To set up buffer zones between his own turf and the outside. Create spheres of influence. Vacant flats become satellites which, while independent of him, are controlled through an aggressive foreign policy. He aims for a wall of science. His strategy is to concentrate on one flat at a time. Feigning friendship with his other neighbours so as to maximise his energies for the attack on his primary target. Disinformation, espionage and aggressive assaults, followed by rapid withdrawals, are his tactics. As a child, he sat on fences and watched his neighbours swimming in their pool. He watched the eldest child sit aside and read books. He watched the eldest child make things in the backyard. He knew 'Four Eyes' didn't like the pool because it was full of germs. He took Four Eyes into the space between the house and the fence to show him a 'thing': he pushed their penises together and said that they'd now had a 'root'. He enjoyed watching them clean up after car accidents. He took Twisties along to snack on, and once had his photo taken doing a wheelie next to the tarped severed head of a motorbike rider. The corner he lived on was a Mecca for accidents. He took his vomit to school and showed it during show and tell, he liked watching cars run over dog shit. He dug little holes and shat in them. He investigated his own faeces with a stick and felt its warmth, watching the steam rise from it on a cold morning. He forced his little sister to show the boys next door her private parts for a dollar and then pushed a stick with crêpe paper into her. He said for another dollar they could smell the stick, but they went home feeling sick. They never talked to her again but felt impelled to talk to him. They heard that the sister wet the bed until she was thirteen. But that was years later. Their mother called him The Ghoul. She said his mother was nice but his father was an authoritarian pig. They were brought up by their mother and her friend. A father was a distant concept. It meant loss, it meant not being able to decide things for yourself. 'Theology is very strict on the following point: there are no werewolves and human beings cannot become animal.' The wolfgirls howled at the moon at Vassar and out of society were propelled, the moon spitting a colleague of Daddy's out over the BwO's great emptiness: skinned alive like a botched phantasy ... my mother won't let me share the place at Vassar my mother won't get out of my face at home she even reads the diary she gave me for my birthday. It's got a map of America on the cover. I want to be a wolfgirl at Vassar and cloak my body in hair and howl at the moon with my sisters. He knew that Freud knew nothing about wolves, or anuses for that matter. The Wolf-Man knew that Freud would soon declare him cured, but that it was not at all the case and his treatment would continue for all eternity under Brunswick, Lacan, Leclaire ... this art of molecular ... reverting to

... Castration with a capital C ... Proposal re 'The Interpretation Of Artworks In The Claisebrook Valley Pedestrian System' for The East Perth Redevelopment Authority: I believe that the 'inscriptions' used to complement the artworks and design of the Claisebrook Valley Pedestrian System should be 'multifunctional'. In a sense they should work like two-way mirrors — meaning one thing as one approaches the city, another as one walks away, toward the river. For example, approaching the freneticism of the city, the language should have a soothing effect, such that one may enter the metropolis 'unburdened'. Enter it hypocritically! The veneration of 'Art' and 'Culture' — besides leading many women into boring, passive activity that distracts from more important and rewarding activities, from cultivating active abilities, and leads to the constant intrusion of our sensibilities of pompous dissertations on the deep beauty of this and that turd. This allows the 'artist' to be set up as one possessing superior feelings, perceptions, insights and judgements, thereby undermining the faith of insecure women in the value and validity of their own feelings, perceptions, insights and judgements. She did not say this but knew it to be so. Like the women who could play Beethoven, she focussed on the blank space of absolute knowledge. He dragged himself slowly through the text, slouched over the couch, reading in a poor light. In the city of Kaks I ate mandrax for breakfast and took a vertiginous walk to another pharmacy and bought more mandrax and a bottle of dexedrine. Dexies. And a few hypodermics, and searched out morphine which I scored in an army camp. I'm addicted to prayer times. The wailing. The Escapee has found a boy. They sleep in the bed opposite mine. I smoke hash, hit morphine. Drop dexedrine to get myself moving. It is curfew and I cannot escape. I'd like to think they look beautiful but can't. I crush dexedrine tablets and snort them. I am getting paranoid. I know this. Can't settle down. It is near 12am and The Escapee has not yet returned from an 'outing' with one of the hotel boys. Yesterday he went in search of a mystic. Today he slept with B. They are conspiring against me. It's because of M., I know this. A rickshaw driver took me to the ruins of some palace or other. He rode past a number of 'high class' hookers and was surprised when I told him I was only interested in morphine. The power struggles and intrigues, double-dealing and backbiting ... the machinations of the Red Oasis Hotel and its satellites. That embassy doctor had said that I must stop using my imagination, that if I wish to write I should simply describe what I see. One of the hotel boys ate a few mandrax tonight and appears to have gone into a coma. It's really scary. He's never had drugs before and we can't work out how much he's taken. Curfew. The effects of the mandies are wearing off. I tell him he is lucky. These things can kill you. Stop your heart. Pow. Just like that. He mentions visions but I tell him he was only dreaming. Dawn, and I watch the mist roll in from the river, over the flat roofs of Dhaka. The kaks cluster about the windows. Kaks are crow-like birds that feed on rotting corpses, forage amongst the rubbish and excrement of the streets. Their caw is deadly. Not lost today. B is going to vote for the President because he goes out into the villages and has good business sense. Had an argument with The Escapee. He ran off in search of peth. I prefer morphine au naturel. This accords with the notion of water (and associated sounds) as a calming effect. Conversely, as one approaches the river there is a desire to leave the intensities and 'rush' of the business district behind, but, at the same time, create a lively sense of 'recreation' — pace linked with calm, as opposed to calm linked with pace, if you like. The same inscriptions, skilfully written, could achieve this result. I have identified six areas I would approach in writing the desired texts. They deal with reclamation of scape and history, the stillness (oasis) of the place in the lively location, incursion and resurrection, flow, the journey (the picaresque, the linking of disparate things by a common thread — water), and the rejuvenating aspects of art. Below is a brief outline. 'The Phantom Logic of Flow' 1. The motion of 'unseen' water flowing into the heart, pumped into the body of the river. Water, the blood of the soil. The irony of secure footholds, feet firmly on the ground but ... the transience of settlement, those tent-camps in the gold rush days, moving up river, against the flow. 'A legacy of pipes, connections and buildings ... ': the flow, the links. 2. Signifiers. Sculpture as a natural extension of nature. As elemental forces shape the land so the sculptor shapes an environment. When the two interact, a 'monumental' artform is created. In the same way that the tortoise shells sink into the 'earth', the project as a whole has a feel of 'fringe' about it — ie. a place where the natural and urban environments interact. 3. 'Neighbourliness & tolerance': as an integrated 'urban scheme', it is essential that the residents feel part of the landscape. They are, in a sense, the living sculpture of the project. Their 'backyard' is open to all, but is still their backyard. Visitors, pedestrians, etc. should feel as if they have been welcomed into a comfortable, relaxing, though vibrant riverside garden/s. An 'All for one and one for all' kind of philosophy. 4. Aboriginalities. A quote from a Jack Davis play. A line or two from an oral history. The water still flows beneath the surface. The blood-lines intact. 5. Wetlands. The migratory passage of birds. The simple lyrics of flight. The return flight bringing greater 'riches'. The old lake system concentrated. 6. Local history as a magnifying glass to the future. The smallest shop, the largest factory, the cemetery and old picnic spots, all are part of a microcosm that points to the social interaction of humans. What he doesn't know, even if he thinks it so, is that he can't. It's ironical that our most witty poet is in fact our most confessional. It's just that he is so good with language that we don't label him with this pejorative, or if we do we can't quite believe it ourselves. The thing about wit is timing, as Forbes says in 'thin ice', 'I think our sense of timing's/the most important thing/O'Hara taught us?/don't you Ken?' But this is when Forbes is talking to one of his mates and not when his introspective self is witticising its way out of a love sickness. The timing's a little different then. I remember Forbes once being incredulous at a comment that his Odes marked the end of a tradition, that he was writing the epitaph of dedicatory poetry. He argued that he was trying to revive the ode. Here is the key to Forbes' 'newness'. He is in fact a traditional poet, in the clichéd sense of the word, but one who is familiar with the language of his time ... Sure, he hasn't picked up Generation X's speech, but that doesn't stop him reflecting on it through his own. But Forbes is also someone who wants to survive as long as he can, and to this end he wants to remain flexible. He knows that the market wants at least to perceive change in his voice. It wants something new. In lines like these from 'Scottische' (another objective correlative poem) he seems both freer and, in a sense, more wantonly lyrical: grief is a house/with an open fire,/warm bed, swept floor/& up to date magazines —/you're terrific, you're great/you run in the mornings ... The familiar Forbes come-back, or contrary, is there after this, but with a difference: 'not when I see/how much I'm the same'. This is a poem where instead of studying the cultural iconography and looking for the frustrated love poem underneath, we read the forlorn love poem and look for 'political' or cultural (or anti-cultural) underneath. L. reckons that she had her first abortion when she was fifteen. Forbes is aware that no matter how much you poke a stick at society you're directed by its rules, that there is such a thing as a 'permanent record'. 'Scottische' is an example of an 'inverted' Forbes poem, a technique I'd guess we are going to see a lot more of. On the other hand, a poem like 'The Numbers', from *Stalin's Holidays*, makes for an interesting aside, as it's one in which the persona is both recognisably 'Forbes' and very obviously not Forbes himself. It's not a great poem, and this is probably why. But it is 'recognisable'. There's that jar of marbles again, and the television as a complicit means of removal. Unfortunately a poem like this is taken by people as *being* Forbes, despite the obvious use of persona. It's like the poem that hides within it a 'real' Forbes poem but doesn't. I mean those poems in which it's not the 'sunshine and girls' that we think about but rather the extraneous nature of such icon-making. Apparently the pink sunsets are a result of ash in the upper atmosphere. It's like there's a blanket of perfumed poison hovering over us. Forbes once said that 'Sunshine is not weather' (and that Sydney doesn't have weather while Melbourne has; but I'm digressing!). It's a little as if the wonders of America are like sunshine. That is, we can't take them for real. But this doesn't mean they're not good. Sure, Forbes will borrow your money, but part of him will always want to pay it back. This is not the smart part. The poem 'Stalin's Holidays' itself is also a case in point. But it is far more evasive than 'The Numbers' and is a better poem for that: Stalin's Holidays/The quick brown fox jumps over the lazy dog./Juniper berries bloom in the heat. My heart!/'Bottoms up, Comrade.' The nicotine-stained/fingers of our latest defector shake as they/reach for Sholokhov's *Lenin* — the veranda is/littered with copies — no, commies, the ones/in comics like 'Battle Action' or 'Sgt Fury/& His Howling Commandos'. Does form follow/function?

Well, after lunch we hear a speech./It's Stephen Fitzgerald back from 'Red' China./Then, you hear a postie whistle. I hear, without/understanding, two members of Wolverhampton/Wanderers pissed out of their brains, trying/to talk Russian. Try reading your telegram —/'mes vacances sont finies: Stalin'. But we don't/speak French or play soccer in Australia, our/vocabulary and games are lazier by far. Back/in the USSR, we don't know how lucky we are. This is one of those poems that comes in for the limp 'surrealist' treatment. But it is a poem about the difference between language and speech, between format and colloquial speech. Strangely enough, though it is driven by its Cold War imperatives, it's got little to do with concepts of 'freedom', or democracy versus totalitarianism, or even about lines of cultural demarcation. That where several inmates are in one and the same house, and any person in that house happens to be infected, no other person or family of such house shall be suffered to remove him or themselves without a certificate from the examiners of health of that parish; or in default thereof, the house whither he or they so remove shall be shut up as case of visitation. I don't like the old man in number four. He's quiet, not like the weirdos in number three. But he's got a cat. Cats disgust me. Sometimes it comes to my door. I spray it with mace. (Fleas like me.) It is a courier of disease and vermin. It is a poem about cultural self-evaluation — the necessity to have a comparative with which to define the virtues or inadequacies of one's own society. Once again, we see the removed persona, but this is Forbes' ars poetica (and a much better poem than that which bears this expression as its title), it is as much about his own aesthetics as cultural and political plays. This project not only reflects on East Perth and its unique character, but may be used as a pointer for locality-identification in all urban-scapes. A 'new model' that has been created through the lens of the past. A sense of continuity must be maintained in all inscriptions, but with a steady eye to the future. Note: The above points are brief outlines. Factors such as the influence of light, the effects on the scarp of it being night or day, vegetation, the characteristics of homes and business properties, etc. would all have to find a place in the inscriptions. All of the above would flow into each other, there would be no sense of isolation or separation (though humour can easily be achieved by 'lightly' playing these factors off against each other). Kept short, pithy and rhythmical, these inscriptions would remain with the reader a long time after physically leaving the 'place' ... Let us compare this hypothesis as a whole with Clausewitz's formula: War is the continuation of politics by other means. I'm not bullshitting you! This boundary line was fifty metres closer to Jarrahdale a month ago. The Government has appropriated forest outside the original boundaries. I've got friends in the Department of Conservation and Land Management who reckon they're always moving markers and logging when they shouldn't. One of them has taken videos, kept a notebook of dates and details ... As we know, this formula is itself extracted from a theoretical and practical, historic and transhistoric, aggregate whose parts are interconnected. (1) There is a pure concept of war as absolute, unconditioned war, an Idea not given in experience (bring down or 'upset' the enemy, who seemed to have no other determination, with no political, economic, or social considerations entering in.) ... in the proliferation of eyes by the multiplication of insignia/of borders in societies reduced to military enterprise/territorialised humbly and slowly abstracting larger movements/as large bellied men move quantified pieces on a simulation board on a muggy afternoon in Geraldton. The piercing thrusts of the sappers, the logistical follow-ups as nomads tribe the *Pax Mongolica*: 'War is the continuation of politics by other means': corellas are rare in these parts but there's a white feather with a dusting of sulphur on the dresser, a corrupted sign of cowardice in *L'Idea del Teatro*, those speeches in drawers of ... But that doesn't make this something new; rather something imitative. The same applies to those writers who call for a return to 'poems with meaning', to admiring and imitating the traditional canon. It's fine, but it doesn't amount to being a group or movement. Such calls have been heard since 'day one'. This all shows a healthy, desirable debate about what constitutes a poem, what meaning poetry has in our time. One could doubtless list groupings of poets with common interests, create some kind of map of the Australian poetry-scape that would indicate directions in contemporary poetic thought and response to the Australian condition. Yet it's usually those poets who manage to lift themselves outside of these groupings, or define groupings through attracting imitators, who become those voices best identified with the generative side of the age. They possess a desire to explore language and notions of meaning outside the acceptable. Poets like John Tranter, John Forbes, Gig Ryan and Robert Adamson, who in many ways exemplify a whole period of poetry, have really established their own voices that have made them enduring poets. The same can be said of J S Harry, Jennifer Maiden and John A Scott. All inventive, 'hybridised voices', with a consciousness of the canon, but a desire to reinvent it. It's not by chance I group these poets together. They are of the era of factionalism (with Ryan being on the cusp) in Aus Poetry. Edwin Fischer in

Beethoven's Pianoforte Sonatas writes: All these questions of grammar were answered for me by an experience I had when I was on a concert tour in the South. I was in a small town and wanted to practise before my concert. Looking for an instrument, I was given the name of the grocer. I called on him and was shown into a pleasant room where a small girl about fourteen years old opened a grand piano for me to practise on. As she leant against the piano listening, but not looking at me, I asked her to play me something. Without a word she sat down and played Op. 27, No. 1, with a naturalness, gentleness, equanimity and sadness that suggested that this was a true expression of some hidden suffering. She knew nothing about 'subjects on the upbeat' or the metronome marks of various editors, but inside her there beat the heart of Beethoven who composed this sonata. Deeply moved by her playing, I found the solutions to my problems and consequently appropriated the disappointments and oppressions of childhood, approaching youth and financial hardship. She taught piano after he'd gone North, trying to instil her love for the instrument into the neighbourhood children. They wanted to play rock, so she taught them rock tunes. Sometimes they spent the lesson money before they got to her place. His wife realised that they were treading familiar territory and it bothered her. The problem of writing the same experiences wouldn't go away. He'd say the more angles on the one event would be interesting, that it would highlight the reflection. All she could hear were the sounds of Op. 27, No. 1, and she wanted to get away from him. She'd determined a chunk of the market and wasn't going to let it be pilfered by a cultural ghoul. Their daughter was singing in a voice that was shrill, grating. 'Raindrops keep falling on my head ... ' and she wondered who owned the copyright to that song. And she wondered why he liked her to lick his arsehole, and penetrate it with objects. She'd read in the paper a couple of years ago about people having to have bottles, lumps of wood, rubber balls and concrete removed from their rectums in hospital emergency wards. She considered how he always wiped the toilet seat, even if he'd been the last one to use it, how he always thought one of the hotplates and the stove would have been left on, after they'd locked up and got two blocks away. From the original Woldendorp vision of informing and giving value to the artist in their particular place, to make it part of process, the project seems to have fallen victim to the greater forces of the Market and a particular political 'vision' of how art should be represented. Patriarchal in their structure, the book and exhibition subvert the presence of women as predictably hermetic, idiosyncratic, or bright (Dombrovska Larsen!). An exhibition like this should be curated by men and women. Like apportioning blame in the Birnie murder cases. The way *he* was actually responsible, but *she* aided and abetted. What pleasure was derived by each was up for questioning. She relied on him, it was claimed. Catherine was a smack junkie, Dave a sex junkie. He'd met both of them and it seemed they were entirely reliant on each other. Like the guy sitting opposite you in the restaurant who's eyeing off your food and ignoring the food on his own plate. He reaches across with a fork and stabs a piece of broccoli. And again. Eventually he consumes every morsel as you wonder about the filthy dish-washing water. He wonders how much it's a matter of the machine processing different territories of utility. Like *HQ* magazine. The 'slick' and fast chattiness of once- (When?) forbidden subjects: The Woody Allen sperm doesn't know how lucky he was to get a run, even back then. In the 1990s, he might have been in worse shape (literally) or not there at all. Today there are fewer sperm and more abnormal sperm at the starting line ... as the smell of tempeh wafts through his papers. He writes this kind of shit about me. I don't think this way. And he says it's nothing to do with me really, a kind of selective appropriation, like attaching the superfluous to the meaningful — that being me as a set of instinctive REACTIONS to his meaningful reason. Maybe it all depends on how well your books sell. How many grants you've had. It's one of those things that's not actually a question as a statement of potential abuse. It's this newfound prestige within the industry and among the public that Tarantino has used to secure the release of Brian De Palma's *Blow Out* (1981), which failed on its initial commercial release. He thinks (rightly) that it contains one of John Travolta's best performances, but it's also *his* kind of hybrid film. *Blow Out* drew on Antonioni's *Blow Up* (1966), made three years after he was born, and as his mother played tennis he wandered over to the bathtub next to the garden shed at Bateman's farm, climbed up on some bricks, and plunged into the liquid manure. The pine trees quivered with his shrieks, his mother's tennis whites ruined. The river then was cleaner, and occasionally bronze whaler sharks found their way up to Deep Water Point. Even three years later, as the sixties approached their 'end', swimming lessons at the Point were occasionally interrupted by the call of 'Shark!' There was a lot more vegetation around the Bull Creek, the watery border of Bateman's and suburbia ... and Coppola's *The Conversation* (1974) which also drew on *Blow Up* ... It would be assumed, to counter this, I'd place Les Murray, Geoffrey Lehmann, Rosemary Dobson, Robert Gray, and possibly Kevin Hart on the 'other side of the fence' — those poets who apparently represent a more lyrical, meditative ('religious'?), conservative ('traditional'?) poetics. Perhaps some of the Deleuze and Guattari passages could be dispensed with altogether, or possibly replaced by a discussion of Bakhtin, or any number of other writers on heteroglossia. In between we'd have Gwen Harwood. Peter Porter forms a 'school' of his own (European, Augustan, and 'urban-e'), while Dorothy Hewett exists outside all of these, though obviously associated with the new romantic traditions of Adamson and his 'followers'. Yes, it's a nice picture of the fruit bowl. But how do you think Barbie sees it from over there? She's looking at it from a different angle, isn't she? So it won't look the same as you see it. And what about Sailor-doll and Cindy-doll? They're all sitting in different places and see the fruit bowl in different ways. The point is, I don't think even these contrived groupings are relevant now. One can admire any particular association of poets one desires without having to be an 'adherent'. There seems to be a need, as part of creating a literary identity, to create lines of influence in a nation's literature. The influence of anthologies on the shape of Australian poetry has of course been significant. Shapcott's *Australian Poetry Now* redefined what was 'allowable' in anthologies. Experimental and vibrant, it welcomed many new readers and practitioners. It's really a bowl full of fruit. A glass bowl full of fresh fruit. You can see the fruit through the glass. The glass keeps the fruit in place. Yes, the banana is a little mushy. Yes, it will still be a rotten banana no matter which way you look at it. Likewise Kate Jennings' *Mother I'm Rooted*; despite its containing much that would also rate poorly on the scale of 'literary' poetry, it redefined what was readable as poetry, showed that there existed many voices and subject matters outside the patriarchal 'tradition'. Anthologies are of course a regular, expected part of the poetic landscape, with many variations on the canon (and against the canon) out or coming out at any one time. Though from Cindy's point of view it may seem that the banana is okay as only the top is showing. There's a grapefruit in the way. Yes, there is, you walk around and sit behind Cindy and tell me what you see. Of interest in recent years have been the dichotomies between the clear expression of the Lehmann/Gray volumes and the post-modernist touches of Tranter/Mead, both worthy of particular attention, and influential in schools. It's great to see more women's writing in general anthologies, though a natural level of inclusion is still to come: there's still a sense of obligation or tokenism in contents pages. I was asked to write a story on photography and the supernatural and I was fucken nine months pregnant and just not up to it, so I passed it on to him and he wrote about photographing a fucking plinth that wasn't there, but WAS on the print and fucken made such an impression he had a book contract in a week. He told them it wasn't fiction, but an essay. A fucken commentary on appropriation and the investment of sci-fi in popular culture. The trash of illusion. And they bought it. Tarantino's films offer a similar mix of art cinema and full-on genre film-making. Although initially he might seem to be the latest version of David Lynch, trotting out a cool, stylised *petit guignol* of slapstick and slaughter (remember the ear at the start of *Blue Velvet* ... of course you're hip enough, as a reader of this kind of publication, to be au fait with the frustration of watching him, on his knees, ear pressed to the floor, listening to what's going on down below. When I'm not here, he sleeps by the vents. Sometimes he rubs his body with oil and dribbles into the eye of his penis. I don't say anything. He tells me that he hung horseshoe magnets from his penis when he was a child, and sniffed his next door neighbour's cunt after school every day for years. That sometimes she gave him little perfume bottles filled with her 'wee' which he'd drink. When he's got his kids he's always at them about being clean and not talking to boys and not undressing in front of each other. But I'm sure he's safe with them. He avoids them. He can't have them here without me, he doesn't feel it's right. At school one day he'd told a class of kids that his best friend was a robot and that (by pushing his nose) only he could *turn him on*. He was branded *poof* from that day and beaten mercilessly. A list of goals. From A.A. days. What he'd achieved and failed to achieve. As music drifts up through the vents. Dance music. James Brown is dead. It was at La Coste, rather than at Arceuil or Marseilles, that Sade's sexual ambitions were most nearly realised. Behind the menacing walls of the chateau, out of sight and earshot, the victims of his passion were to endure all that he chose to inflict upon them. Nothing was to be denied him. As Sade himself remarked, in his one observation which reached the level of a proverb, Every man is a tyrant when he fornicates. His own tyranny was to be felt by his harem before, during and after the acts by which he contributed to his pleasure. That he said, I do not want to investigate or contribute to popular culture, that post-60s appropriation of social flows, but rather preside over its destruction — nothing more, nothing less. The male, having a very limited range of feelings and, consequently, very limited perceptions, insights and judgements, needs the 'artist' to guide him, to tell him what life is all about. A degenerate can only produce 'degenerate' art. It is inherently evil, it is the advertising agency of Vogued Capitalism. Popular (designed for mass audience), Transient (short term solution), Expendable (easily forgotten) ... that we are all depraved, that it's been one long, inevitable plunge into attributing quotes to those who didn't make them ... Low Cost, Mass-Produced, Young (aimed at Youth), Witty, Sexy, Gimmicky, Glamorous, Big Business ... He had contrived the situation with such care, the setting was perfect and the girls willing, that it seemed impossible that the planned sexual melodrama could turn suddenly into an unpredicted burlesque. But the gloating relish of the regulars at the Globe prodded him on, led him to take up the bucket and scrub the toilets against the most intense and deep revulsion. And clearing blockages, he thrust his hand down into the bowl, and around up into the elbow, peeling away the paper and faeces, removing a syringe, watching the blood pour from his punctured thumb. And he didn't flinch while the guy with the stutter masturbated himself behind him, nor turn around when the warm drops of ejaculatory discharge landed on his exposed back. He scrubbed, and scrubbed. Three bottles of sherry a day, and total dedication to his task. Sometimes she visited him there, and thought how far the mighty had fallen. That the Red Cross gave him vegetables which he ate raw, that poets visited him and gave him Hopi talismans, that street kids drove him from his room to the park and vomited over his bed, that he stared at a television that showed nothing but static, that he wouldn't sleep with her because he was sure the infection had got him, that he pissed in sherry bottles because it was a long walk to the toilet late at night, that he occasionally drank from these very same bottles and didn't flinch, just putting them aside and searching out the genuine product ... But the gloating relish of the cruel libertines in *The 120 Days of Sodom* was not destined to survive the hazards of everyday living. Nanon became pregnant, swearing that it was her husband who was responsible, though her husband might look angrily at Sade. And then, unthinkable in any well-organised novel of debauchery and torture, one of the girls of the harem ran off. He heard her voice resounding through the fetid air: Sex is the refuge of the mindless. Become clandestine, make rhizomes everywhere, for the wonder of nonhuman life to be created. Face it, my love, you have finally become a probe-head Year zen year omega, year w ... Must we leave it at that, three states, and no more: primitive heads, Christ-face, and probe heads as quote marks are the territorialisation of speech, as if words are owned by the utterer, that without licensing fees and recognition, the to-be-born child should be aborted because it displays tendencies and possesses features that are, or have been, in use? senseless stories, idle tales, Dreams, whimsies and no more. Our sphere of action is life's happiness,

And he who thinks beyond thinks like an ass. Or having to pay his bloody book fines at the University library. *Annotations to Finnegan's bloody Wake*. He'd spent two days going through it with a fine-toothed comb looking for every reference to Australia, pasting them together, and then presenting it as a paper entitled 'Australia and the Mapping of *Finnegan's Wake*'. 'You forget all that a skilled vivisector can do.' In some ways, ladies and gentleman, it was H G Wells' book that led me to think about veganism. The girl above me never says anything. Sometimes I'm aching to speak to her but she avoids me. She leaves every morning at eight and is back at four. She might be a school teacher, though a new one. She couldn't be more than twenty-two or -three. She dresses conservative and plays the flute. Very quietly though, sometimes I hear her. I know she's playing it from the mistakes. She must be learning. Sometimes I hear *Greensleeves*. He's out scoring and I'm reading *HQ* magazine. One of the 'dance girls' from number two gave it to me. She reckons someone from number three gave it to her, but she was a bit vague about it. I got the feeling that she might have found it in their recycling bin because I see lots of magazines in their bin. They say you shouldn't recycle glossy magazines. Anyway, there's this advert that I've got stuck on. It's got Lucifer and his fire. I like it because it says: 'Who's for a Drambuie on ice? Hey, just kidding!' You've got to laugh at these things, especially when you've got a little bastard of a son who'll probably end up with a job in Hell. There's a recipe for *biscotti* with chocolate and black pepper. I might make some and offer them to the girl upstairs, that might break ... the ice: These biscuits can be stored for weeks in a jar. They are good with cheese, particularly soft blue cheese. Like the way he told them all they were in his book and they read it and found themselves despite the fact he was bullshitting them. That's the sort of person he is. And he laughs so damned quietly about it. As if it's just the way it is, and he's being impelled by the causality of it all to do such fucking abusive things. It's a kind of hubris, and he'll end up with me gone and the Furies at his door. 2.5 cups plain flour with 1 tsp baking powder, 2 tbsp cocoa, sifted, 1.5 cups caster sugar, 4 eggs, 1 cup almonds, toasted in the oven, 1.5 tsp coarsely ground black pepper. Sift together the flour and cocoa, sugar and eggs. (If you need to add a little water, use sparingly.) Chop the almonds roughly. On a floured board, incorporate the almonds and pepper into the dough. This recipe is about making things fit together that normally don't, or 'shouldn't' according to popular belief. He's been clinically dead twice and he's still kicking. The art of food preparation. A foodie and a junkie. The true artist is every self-confident, healthy female, and in a female society the only Art, the only Culture, will be conceited, kookie, funky females grooving on each other and on everything else in the universe. I tell him this but he doesn't hear. He likes tie-dye and op art. Scummy bastard. Tells me there's just an absolute awareness of nothing. That's it. As if you are entirely awake but there's nothing to be seen and no one to hear you. As if there's only you and your conscience. He *tries*. He's afraid of his conscience. He wants to give it up. Divide the dough into three pieces and roll into 'baguettes'. Bake in a moderate oven (180° C) for about 20 minutes. Allow to cool enough to cut into 0.75cm slices. Lay the slices on a baking tray. Lower the oven to 120° C and dry out for a further 20–30 minutes. The 'academy' still needs to broaden its reading outside the inherited, patriarchal way of seeing that comes with English Lit, an ostensibly male tradition. Doll Position 1: *The Oxford Book of Australian Women's Verse* (Ed. Susan Lever) will be a welcome addition to *The Penguin Book of Australian Women Poets* (Ed. Kate Llewellyn and Susan Hampton). Doll Position 2: Aboriginal poets too are inventing almost a new language to communicate between cultures: Lionel Fogarty, for instance. His *New and Selected* was recently awarded the inaugural Poetry Book Club Award for best volume of poetry in the quarter: much deserved. I met him when we were both on a panel at last year's Melbourne Writers' Festival, and he was mercurial. His influences are many, but he is entirely unique. He will influence many in turn. Doll Position 3: Then there's the east-west state dichotomy. Many poets here complain of this schism. There's undeniably a belief in Sydney and Melbourne that those outside are poor country cousins, but it's something of the old English-Australian cultural cringe to let it affect the way you work; I feel it's the responsibility of the writer to overcome this. And the publisher: Fremantle Arts Centre Press, for example, has placed many WA writers on the national stage and helped bridge this 'factional' gap. And the Five Islands Press New Poets series is bridging all sorts of gaps: cultural, social, gender, and regional. Child Seated Here: Perhaps the growth of pluralism in Australian poetry means that it is successfully negotiating its 'transitional period', that personality-based factionalism is a thing of the past. Cambridge Conference on Aesthetics: A Report. I trod in dog shit this morning. Foul stuff. There was a chewed-up condom in it. I can still smell it, despite scrubbing my shoes. It's the sort of smell that never leaves. Processed dead animals plus rubber and a squirt of human sperm. Stand up come closer the spaces between closer what do you want I don't know Don't move Don't look at me (suck you) you like that? You like that. Don't touch me or I'll kill you Knife cocked up ... like 20s in fifty shlock takes him on the couch ... Knock don't say anything or he'll kill you KNOCK KNOCK Frank Hello baby SHUTUP it's Daddy youshithead where's my bourbon don't you fucken remember anything behind him the cone of light spread your legs (now it's dark) wider now show it to me drinks twists head and hand swirls don't you fucken look at me Inhales eclipsed by her head alters his voice Mummy mummy mummy bubby wants to fuck hits her in face don't you fucken look at me inhales ... baby wants blue velvet inserts in mouth throws to ground scissors ... daddy's come home cloth in mouth rams hand fucks bash don't you fucking look at me. Yes, I've seen them both down there. And I've seen her on her own. Once you see them, you own them for good. They become part of the big picture. Their little story is only one chapter: KNOCK KNOCK bubby wants either of us to admit to being paranoid. And we were! What if we were seen? What if? I probably wanted it a lot more than her. Neither of us are anything to look at but I insisted that it didn't matter down there. How do you know? she asked. I went once when I was young and it'll be the same now. Bodies are the same regardless of the era. Basically. We decided to go early when it was less crowded. And there was less chance of skin cancer, we assured each other. Driving down I suggested that we put on accents to disguise ourselves. This made her much more comfortable and we loosened up, imitating French, Italian and German accents. After years of *Hogan's Heroes* re-runs we decided German was easiest. There was a moment when it nearly came unstuck however, when I was imitating Klink and she suddenly recalled that the guy who played Hogan had been murdered while involved in some sexual perversion. I quickly swung the conversation to the therapeutic value of the sea, how it would cleanse our bodies. When she next spoke it was with a German accent so I knew it would be all right. *The beaches of Perth are renowned for their beauty. And cleanliness. No shit washed up from the sewers, no needles under the white sand. Drenched in sun with long lazy sunsets. Changing from yellow to magenta to red. Even the moon gives a tan. If you want gentle lapping waves of green water you can have them. Black reefs with surging swell, you can have them. Deep clear blue water, it's there as well. Once you've tasted it, once it has caressed your body, you'll be addicted. Even during the height of the summer season you'll always find a place to spread your towel. And the natives are friendly. If you want to walk your dog, there are places set aside. If you want to swim au naturel, no problem. There's regular pervert patrols so only those true-blue sun-lovers will occupy the piece of sand next to you and lap up the Mediterranean clime. And from Scarborough to*

Safety Bay there are first class facilities. Clean changerooms, places to grab a bite or cook your own meat, sink a cold beer, or let the kids loose. The beaches of Western Australia. One of the natural wonders of the world! Discover them for yourself! In *troubador* we find two poems of relevance: 'Lessons For Young Poets' and 'Ode To Karl Marx'. 'Lessons for Young Poets' reminds me a little of Vladimir Mayakovsky's 'How are Verses Made?' There's a link despite the differences in tone if only in that Forbes knows that what Mayakovsky says is true, 'A poet regards every meeting, every signpost, every event in whatever circumstances simply as material to be shaped into words.' It's funny, the interior tone of Forbes suggests he'd give up poetry for love. But then he knows love *and* political freedom are unobtainable *complet*, so, poetry has its inedible cake ... Ode to Karl Marx/Old father of the horrible bride whose/wedding cake has finally collapsed, you/spoke the truth that doesn't set us free — /it's like a lever made of words no one's/learnt to operate. So the machine it once/connected just accelerates & each new/rap dance video's a perfect image of this,/bodies going faster and faster but dancing/on the spot. At the moment tho' this set up/works for me, being paid to sit & write &/smoke, thumbing through Adorno like *New Idea*/on a cold working day in Ballarat, where/adult unemployment is 22% & all your grand/schemata of intricate cause & effect/work out like this: take a muscle car &/wire its accelerator to the floor, take out/the brakes, the gears the steering wheel/& let it rip. The dumbest tattooed hoon/in Ug boots — mortal diamond hanging round the Mall — /knows what happens next. It's fun unless/you're strapped inside the car. I'm not/but the dummies we use for testing are. The obvious problem here is that the poet separates himself from the masses, but this is playing the expected role of satirist or social commentator. By his position as an inside outsider he is 'allowed' to observe, though of courser the irony indicates he's as much a victim as the 'dummies we use for testing are.' Forbes is a metaphysician and not an Augustan, and definitely not a Symbolist! Working on the theorem reductio ad absurdum, Forbes takes the serious and turns it into the ridiculous. But the component parts of society are absurd. To be as the dumb hoons or the poet himself is not to prevent the crash, but if you're not the victim should you really care? Irony dictates we should, but then, that's moralising ... and aesthetics would have us interested in the results of the crash ... Talking of the difference between French and English poetry Michael Hamburger in *The Truth of Poetry* refers to Yves Bonnefoy: Bonnefoy sums them up when he points out that English poetry arises from tension between multiple appearances and the desire to discover essences. He quotes Coleridge's remark: 'Beautiful is that in which the many still seen as many becomes one.' With John Donne in mind, Bonnefoy writes: 'People often repeat that English poetry "begins with a flea and ends with God." To that I reply that French poetry reverses the process, beginning with God, when it can, to end with love of no matter what.' The poetry of Forbes sits between the two, if you like. Forbes starts with Love and ends with Love (surely his God-substitute since he 'stopped believing in God when he was 21') but his entire poem seems to be about a flea. This is his objective correlative. A fascinating aspect of Forbes' work is his colloquial language with its classical bent. He is traditionally schooled in the construction of his language but his speech is colloquial. Somehow the two sit together and the paradox produces an anxiety that is generative. While remaining true to tradition, forms can subsume it to the immediate. This is how his Odes can be misinterpreted as being the end of a tradition rather than an effort to rejuvenate it. It's the deconstruction of form through the immediate that leads to uncertainty. But Forbes knows that all good poets build their poems out of scraps of the past. In this way he reminds one of the language of Swift. Paul Goodman in *Speaking and Language* says: But colloquial speech is quite impervious to corruption by format. It has an irrepressible vitality to defy, ridicule or appropriate. It gobbles up format like everything else. There are too many immediate occasions, face-to-face meetings, eye-witnessings, common sense problems, for common speech to be regimented. People who can talk can be oppressed but not brainwashed. Modern cities are depressing and unhealthy, but people are not mechanical. Forbes is both of this idea and its antithesis. In 'Ode To Tropical Skiing' the appropriate refrain to this would be '& it's a total fucking gas', and in poems such as this we see Forbes actually regimenting colloquial speech. But he'd say that's what makes it poetry, and nothing else. I recall him saying that what makes a poem a poem is line length. That is metrics. The rendering of real talk into a portable valise! But here I am playing the game. Form-wise, Forbes is more conscious of sound effects than internalised visuals. It is the package of words that matters. There exists the kind of dualism that existed in the metaphysicals. The influence of the modern Americans on Forbes has been pointed out many times. O'Hara, Ashbery (on whom he wrote a dissertation), and that Englishman-cum-American, W H Auden, were and remain major influences. But this is more in spirit and the use of diction than in technique — more in voice than in structure. Forbes will say that a poem like 'Toposthesia' was a very feeble attempt to imitate John Ashbery's 'Clepsydra'. Brilliant poem, magnificent poem. That dominated that poem entirely. But the rhythms of his poem are quite different to Ashbery's. Maybe it's because Forbes has a particularly Australian diction, a kind of Australianised Classical diction, which means he couldn't have come from anywhere else. One could also imagine that the American conception of 'fame' is both appealing in its 'bobby dazzler' simplicity and naivety to Forbes. It is the land of nostalgia that has covered (if not 'understood') all possibilities — maybe unlike Europe which has understood but staunchly ignored the truth: No doubt some thorough American manual/can give you the lowdown on Europe's margins/but mine, designed for only one traveller,/is better written & much shorter./Besides, if you remove the art, Europe's/like the US, more or less a dead loss ... But one gets the feeling it wouldn't matter where Forbes was travelling as long as it was with a 'you' who wouldn't double-take on him. Once again, the bluff of the poem is a kind of ironic cultural reference guide. The anxiety, the inner poem, is isolation, and loneliness, despite the busy schedule. A kind of internalised exile that, even if vaguely hinted at, reconciles itself in an affirmation of cultural defamation: not standard? I can't advise you on this/but I know how I enjoyed myself: though/knocked out by what convinced me/'Great Art' without inverted commas is/(but not because of this) I hung around/with other Australians & hit the piss. The 1995 Cambridge Conference on Aesthetics was considered one of the best by many participants. Discussions of artistic practice and vibrant readings were its hallmark. As part of the program, I performed on the last night to a packed theatre in ... College, receiving generous applause, and was much in demand after the event to discuss my work and aesthetics. I was also able to discuss, over the three days, general trends in Australian aesthetics and 'what the future holds'. As a result of this Conference, I have received invitations to contribute to numerous avant-garde English arts journals, an invitation to deliver a series of seminars on Australian art at ... The Conference was well advertised (in places such as *The London Arts Review* — recently a Canadian friend contacted me saying how good it was to see an Australian name in among the English avant-garde) and extremely well attended. People were intrigued by there being an Australian who was working in similar fields to themselves. Courtesy extended to invitations to attend other conferences in addition to open invitations to speak at various venues in Cambridge and London on my next visit. I was well catered for in rooms at ... College, under the patronage of ... , head of the College. Dear

Sir/Madam, I would like to express concern at the application for Review of Assessment made by my former partner, ... , for which forms were issued to me by your office. Ms ... made this application on Ground 8 of your form, ie. on the grounds that my income had increased, without providing to your office any evidence that this was a fact. I notice the form forwarded to me states that your office decides on the validity of her claim and then contacts me to reply. On what ground was her claim assessed as valid (since it is not) if no hard evidence was provided? Hearsay from newspaper articles has never been considered a valid ground to my knowledge (papers are often wrong or inaccurate, as in this case — I did not receive both grants). Theoretically, it seems, she could make these claims as often as she pleased and I would have to continue providing details. My annual income as stated in Section A will be much lower after tax deductions — as shown by previous tax assessments, almost half my wage goes on tax-deductible related expenses. Theoretically my annual assessable income should be more in the region of ... than ... , so I feel I have more than paid my dues. I will be submitting my new assessed income with the new financial year. The income Ms ... claims as 'further', ie. extra over and above my previous assessment, is in fact my only income for this year, and as I have stated on the form I am returning to you,

I am more than happy to pay maintenance as owed. However, I consider that being required to provide personal details to a former de facto — whenever it pleases her to claim that my income has increased! — constitutes a form of harassment. I object to having to detail my expenses (as in Section 21) for her perusal, as it reveals to the informed reader what my plans for the year are and is an invasion of privacy (I have since married and have a stepdaughter to support). Thus I have provided only a general breakdown in that Section of the form. I believe wholeheartedly that I should pay maintenance to support my son, but I do not see why details of my private life should not be kept confidential, or why your office should treat Ms ... 's claim seriously without real evidence to support it. Sincerely, Dear ... , It's a glorious Saturday morning in Perth. I was going to head down to the University library to get some research work done but have decided there are probably 'better' things to do given the circumstances. I rang the other day and heard, c/- your answering machine, that you are taking a rest from the interruptions of the outside world. Now this I can understand! Still, I thought I'd fax this while the 'mood' to write is with me despite knowing it will probably be a while before you read it. I received a fax from the Canadian poet L L last night in which he talked highly of your work. He also mentioned that you were resurrecting your old Press. Is this true? Sounds great! I've just been reading one of Rita Dove's Library of Congress lectures (she posted them to me last week) in which she says: ... It reminds me of another litany, this one written shortly after the end of World War II — that point in history which Theodor Adorno called 'Ground zero.' Adorno posed the question: 'After Auschwitz, is poetry possible?' The following poem was Günter Eich's chilling answer: Inventory This is my cap, this is my coat, here my shaving things in a pouch of linen. Tin can: my plate, my cup: in the tin dish I've scratched my name. Scratched here with this precious nail, which I hide from jealous eyes. In the bread bag is a pair of wool socks and stuff I'll tell no one about — it serves as a pillow nights for my head. This cardboard here lies between me and the earth. Most of all I love the lead in the pencil: it writes poems by day that I thought up at night. This is my notebook, this is my ground sheet, this is my hand towel, this is my twine. The translation is Dove's own (I assume). It is interesting in that her use of it suggests (I believe) that the lyric IS transcendental under any circumstances, that even the matter-of-factness of horror cannot corrupt it. I think the basic problem with this notion is that the lyric is actually being used as a tool for 'liberation' and is not an end in itself. One has to be careful not to invest too much power in the medium rather than in the notion itself. What do you think? Some 'good' news — I have been sending letters of protest to French ideas and literary journals. Well, it's off to the hills now. Up into the jarrah forest for a few hours. Lots of love, She says it keeps your weight down. I know it does because I'm losing weight. You don't want to eat as much, but you can and want to drink heaps. I drink spirits because that keeps the weight down as well. L's got beautiful legs. They look so smooth. I'd like to run my hand all the way up the inside of her leg. Not touching her panties, but just about. Just close enough to feel its warmth. I've always found it difficult to give it a name. She calls it a 'pussy'. I kind of like that when she says it. Dear Alan, Great to receive your letter/work. I'll take the piece gladly — I'm not sure if the poem's on offer, but I reckon it's great. This material will appear along with the Poe review in *Poetry Journal* 20. This will be published in a few months so if you have anything else you'd like to submit for consideration please get it to me as soon as possible. My wife tells me there's evidence to suggest that Poe might have been responsible for a number of murders during his life. Some of the things he wrote about were uncannily close to actual events; there were things he could have only known if he had been the murderer or had known the murderer. After all, he fucked his thirteen-year-old cousin after she'd died of pneumonia. There's a novel in that! Actually, come to think of it, I might enclose a 'new' volume for you to review. It might not be to your liking, but who knows, something might spark your interest. It's M's *Selected Poems*. An interesting guy — Professor of Philosophy and Comparative Literature at ... (amongst other things) — who has some interesting notions on poetry and The Academy. I'll discuss them after you've done the review, so as not to 'flavour' your response, not that this would be likely! I feel inclined to include JS Harry's new volume but might wait until I've got a bundle of interesting material together to send you. Oh, and maybe Adamson's new one, *Waving at Hart Crane*. A list of Australian publications? Yes, I must get to that. I've been silent as I wasn't sure if you were going to reply, or if my cards had in fact reached you. I must add, at this point, that I thoroughly enjoyed (a fatuous word, but I'm sure you appreciate the vitalising nature of the irony) your company when I was at the Conference. I've enclosed a new essay: it is an expression of my anger at the 'death of the lyric' debate that's simmering away down here. There are plenty of fuckwits who rave about the lyric as ego-compromising and unwittingly write lyrics! Instead of anthropomorphising Nature they egotise notions of Nature. Six of one and half-a-dozen of the other, when all is said and done. They're still writing fucking lyrics but don't recognise the shadow behind their own best (anti)efforts. Ludicrous. And of course, this is grist for the 'trad' mills — playing straight into their eager (right-wing) hands. I recently wrote an article for the L on American Language poetry in which I wrote (following a quote from Kristeva's *Revolution in Poetic Language* — 'The regulation of the semiotic in the symbolic through the thetic break ... society is founded on a complicity in a common crime.'): 'In the same way, the 'romantic' poet exploits our complicities to reference his/her self and divert our attentions from the commonweal ... ' and all Hell let loose. Why? Anyway, I'm sorry to have digressed. If you are interested I'll write at length on the issue. I'm by nature a long letter-writer and tend to get carried away. I'll resist a new paragraph. The other essay is the first section of a long work 'Graphology'— it pretty well speaks for itself. There are some other essays I'd like to offer you but they're part of my new volume which will be published in a couple of weeks. I'll also enclose an extract from an interpretation from the French of Lucienne Durollet, a Québecoise poet I met some years ago during my travels. She's not published a great deal, having, in her words, 'an overwhelming disgust for all things "littéraires" '. Anyway, I reckon she's pretty interesting and am at present working with my wife on a complete translation of *Muette*. Maybe you're interested in seeing more? Well, looking forward to hearing from you. All the best, Yours, Dear ... , It seems such a long time since I've heard from you. It has been a silence I've found somewhat disturbing in that I greatly value the quality of your friendship. Still, as it takes two to tango, here I am making the first step in the next dance sequence. Things have been quite strange (what's unusual about that I hear you say!) for me in recent times. We are both well these days. As you would have guessed, we've had a hiccup or two, but things are great now and we are really enjoying each other's company. The household is happy! Please give my love to June. What is she up to at the moment? Is she writing poetry? Please write and let me know. Looking forward to hearing from you. All the best. Yours, The Vegetarian and The Meatpacker. A vegan — the absolute vegetarian. No animal products worn, eaten, used in any fashion. But there are always those unseen, unknown usages. The inhalation of micro-insects. The Jains, who are not vegans, cover their mouths, sweep the ground before them. That is, the human is no more of an animal than the animal. As such to eat animal would be a kind of cannibalism. But to be human is to be possessed by the demons of unliving. These demons suggest conscience. A knowledge of 'right' and 'wrong' is what we call ethics. We are guided by our ethics lest we lose our demons and become unconscious of unliving. But then, this is what all hedonists hope to attain. Veganism and hedonism are contradictory terms. The vegan is a moralist; if not, then vegan is only a terminology of supply and demand. The vegan requires or does not require in the market-place. The vegan self-labels as part of a spiritual defining. There is always the implicit desire to encourage others to veganism. The vegan usually plays this down to coexist, otherwise the meat-eaters will stamp him or her out. In the landscape of rural Western Australia the vegan treads carefully. Farmboys drive pickups with 'Shoot Ferals' as bumper stickers. Kangaroo and rabbit shoots are nightly occurrences. The land is generally harsh and forbidding and doesn't allow for 'softness'. It is also a landscape ridden with guilt. It is re-territorialised land. It has been usurped from its indigenous occupants. And the way to placate this guilt is with violent arrogance, manifesting itself as both overt and indirect racism. It's impossible to say 'subtle racism', it is never that. In the hobby farmer communities, the arty towns, or those with strong religious pastoral shepherd-flock persuasions, there may be a patronising acceptance of the black indigene. But it despoils on grounds of 'the only real one is a full blood and in the same breath they've got to integrate' mentality.

Its complexity is doubled in that the re-territorialisation is so complete, so absolute, that the children of farming families are as much part of the land as any other. The Europeanisation of the scape has made it part of their learning. It is no longer alien to them. The green fields of England are scarcely schoolbook notions. So, to adjust the wrongs, a kind of collectivisation has to take place, whereby traditional lands and post-traditional lands are reconciled. Mabo must meet private property head on. The need for this is the result of the all-pervasive capitalist occupation of the decorative. Embellishment, that is, the eating and disposal of waste, the peripheries to these processes, are controlled by the market. If the market could, collectively (the totality of the capitalist ethos is reflected in the functionality of this term in this context) value the indigenous occupation of the land above that of the post-invasion European inheritance, then, without equivocation, it would dispense with notions of European 'ownership'. But, of course, the market is of the European, and therefore cannot allow such a valuation to occur. All the devices of empowerment the State possesses would be put into action to prevent such a market redirection. Government becomes a front for vested interests within the market, behind it the controls are wielded by enterprise — the state being a conduit for the profits of enterprise. So it's not a question of morality, who has rights to the land, whether it should be Palestine or Israel. But rather which profits enterprise the most. Judgement is suppressed by the acceptance that things are directly unchangeable. The animals will be slaughtered, the pesticides showered, and so on. But in the territory of the poem s/he works subtly. Propaganda only converts those with an idea already sown in their head. To seed the idea you work in laterals and intangibles. The demons must be evoked and sent out into every heart. Or evoked from the heart. For morality defines goodness as existing as a thing-in-itself. It is not contrived, it is. I'm really ill. Can't stomach anything more than watermelon and rice. Woke up in a bed full of blood. My chest is getting worse. Went down to the New Market but collapsed on the way back. I am propped up in bed. The floors are covered in filth. The toilet is blocked with watermelon rind and stinks. I've painted anarchy signs on the walls with blood. I bought a copy of Milton's *Samson Agonistes* from the market. I couldn't resist the irony. It is filthy overcast. I should have that X-ray. I've developed a fierce morphine addiction. What freedom of choice do I have — a plane ticket, money? Looking across from my window I see a man pouring cement. Just one man building a five-storey building with two buckets and a shovel. And always the kaks, laughing. Three days until the referendum. The military is active. American jets that probably saw service in Korea fly low and slow over the city. They wilt in the sun. They carry pestilence and disease for weapons. An electrical storm. In the surreal light a red pilot light beckons through the palm trees. The Escapee is fucking somebody in the alleyway below. The roofs of these buildings are left unfinished so new storeys can be added when needed — slowly, slowly the towers rise — towards the lightning, the red effusions of a distorted sun. Stepping over a beggar's hardening corpse, the troupe of Catholic private schoolers make their neat and orderly way home from school. And man shall be as an hiding place from the wind, and a covert from the tempest: as rivers of water in a dry place, as the shadow of a great rock in a weary land. 'Woe to the land shadowing with wings, what is beyond the rivers of Ethiopia.' Referendum. Many explosions in old Dhaka. I don't know why. People in Australia are probably better informed. Pathetic. A hailstorm blends with the morphine. The Custody of Bodily Functions. If the body were fed exactly what it required it would issue no waste. But the machinery is designed to extract, to extract goodness from a neutral mass, to leave waste. Experience is processed in the same way. As the nun walks the street with her eyes averted, so does the girl brought up within the patriarchal family unit. The mother, aware of the need to deter the intrusions of men, teaches, consciously or unconsciously, her daughter not to intrude or allow intrusion into the respective spaces between herself and men. The clichés of 'she wanted it', 'led him on', or taking it into material manifestations, 'dressed provocatively', are the products of such teaching. Perpetuating behavioural patterns also encourages reciprocal ones. This is a double-edged sword, and this is a field fraught with piercings — such as the desire for body piercing as contradiction re the desire to penetrate from outside ie. outpiercing, breaking the hymen before the male can deflower — as the misogynist would argue that for every reaction there is an equal and opposite reaction so the appropriateness (and, against logic ironically, the instinct to react). Male history talks about power coming from the ability to stare someone down. Or even to soothe an animal by confrontation. It is no coincidence that the most mysterious of arts, hypnotism and the such, source from the eyes. And the myths of male fear, such as the Gorgons, centre on the woman usurping such power, of being able to bewitch with a long look. Such women were/are to be avoided at all costs. Mothers should teach their girls to look everything in the eye. This would disarm the aggressor. But it must be done en masse. The movement must be rhizomic, working away at the roots of the capitalist patriarchy.

In truth, the woman is brought up in custody of all bodily functions. Myths have denoted her sexuality as mysteries to be protected. But this is playing into the hands of men. It's as if withholding something allows for invasion — every reaction ... It is men who are kicking against the pricks! This is why the best gender revolution is that meted out by the Mother. It is the children who will change and eventually bring down the patriarchy. All differences are equal. Given the case of boys being brought up solely by women. Blows out candle now it's dark stay alive baby do it for van Gogh (whole times no custody of the eyes from closet) Are you all right (doesn't like being covered with shawl on couch) hold me hold me I'm scared I'm scared I'm scared do you like me yes embrace repose do you like the way I feel? see my breasts you can feel it do you like the way I feel mouth and nostril close-up — lips alive and wet hate me hate me hate me corridor back to bathroom and mirror I'm leaving now eyes down to patch of blue velvet ripped from her gown ... She reads 'I can't get it out of my head, she reminds me of you.' The bastard. I thought so, I knew it! The reconciliation of vegan morality with the inherent 'rights' of indigenous populations is another argument. See chapt ... If the dream-state is a cleaning device for the conscious state's indissolubles, that waking in the morning and analysing, often with horror, the mania of your post-modern video onslaught of REM sleep, is the scrubbing (cleaning the tape) process necessary for the next day's recording process to begin anew, then it is interesting to consider the corruption of the object of conveyances (the self or another) experiences in being exposed to the detritus of another's ablutions. It is necessary for the dreamer to consider or convey those dreams which have persisted beyond the 'forgotten' or lost chunks, or are remembered only in glimpses. But like all subliminals, the receiver incorporates another's experience into the consciousness and consequently subconscious. In this cycle of ingestions and expulsion they become recomposed on the waste of another. In a sense, all art is like this. We allow ourselves, willingly or unknowingly, to be supped on by another's demon of the heart or delirium or mania. A collectivisation of these excretions makes for a movement. And of course, all are decoration to the physical acts of eating, drinking, breathing, sleeping. But, as they are a spiritual and mental consuming process, they could also be considered part of the essential core process of survival. Herein the eternal contradiction of perpetuation of the individual. The body is not mere flesh, it requires alternative food. But largely it is fed what it doesn't need to survive. Logically, life itself is decoration. What the poem attempts to do is distil, literally or in an antithetical way, the properties which exist outside decoration. Decoration is the machine, is the aspect of process that brings it into being. Makes it life so that the living can read it. The sacred heart, outside the poem, will decompose into mania and delirium, if not given an outlet for consolidation into object. It must become decoration. The devices of its torture should become museum pieces, the items of examination and interpretation by the hungry. It should be excreted. A particularly abject image — and all processes of living must be abject — is that of the shit eater on the Ghats in Varanasi. Eating nothing but shit, he grows to gargantuan proportions. But he is revered as a holy man. He openly absorbs the wastes of others. In turn, he gives them food for thought. He is the living machine processing the decoration of spiritual longing. He is the product of the desire to be unliving, to be only the sacred heart. The mania and delirium come with a loss of spirit. A loss of acceptance that life is decoration. A belief that beauty exists as a thing in itself, that not all is abject in the state of the living. Territory is the consciousness applied to space. It is concept, as opposed to spirit. It is consequently decoration. Landscape is the product of notions of territory. The process is called territorialisation. It involves a concept of place and the position of the body and the collectivised body in it. It may alter the space, rearranging its internal perimeters, but this is not necessary. It may leave it untouched, but this is still territorialisation. It is part of the process of obligation and guilt. Guilt is the necessity to maintain something. It is considered to come from the spiritual, but is in fact a product of the decorative. That is, there is a logic within the actualness of living for it to be so. The forest left untouched has a logic to it. Cleaner air — general environmental benefits, resources, the necessity of other life to validate our own life-lust, that is, a foil to lapsing into delirium and mania. Landscape poetry is a paradox. The demon of the heart attempts to manifest itself outside the decorations. The framework is not built around it. It already exists. But this is only insofar as an acceptance of existence is a conscious part of the 'form'. It is a process of finding windows within the territorialised, through the living, into notions of the spirit. The writing process can only be about notions of the spirit. Notion is the decoration of the unconscious. It is the conscious manifestation of the anti-living. The landscape poem references the decorations as kinds of spiritual markers. As signifiers of particular demons. It appropriates associations that have been established in the museum of experience. That compilation of inherited awarenesses. The video libraries' magnetic storage. The cesspit of all excreta. The luminous pout of a salt lake on land recently thick with scrub speaks of the late twentieth century, the post-Warhol visions of female sexuality. Inherent is defilement, the rape of the land, of patriarchy. It may also speak of lust, and desire, the poem's demons gasping in the intertextual, the referenced Tree. The rhizomes working below the tree, which salinity, of its own making, is killing, though it looks bold and 'intriguing' in the morning light. So easily can decoration, notions of beauty, deceive. Even within the realm of decoration, there are those things invested with false embellishment, meant to deceive and corrupt the windows into the spirit, and those which sit, often ignored, unadulterated. These are the aspects of truth and wish-fulfilment. Wish-fulfilment is about overeating, indulgence. The honest are anorexic, but both gluttony and starvation lead to death. Though not anti-life. Knowledge of the existence (though not of its nature, which is hidden to the living, except by conjecture or notion) of anti-life is about an awareness of decoration. Photo under couch — marriage certificate — she's married — back to bathroom shot blades of plant on cistern top. Here Puss, come on, here's some tuna. Fish tonight. Come on, meow louder so I can hear you. Come on, meow as loud as you can. Stinky old tuna, we'll have the whole place smelling of dead fish. And it feels just like it smells! bowel noises leaving building like he's being expelled then bending of mouth and Frank howling beast-like in living memory and darkness and the sexually perverted flame flickering like votive candle of prayer into her mouth hit me hit me- OOOOOWWW from sleep pyjamaed and object on bedroom wall hardware shop as oddity, normal — can't be a blind man — operates the cash register — she's out with him in car and looks like a prom queen he's been inducted into strange worlds strange world married to a man named Don with a son forces Dorothy to do things thinks she wants to die Frank is a very dangerous man. Here Puss, let me watch you gnaw the tuna. I can see you gnawing. It's like you've spent your whole life, your entire little life gnawing the smelly tuna. After that I considered which were the primary and most ordinary effects which might be deduced from these causes, and it seems to me that in this way I discovered the heavens, the stars, and earth ... can't do that can't prove it found out my information illegally it's a strange world why are there people like Frank why is there so much trouble in the world? Church organ slowly bleating in the background as her perfectly clean face looks over the car seat carrying the suffering of humanity the pensive I HAD A DREAM there was our world and the world was dark because there weren't any robins and the robins represented love as her hands curve and pose like angels and for the longest time there was just this darkness and then suddenly thousands of robins were set free. I went down early in the morning, before sunrise. Suntan lotion, binoculars, towel, condoms — all in a sports bag. I found my place in the hills, deposited my stuff under some saltbush and jogged naked down onto the beach. I noticed a guy jogging towards me, but a long way off. I knew it was a guy because women never come down at this time. Never. I rushed back up to my stuff and squirted some lotion over my prick. I let the white cream just hang there in a thick white stripe. It's the sign. I went down and the guy was getting close. I jogged towards him. We went up into the hills and jerked each other off. We ran down on to the beach, forking like lightning, conducting ourselves into the sea where all the negative ions were swept from our bodies. My mind turned to business and I remembered that I was expected at a meeting sometime around three. But sales were up this month so it wouldn't matter if I skipped. I went back up to the hills, spread my towel, and lay down as the sun emerged. It being high summer, this was the most pleasant part of the day. I dozed off and when I came to I could hear voices down on the beach. I took out my binoculars and watched. Occasionally people would cruise past but I ignored them. I had friends and I knew no cops were due for a couple of weeks. I could relax. I was really in luck. Two ugly ducks and a svelte young blonde had picked each other up. They moved into the hills nearby. He blew his load over her belly. I squirted and rolled the cum and sand into balls which dried with the rising heat. *The beaches of Perth are renowned for their beauty. And cleanliness. No shit washed up from the sewers, no needles under the white sand. Drenched in sun with long lazy sunsets. Changing from yellow to magenta to red. Even the moon gives a tan. If you want gentle lapping waves of green water you can have them. Black reefs with surging swell, you can have them. Deep clear blue water, it's there as well. Once you've tasted it, once it has caressed your body, you'll be addicted. Even during the height of the summer season you'll always find a place to spread your towel. And the natives are friendly. If you want to walk your dog, there are places set aside. If you want to swim au naturel, no problem. There's regular pervert patrols so only those true-blue sun-lovers will occupy the piece of sand next to you and lap up the Mediterranean clime. And from Scarborough to Safety Bay there are first class facilities. Clean changerooms, places to grab a bite or cook your own meat, sink a cold beer, or let the kids loose. The beaches of Western Australia. One of the natural wonders of the world! Discover them for yourself!* There is a strange onomatopoeia at work in a Forbes poem (such as the 'plunging jet' or the 'so loved drawn-out death-bed scenes' or 'huddled before' of 'Death, an Ode'; or the curvature and impressions sub-texted in 'opening each degree of arc to pressure' from 'Phaenomena'). Maybe it's as Paul Goodman says of Saussure — Ferdinand de Saussure points out that onomatopoeic words are never organic elements of a linguistic system. I doubt that this is absolutely true — I cannot think of a good example of syntax governed by onomatopoeia: 'Ah that he were alive!' the example is factitious, and there might be a better one. But surely Saussure's remark is largely true.[1] Forbes' use of onomatopoeia is often iconic with his setting up a juxtaposition or conceit (if we can use the term in a purely linguistic sense) between his rhythms/cadences and the iconicity of his speech. There is a case for saying Forbes takes to task his own propositions by his overwhelming feeling that commonsense is what it boils down to at the end of the day. In 'Love Poem' (*Stalin's Holidays*) it is almost commonsense for the object of his desires to come with another, to defeat or foil his love. If there is

1. Goodman, op. cit., p. 39. The passage continues, 'Its importance, however, is that it points to a serious defect in language — at least modern language — not because onomatopoeia is important, but because the animal basis of interjections is important and ought to be able to be said structurally. Poets contrive to make interjections an organic part of their language by inverting the word order, distorting the syntax, and adding rhythm and resonance. Ordinary folk in a passion give up on the language.'

persuasion in this it is as a statement along the lines of 'I know that's what you'll do and I understand but all the same I wish you wouldn't — and maybe you won't because you know I know.' In the synchronics of Forbes' '70s (via the '50s and '60s of the Americans, but not with a diachronic awareness of change — it's more a matter of hijacking) language usage there is persuasion: 'I speak the same language as you.' Forbes may be lonely, but he is never alone. He doesn't lament his isolation, he gets out and mixes it with them despite his anxieties. It's like the breath in his work, the incidentals, his sense of obiter dicta. He might be smart but it's a casual smartness that allows familiarity. This is why his poetry is widely read, despite its apparent cleverness. In 'Ode To Death' we see Forbes at his most dynamic. Donne says in his 'Holy Sonnet No. 10': One short sleep past, we wake eternally/And death shall be no more; Death, thou shalt die, while we find Forbes writing Death, you're more succesful than America,/even if we don't choose to join you, we do. Regardless of religious pedagogy there is no avoiding the completeness of it — it wins hands down regardless of belief ('what gets me is how compulsory it is'). It also interesting to note that this America, the America of the Cold War, is as much a military entity as it is a cultural amalgam. Death and the Cold War, and death as a kind of failed love in the sexual vocabulary of the metaphysicals and their contemporaries. That Donne says death cannot win because we move on to something greater, more alive if you like, prompts Forbes to respond in the opposite way. But I'd argue the Catholic-guilt-line here. The subtext *wishes* what Donne says were the case. In a line like: 'I've just become aware of this conscription/where no one's marble doesn't come up', Forbes doesn't like the idea of death winning like this any more than he'd like to be conscripted. And though it's inevitable, the marble game is still exactly that, a game of chance. The contradiction works both as irony and paradox. This is the epigrammatic Forbes, questioning his own acceptance of the inevitable. It is worth remembering, Forbes is never convinced what he states in the outer poem is true. His sure tone is always open to question. It is because of this disparity that certain critics have observed the 'surreal' in his work. But surrealism is more confident in its disassociations, if not its origins. Forbes can never be this. It's a matter of style. Style in literature is about keeping the best models and reinventing them; style in society is about capturing the idiom of the moment and concentrating it. There is an obvious overlap between the two, but a fundamental difference. Functional aspects remain constant, but the social style does not carry with it the necessity to comment on what has come before (though it can, of course). Literary style relies on what has come before and must make constant reference to it to qualify itself as something different from cultural ephemera. Forbes moves between both worlds, transporting elements of social style into his poems, and bestowing literary style on his society. In his search for credibility, both in his desire to convince someone that he is worthy of their love and that he is aware of society's soft sell, Forbes is opening up his poems. The external bluff and internal anxiety are approaching a sense of closure, even if he can never truly escape them. There are firm indications in poems such as 'Scottische', 'Entartete Kunst', 'Admonition', and 'Humidity' that the next period in his writing will be the most interesting, There's that new freedom, even relaxation in his verse (if not his love life?!) that makes it more 'inviting', but without any dilution of its ironic clout and intelligence. John Forbes might never write an 'Ode to Generation X' but I'm sure he's considered it. Still a child of the Cold War, he's at least aware that it's been over for about six years. It seems fitting to end with a quote from the poet Forbes most admires — Frank O'Hara: ... Now I am quietly waiting for/the catastrophe of my personality/to seem beautiful again,/and interesting, and modern. Dear Alan, We're having real problems with copyright re the Hopper book. They want exorbitant fees and my publishers aren't willing to pay. Strange situation, considering it's a book which purports to stand against the 'occupation of language by market forces'. I'd like to publish it myself, distribute it to every household free, and do a bunk! Yours, and they flew down and brought this blinding light of love and it seemed like love would be the only thing that would make any difference I guess it means there's trouble until the robins come you're a neat girl I'd better go I guess so camera rests on church as she drives them home The first thing her last boyfriend said to me was You look fuckable, but your tits look tight. She laughed her slow deep laugh, her eyes wild with speed. She's a contradiction. I wanted to ask her what he meant by tight tits but didn't know how to. He was a big jock but had heaps of dough and drove a Jensen Interceptor. The guy from next door asked me if I was interested in Dennis Hopper. That was a couple of weeks ago. At least I think he asked me; I might have overheard him talking to his wife. I've just read an article in *Face* about Dennis Hopper's house. It's in a slum in L.A. I wonder if she thinks of other things when they're fucking. I can't think of anything. It's just darkness and weight. Mostly it's odourless. They tell me my ... pussy ... smells and tastes sweet. I think of that new song by Corpus Christi — he laid me down with a little bowl of candy ... Flat 7 She's out. I shift across the floor. The light is strong on the curtain's outer side. I move to the taps. Sometimes I picture myself cutting off a big jock's prick. I'm hiding in a male's body. I have a mythological physique. Herculean. I keep moving towards him even though the idea revolts me. I can see his prick and want to cut it off. I've done that before. He looks like a fucking clown with the white shit on his prick but I know I'll jerk off all over it. The seasons will roll on. I will be his shepherd and will be a black dot on his calendar. On his biorhythms. I could tell him how yesterday I gutted a dog I picked up just down the road. How I chopped it up in the kitchen just for the hell of it. A dry run. A very wet dry run. The things I'd like to do to him. And of course I could. And one day will. If not to him, then one of his type. Filthy fucking mongrel, like the stray I cut up. *The beaches of Perth are renowned for their beauty. And cleanliness. No shit washed up from the sewers, no needles under the white sand. Just a copy of Bullfinch's Mythology flickering in the light breeze ...* The Poets of The Age of Fable If no other knowledge deserves to be called useful but that which helps to enlarge our possessions or to raise our station in society, then Mythology has no claim to the appellation. But if that which tends to make us happier and better can be called useful, then we claim that epithet for our subject. For Mythology is the handmaid of literature; and literature is one of the best allies of virtue and promoters of happiness — Author's Preface, *Bullfinch's Mythology*. In the story of Psyche and Cupid we are shown how curiosity — the desire to know more than one should — will inevitably bring downfall. That through trials and tribulations what is lost can be regained, and regained with territory added. The decoration of life has been enriched, but not by mere gauche addition. Rather reinforced and improved. The ultimate reward, as in the case of Psyche, is to have the window to unliving, or, rather, eternal life, opened. To eat and drink of ambrosia and nectar, to be transubstantiated into something eternal and absolute. But Psyche's flight to Heaven on beautiful butterfly wings is a suspect one. Initially she is the target of spite from Aphrodite, jealous of her famed and acclaimed beauty, and then the victim of jealous sisters plotting to usurp her place. It is the imagined male monster, the beautiful Cupid, messenger of the temperamental Aphrodite, his Mother (who else would be beautiful enough to carry out her tasks), who eases her tasks, who restores the secret of beauty — sleep — given by Persephone to the vessel of Aphrodite, and transports her to the folds of Heaven. This, despite his having wounded, doubted, and generally having given her a hard time. From this story, as lovingly recounted by Thomas Bullfinch in

'The Age of Fable' (1855), we see that it is in the interest of modern man to perpetuate the archetypes of myth. Mythology, rather than enriching and informing our lives (through literature) as claimed by Bullfinch, really seeks to keep women as the 'handmaidens' of virtue and happiness. Virtue and happiness are undoubtedly the stuff Bullfinch sees through the window into the unliving, the staples of eternity. But they are concepts formulated to support a hierarchical (read patriarchal) interpretation of the World. They are perpetual rather than cyclical concepts. They consume constantly, believing themselves immune to the need to excrete. The wastes are the opposite of their afforded values. They are pure. But, of course, they are mere words replicating quarks of behaviour. They work in the same space (collision theory) and are quantitative. How much applies. The unliving is the immeasurable. They are, in truth, baubles, on the tree of living. Bullfinch's idolisation of poets is of the order of the Psyche-Cupid myth. The symbolist movement toward the realm of the absolute and eternal on the metempsychotic wings of poesy are found in his Romantic view of the poet as purveyor of a vehicle that will transport the listener/reader to the realms of virtue and happiness. The poet, even Sappho, is the spirit of patriarchy, cloyingly coupled with the trusteeship of guardian of freedom. The association of 'freedom' with patriarchy is the central agenda in the premodernist presentation of these myths. Orpheus and Eurydice: the essayist as would-be poet: a ghoulish story. If only he knew how much I despise him. He's too arrogant even to contemplate it might be the case. His feet and hands are always cold. He degrades culture and feeds on its corpse. It is a child to ignore or push around as he chooses. This book of interviews with Australian poets. I'm going to make an essay out of the questions answering the questions. Get rid of the middle man. I'll conduct the dialogue between interviews, removing the poets. They all say the same things anyway. The implication may be reciprocal, as with the wasp and the orchid, or the snapdragon and the bumblebee. Jakob von Uexküll has elaborated an admirable [as we wander through the gardens of Varuna, tacky K-Mart umbrella in hand, considering what it would have been like playing tennis on the courts that used to be here] theory of transcodings. He sees the components as melodies in counterpoint, each of which serves as a motif for another: Nature as music. (See *Grove*.) Sonata In B Flat Major, Op. 106: The way Beethoven leads into the last movement is one of his greatest strokes of genius: leading the player away from the sublimities back to the earthly conflict of the fugue, forgoing barlines, starting four times over and finally, after

the great outburst in A major, attaining the F,
which had begun as in a dream, establishing it
now as the dominant of B flat — all this is psy-
chologically magnificent. The strip of paper
pasted on the wall under the ceiling. There are
arrows marked at intervals of five centimetres
down it. It looks like a photocopied sheet of a
school history text. Or it could be historical
notes for some other subject. Physics?
Literature? It is impossible to tell. It has been
stained with water. The roof leaks. She is
tracking the flow. Arrow by arrow. Alone. (2)
What is given are real wars ... He punishes me
with paranoia ... with his non-understanding
... he is full of doubt because his doubt
consumes me ... as submitted to State aims;
States are better or worse 'conductors' in
relation to absolute war, and in any case condition its realisation in experience. (3) Real
wars swing between two poles, both subject to
State politics: the war of annihilation ... if she
publishes that book it will rise up and eat her
— I can't tell her that it will do this because
she will think I'm oppressing her, denying her
right to speak. One just awaits the inevitable.
The arrogant bastard. And on a scummy scrap
of paper at that. Not even an attempt at a
reasoned discourse, just a scummy scrap of
paper among his documents — which can
escalate to total war (depending on the objec-
tives of the annihilation) and tends to
approach the unconditioned concept via an

ascent to extremes; the schizo's loss of face is the loss of landscape's sense/find your black holes and white walls, know them/as off your face you stagger over the Rottnest graves/terrestrial signifying despotic face/maritime subjective passional authoritarian face/the desert can also be a land of sea/the nomads are there, on the land, wherever there forms/grazing fluid sand/rhizomatic patterns/crosshatched absolutes/a smooth space that gnaws, and tends to grow, in all directions/the local absolute. Potentially a destination in the oasis growing with productivity, burgeoning with potential as advertised whole new realms of clients seek to possess a small piece of temporal territory, as it positions within the larger territory within whose boundaries they wander, except for when the Soviet Space Agency suggested flights for American millionaires 'cross the vectors, desert to desert as within the still greater territory of the Cosmos as for monotheistic religion, at the deepest level of its tendency to project a universal or spiritual State over the entire ecumenon, it is not without ambivalence or fringe areas ... Otherwise the entire human race would have been wiped out there and then instead of being propagated, generation after generation, down to the present day/as becoming the speaker of 'Aide-toi, le ciel t'aidera'/facies totius universi/'Par miracle et soudain devinrent des épées ... ' ... and limited war, which is no 'less' a war, but one that effects a descent toward limiting conditions, and de-escalate to mere 'armed observation': the pseudo-paranoia of hypochondria, mild — the uncertainty of possessing space, of knowing on whose ground one treads. The occupation of the body by an outside force, the threat of colonisation, leads to overactive defences. On edge constantly, morale falls and the paranoid actually becomes vulnerable to that which s/he is constantly on guard against. Traveling in a bus a cough is heard coming from the back of the bus. It's not just a cough, a clearing of the throat, it's a bacterial cough. You cover your mouth and nose with the inside of your jumper. You kind of half-breathe, making gasping sounds that have the person sitting next to you wondering. You try to place yourself in a stream of fresh air. Your day is ruined, knowing that it's inevitable you'll wake up sick in two days' time. And your intelligence is always accurate, the war machine, the defence mechanisms of your Fear, are highly tuned and devastatingly accurate! Harry: They're filthy, useless bastards ... and I don't care what you say! A bunch of dickless wonders. They've got dreadlocks as a sign of penis envy! Hooks: I'm sick of hearing about Freud. It's just an example of the virus that is capitalism. These people are more of your kind, Harry. They want the benefits of the marketplace without moral responsibility. They've ignored the spiritual callings of collective living and decentralisation, respect for the environment and natural communion, for the image of such, while really caring about what they can get. It's just commodifying something that was a threat to the virus' continued multiplication. That is the face of capitalism — whatever threatens it, it coerces and consumes. As soon as it gets a commercial hook into an idea it imagifies it, makes it marketable. You can have a bit of that but still remain safe in the mainstream, in the sale-or-return market-driven society. You can be both in and out, or at least present the illusion of being so. Harry: What a load of bullshit. The only thing that remains consistent is that they are lazy bastards led by other lazy bastards like sheep. They eat and shit ... and shit anywhere, as far as that goes. Even in the main street of town. Lance: Showing their contempt for bourgeois society, for the state. The problem is they are as much a part of the system as anyone else. They are the trend, the vitalising element of capitalism. All they are doing is infecting the common health, not the mechanics of the system they deplore by necessity. Harry: Well, give me those rednecks with their 'Shoot Ferals' stickers any time! Lance: I hope you don't mean that, Harry. Those are dangerous. Their attempts at humour disguise deep emotional instability.

They require a concept of normality to suppress their deeply-felt hatreds. They have shit fetishes; the sight of shit sends them crazy because they are secretly obsessed and attracted to it. They'll wallow in the blood and shit of a dead animal and then drunkenly tell the world how they'd like to clean away the feral 'shits'. (Harry spills equipment over the ground.) Jan: Okay, now that's enough. Concentrate on what you're doing and give it a break. I want to be set up by nightfall. Tomorrow morning we'll start marking territory and looking for evidence. Lance: Good sense is of all things in the world the most equally distributed, for everybody thinks himself so abundantly provided with it, that even those most difficult to please in all other matters do not commonly desire more of it than they already possess. Watching the storekeeper display his 5 taka soft drink bottles in the window of his shop reminds me of working in a stamp shop during school holidays. His son helps him. They seem to respect certain brands more than others. Pepsi bottles are handled with reverence. Not in their idol worship, but by labour. Honest, and lawful to deserve my food. Of those who have me in their civil power. I'm reminded of Victor Mature. Serepax: animal pharmacology, indications, toxicology, contraindications and warnings, adverse reactions, dosage and administration and availability. The one-eyed watermelon dealer serves the sticky fruitflesh under the eyes of soldiers, their heavy machine guns almost humorous. Old Dhaka lives! And the river, the waterways of Bangladesh. Food and building materials and goods of all kinds. Heavily laden vessels avoid sinking only by constant draining. The crew of the larger vessels spend their time bucketing water back into the great river. The breeze slices patchwork sails and the oars and the smell of the flood. The banks writhe. S has just asked if there is any risk of his having a baby after being fucked up the arse. Outside a one-armed beggar is fighting a small boy. Dhaka Museum during a storm. The War of Independence, 1971. The first shell fired, skulls as evidence of genocide. A large poster advertising the Concert for Bangladesh. A stuffed Bengal tiger. Hindu, Buddhist and Islamic religious relics. The Gallery of National Portraits. The face of a poet. Morning Star and Demon's Mace. Hashish hookah. An ornamental bed — a tiger holding an elephant's trunk in its mouth. Tried to get a copy of Genet's poetry from the Dhaka University library today. My chest has been feeling a little better. No problem going places. Take a handful of mandrax and a few dexies in case I feel like I'm going to pass out. Entertained myself baiting silk-vendors today. Went into their shops claiming I was a buyer of silk — it amused me to see them carefully spread their wares, attempt to impress me with their wealth. I enjoyed walking out, leaving them with the impression that I would return tomorrow with enough money to buy their entire stock. The Escapee says he is proud of me. The joke's on me. The Escapee told B who told the silk-vendors. Seem they control most of the morphine supply in Dhaka. Within hours the word was out. Nobody will sell me morphine. I approach the first pharmacist I visited when I arrived. He knows me. He sees I have morphine sickness. He promises a regular supply, for medical reasons. He won't tell me why but the price has doubled. Okay. As Mary pulled the handbrake on, the kids jumped out of the car and ran to see their uncle. As he bent down to greet them she thought, I *know* Peter can tell me something about this. He knows his brother. Peter went to kiss her on the cheek but she caught him with a quick, What do you know? He glanced around. The kids were hurling themselves down the track towards the shearing shed, a favourite haunt. Then he paused, as was his manner, and said, Well, it's been raining solid. Bit of a break at the moment, but I reckon it'll be back in half an hour. Might as well let the kids have a look around. Be pissing down in a while. Nice fire inside; come in. Have a cuppa. A dog is at his ankles. This is Zoe, crazy mutt. Bill up the road was going to put a bullet in her last week. She'd run a mob of sheep through a fence. She's a bit of a pain in the arse, but she's worth more than a bullet from Bill's rifle. Danny? she ventured. Yeah, Danny, Danny's a bit of a problem. Yeah, well come in and have a cuppa. I wouldn't really know, that's the problem. But you know, it was kind of inevitable really. I mean, he was tampering with things that are best left untouched. In the distance there was a flash of lightning. They hesitated. They waited for the follow-up — a clap of thunder. And then it was still. The eye of an indecisive squall. They went inside. Have you ever considered that set of bellows that's down in the old shed? Peter asked. No; why do you ask? she replied. Well, they've two dirty great lumps of wood with a large iron beak, and half a dead cow in between. So we've got wood, which is a natural substance, a metal beak — which is man-made — and a cow in between. The cow being a natural substance. But, like the metal, the wood and the cow have undergone a transformation. I mean they've been worked and altered from their original form. They've been man-made. Mary looked at him curiously. Peter had always been idiosyncratic and inclined to his own perceptions, but this was slightly ludicrous. He continued, You see, I look at it this way — he's always had this thing about eyes. Since he was a kid. He wanted to make eyes. He'd mix light bulbs, jelly, and those plastic shells toys in lolly machines are packaged in. I used to think he was the sickest bastard on the face of the earth. And he was always pulling the eyes out of dead animals, and 'experimenting' on them. Fortunately, at least as far as I'm aware, they were always dead animals. He used to say: eyes are more complex than the most sophisticated camera. In a sense they're also much more vulnerable than the most sophisticated camera. The camera can only see as well as the eye. And the camera, even the X-ray camera, can never 'see' inside things the way the eye does. I'd like to adapt the eye, to turn it into a tool. Let me explain. If we shape a piece of metal we can use it to dig the earth — but wouldn't it be interesting if we could shape our hand to do precisely the same job. Not just a tool to scrape and delicately hollow the ground, but to excavate with the same degree of proficiency as a shovel. The idea is that the organic could be manipulated like the inorganic. He'd go on about these things for hours. It never made a lot of sense, but looking back I think he was struggling to formulate some kind of theory of cybernetics. When I think about his work with cameras and eyes I think about his obsession with this notion. I think he's gone not because of the eyes, but because of the principle behind his obsession with them. I don't think this is a case of industrial espionage. He used to tell me he had a 'key'. I think it was the key that took him away. This key is not a device, a formula, or even a process. It's a simple principle that allows for the organic to act in an inorganic way. Like the hand become a metal shovel. A kind of metaphysical karate, if we consider the military possibilities of such a concept. So we're dealing here with ideas as much as facts and actualities, in the same way that those bellows are really no more than pieces of a tree, ore and a cow. It's the form which arises, or is manufactured from these base components that makes it what we recognise as a set of bellows. Once we place them in a certain pattern, manipulate them into a specific shape, the combination of organics and inorganics becomes a useful device. Anyway, that's what's at the basis of it, as far as I can say. I think it's much safer and far more interesting shearing sheep. Mary stared at the fire for a while. She was thinking about Plato. Danny'd like her to be thinking about Plato. But it wasn't because of him that she was. She reached for the poker and stirred the embers, as if it were something she had to do. She glanced up to the mantelpiece over the fire well. It was chock-full of bottles. Peter had dug them out of the rubbish tips around the place, many of them blue with the sun. They were the detritus of a past civilisation, she couldn't help thinking. That Peter, like his brother, was a plunderer of the dead. Hanging on the walls were charcoal drawings, a few locks of wool. A pretty down-to-earth place, really. Kind of like Danny's lab in a way. It was like a laboratory of lifestyle. I'm not too sure about your bellows analogy. A long pause. The kids were heard yelling in the distance, muffled by the stone walls. The military? Maybe she was just thinking aloud. The question is, where can a manuscript like this go? It's a victim of the genre. If it extends itself into something that ironises the process, then it will lose its genre appeal. She scribbled a note in the margin. It's dying, take it somewhere else. She skipped through the next dozen or so pages, satisfied that she'd placed the perfect comment in the right place. Another conversation between Peter and Mary. You've got to be joking. We're talking about the world's greatest fence-sitter here, Peter; you know that! Oh, don't kid yourself, said Peter. I think he cares a great deal more than you think. Don't you worry, every time he cuts one of those eyes out, I see a shudder — and it's not a shudder of squeamishness. It's a shudder because, as he says, it's a violation of the natural laws. She forces her pen through the paper and wonders if it is more of an act of defiance than accident. She draws rings around it so that it looks like a target. He believes all that stuff. L says he is devout and will marry accordingly. But he still sleeps with The Escapee. He says it's okay as long as he doesn't surrender his bronze eye or stick his tongue in The Escapee's mouth. L does all the fucking. The Escapee doesn't mind this and I prefer it because he is more experienced at keeping things quiet when being shafted. L says he'd like to fuck me and The Escapee laughs. He picks his toenails and smells his toe jam. I hate him and he knows it. I decline the offer and The Escapee walks to the end of my bed, crouches, and shits. An exhibition of photographs depicting atrocities committed during the 1971 war opened at the museum today. Vultures ripping the flesh from corpses, martyrs hanged by the neck, skulls in pools of blood ... It is raining. The morphine is just beginning to work. It takes longer now. I shall have to increase the dosage. Found a copy of Conrad's *Heart of Darkness* at the New Market today. Celebrated by getting the pharmacist to shoot me up. It was quite a novelty. He was really nervous, applying an alcohol rub half-a-dozen times. He didn't feel confident doing an intravenous so I settled on intramuscular with an increased dosage. Pity, I'd like to have seen his face when I got him to pull blood back into the pick. Backwash. He moaned about infection and addiction so I told him to piss off. 'Mr Kurtz, he dead.' I wash my hands in snow water and wonder about hookworms. I'm attracted to the blue suit Kalid, the hotel manager, wears. The Escapee tells one of his boys not to worry about me, that I'm not really in the room at all. It was very simple, and at the end of that moving appeal to every altruistic sentiment it blazed at you, luminous and terrifying, like a flash of lightning in a serene sky. S: Where did you get that hash? Me: It's better than the stuff you've been selling me. S: Where did you get it from? A large dose. Me: A rickshaw driver. S: Let me smell it. Me: What do you think? S: How much did you pay? Me: 200 takas for six grams. S: Much too expensive. Me: But it's the best. S: Too expensive. S stares at me. You can't deny he's handsome. Fine limbed, a shock of obsidian hair. Wide-eyed with a strong chin and nose. Lips almost sensuous. He pouts consciously. His voice lilts. Cats have nine lives — I'm on my tenth. Yeah, double agents do exist. A note of regret and thanks. On the first day. On the seventh day. The seventh seal. The Symposium and its Ethics. Waiting for doctor and counsellor. She and I were married at 3pm Friday 22 July. She was saying last night that I was helping her to 'see' things, that is, not merely emotions but the images that can be used to shape them into real poetry. She's like a cross between Sexton and Plath. I feel she'll soon take on the virtues of a Laura Riding: she hasn't read — I'll get it for her. Sounds patronising all of this doesn't it. It's not meant to be. I feel she'll become a great writer over the next few years (if not already). To retain her own voice but learn that symbolism requires imagism to keep in that great void of storage — the subconscious. Emotions are always there and alive and can simultaneously live in the unconscious, but images do *both* the abovementioned. Approx 1.50pm Train to F after rehab appointment. Meeting at rehab with BD and Dr X was civil, informative but horrific! Medically good etc but the TH case has got out of hand. I think she must be mad or truly *suffering*? from delusions. She is either *suffering*? from this/these or is a pathological liar. She is going out of her way to crucify me. I don't mean her (or anybody else for that matter) any harm. But TRUTH (as opposed to shamming) is truth. She'll try to close down all avenues of access to evidence re our relationship. That I know she cannot do! All I want is an acceptance that a relationship did take place between us. Sure, I've had hallucinations before, but not delusions. I hope, for her own mental well-being, she accepts and pulls out before she emotionally self-destructs. 2-hour talk to A will have to be transcribed over the next few days. Flat out with article for *RQB* and poems for special edition on WC's retirement from the university. As usual, over deadline — but hope they get in. A quick note: Ghoul film on at 1am. Missed *Gentlemen Prefer Blondes* last night much to my annoyance — though I've seen it a couple of times already. But then again, I watched *Blue Velvet* 12x in a row on video once and would have done so with *Eraserhead* if it were available outside the confines of the Lumière. 3 poems due *Blue Velvet* (already written quite a lot on this over the last couple of years), *Eraserhead*, and possibly *Battleship Potemkin*. Eisenstein and Lynch make good bedfellows. Tonight's ghoul film is *Ghouls from Beyond the Grave*; last week's had a Leslie Howard lookalike in it (name gone at the moment — Doloxene/Valium don't help memory a great deal) — bizarre spoof. Still like Warhol's (really Paul Morrisey's) films *Flesh for Frankenstein* and *Blood for Dracula*. It's great to have married someone with my same obsessional interest in the humour of horror (the liberation of being emptied). Fassbinder *is* horror! Can't wait for her to see Veronica Voss. Going to rewrite that fantasy novel I wrote (and then burnt) in my late teens — *The Staffs of Kwarn*. Awaiting *Dracula has Risen from the Grave* She reckons there's a connection — via the eyes — between Perry Mason and Dracula. Nah, I reckon it's just between Mason and Christopher Lee. 'You deny the existence of God? Then sir, you are an Atheist!' 'I don't deny it but I don't believe in it.' Sex aids and horror films. Vampire's eyes to victim's. Vampire eyes to victim's nipples. Nipples as eyes. Well, it took a Hell of a lot to wipe this one out. Poor Christopher with his tears of blood. At least he didn't have to listen to a stream of all too obvious commentary. And he wept tears of blood in his final moments as the clouds cleared to reveal the full moon and the corrupted priest was redeemed through Latin and acceptance of his weakness. Last year, in recovery, X'd got him to sign a document that would give them access to all hospital and medical records. This dark is everywhere we said, and called it light, coming to ourselves. (Orpheus and Eurydice, from Jean Valentine). Adrienne Rich writes: He thought there would be a limit and that it could stop him. X never defined but rather expanded the limits — the boundaries — until the fear of 'discovery' overwhelmed her. That really hurt. Her saying that their having children would be 'genetically' interesting. He should have realised that with a statement like that she was merely playing with him. He hopes she will find love outside of her love for herself. Being a doctor and 'helping' others is a foil. A play in which the characters are meant as no more than puppets. Art, it seems, is an Epicurean dalliance, to her. B was right when she called her a ghoul. She won't show me a word of her novel. I feel that my flesh is being consumed and I've no recourse to a cure. 4.40am. Had to wake her for some sleepers (she 'controls' my rehab medicines). She married him because he 'looked good on the beach.' But he couldn't swim. Much to say but the soul is laden with loss. The enemy of my enemy is my friend. The worm turned via a telephone call from London to ... The forecasters were wrong.

Next morning they awoke to brilliant sunshine: the sky was entirely clear. In fact, things were too bright. You almost had to squint. The moisture on the crops, emerald green, glinted like millions of prisms. It was as if a huge crystal had been shattered over the landscape and lit up by a very carefully angled light. A floodlight. Well, I'll be working tomorrow, I reckon, said Peter. The sheep'll be too wet to work today. But tomorrow I'll be working even if it rains tonight. We'll have a shed full. You can look after yourselves, I dare say. Take a walk down the back dam. There's a family of ducks down there at the moment — quite a few birds around generally. Actually I might go for that walk now, Peter. On my own, if you don't mind. I just feel like a bit of space. No worries, we'll look after ourselves. She walked out into the fields, skirting the crops. The water crept up through her sandshoes and into her socks. A strange, centring feeling, like a cold, moist hand touching her, and then warming with action. It reminded her of her husband. It struck her they rarely ever made love in the light. They were busy during the week, and the kids were usually there on the weekends. When they went to bed they just turned the light out. It struck her that she knew him by touch better than she did by sight. And she wondered: if she didn't see him for a couple of years, would she remember what he looked like? Roughly, of course, but not really. Not below the skin. But she'd remember what he felt like. She wondered about him: would *he* remember *her*? Would he remember her touch? Would he remember her touch? What she looked like? It bothered her a little. Her shoes squelched towards the dam, leading her on as if they had a mind of their own. The atmosphere felt like the jelly that surrounded the lens. That's how it felt to Danny, as he made his way, blindfolded, into what he imagined was a large room. It had that feel about it, it had the sound of a large room; as he trod on wooden floorboards, his steps echoed. It was an empty room; they echoed without obstacle. And the footsteps behind him, telling him to turn left or right. Then eventually to sit down. He waited, expecting the blindfold to be taken off, now that he'd been taken to the hidden destination. But it wasn't taken off; nothing else was said. People just walked out of the room, shut the door. He couldn't undo the blindfold because his hands were tied and latched to his belt. His feet were free, so he could get up. Which he did, and walked around. He just bumped into walls, and at one stage tripped over. Eventually he walked into the chair and tripped over that. He sat down again. There didn't seem much else to do. He hadn't thought a great deal about anything very much since being taken. He'd been in the car, he'd pulled over, they'd had a few drinks.

Then he'd woken up again, blindfolded, in a car. He didn't know if it was the same car, or if he was with the same people. He hadn't thought about much — just about how he couldn't see anything. What it was like to be blind. It wasn't at all like being trapped in a dark room, or lying in bed at night, or closing your eyes. It was *absolute*: he wanted to see, he could feel the life around him and wanted to see what it was that surrounded him. He hadn't thought about anything, he'd just *felt* that. He sat there for a long time; he couldn't quite work out how long, it wasn't like he'd been counting the minutes. The seconds. He'd always expected that was what you'd do if you couldn't see and you were tied up, you'd just think about time. You'd find a specific way of measuring time; maybe you'd hear your heartbeats or something, keep track of them. He didn't know how long it was. But he sensed it was no longer light. There was a noise: the door was opened. She'd just lectured on medical ethics. He joked about it. The joke turned in on itself. The perfect affair, to satisfy vanity, had collapsed. That she'd said 'If I fall, I fall entirely.' Today is the day the exile has returned. The rites of Spring. Re-ordained. He realises he was an amusement, a kind of 'artistic' conquest to compensate for artistic inadequacy. And no one would believe it. He woke up with his new wife, stepchild already watching television. The old green

Falcon ute is still on T's road near the fence, the lawns thickly breathing. A dead bird lies beneath the power pylon. In the *Theatre of the Imagination* characters move from stage to stage, become different characters. The written becomes the actual and vice versa. The victim becomes the oppressor. L becomes a man. But then, she's been a man before. Flat 3 is now above flat 6 but not in the minds of the inhabitants. *Blue Velvet* is stuck in the video machine. The dialogue, the script, is only subtext. It has no relevance to commentary. To the general aesthetics. Dear Mr L S, You ask me what it was that drew me to writing, ie. I assume, being a writer. Well, I'll tell you — sex. I wrote my first piece of ficto-criticism when I was thirteen. At school. It was a 'description' of cunnilingus for a girl I had the hots for. Some of the boys in the class had been passing their fathers' dirty magazines around and this girl caught a glimpse of one. Of course, to keep it all sacred and to retain the power of mystique, they refused her access. Actually, I think it was more about embarrassment than anything else. Anyway, she said to me that she'd like to see some. I didn't have a father to pinch them from — my last memory of him was peeling the sunburnt skin from his back and squeezing the blackheads on his shoulders — nor the money or courage to buy one, and wasn't *in* enough with the other boys to borrow one. Ultimately, they were markers of power, and none was about to cede territory, especially to a bookish non-entity like myself whose changeroom masculinity was questionable. So I wrote her a story about a bloke — myself I suppose, looking back — licking the cunt of a woman — her I suppose. What was fascinating, and what she commented on, was my embellishment of the clichéd renderings of the act. I was obsessed with chafed skin and drool, pimples and odours, possible discharges and sickness. It put her off entirely, and her reaction merely confirmed my scepticism of the entire process. Not only did this girl avoid me for the rest of the year but every girl in my class held their nose when I came near. I hope this response has satisfied your curiosity. And I'm glad you enjoyed *Blue Bête Noire*. Please don't write to me again! All the best, Yours As he was leaving, how we should get to hear, to read ... his incomplete narrative? To many, the handing over of a prescription by the doctor to the patient signifies that the doctor cares, that he (sic) has recognised that a problem does exist and has understood its nature, that the transaction is complete and that recovery from the dysfunction can be expected ... in many cases the medicinal benefit is probably minimal but the psychological benefit of a caring gesture has very strong placebo implications. (Senate Standing Committee on Social Welfare, 1981, p. 118). Dear L, I've looked at the opening scenes of your play. I like the idea and would be happy to pass it on, if you like. Please understand that this is not really my area. I'd actually recommend you approach Thomas instead, he's a playwright, he's good and he's got contacts. I'm returning the draft. Good luck if I don't hear from you! Yours, P.S. I'm thinking of writing a crime novel-cum-thriller set in Bangladesh. Maybe I'll send you a copy if I ever get around to it. A Juxtaposition of Essences: the critic tends towards language poetic. He might, or might have, take/n a visit to the country. He is intrigued by desolation. By salinity. One of the girls has a disease that has yet to be diagnosed. It may or may not be a social disease. *Sequestration of the Sick*: 'As soon as any man shall be found by this examiner, chirurgeon, or searcher to be sick of the plague, he shall the same night be sequestered in the same house; *The Language of Oysters* brings together the metaphysical lyrics of poet Robert Adamson and the deeply layered photographs of Juno Gemes. The theme is the river, specifically the Hawkesbury. It is a metaphorical work that deals with the essences of place. The metaphors are built out of comparisons, or juxtapositions, made between the myriad elements that give it identity. The mist (Serpent's Breath) rises over a black glass river which meanders by an old oyster farmer's hut. There is continuity, but also change.

Things are working for and against each other. Beauty can be found in the toughest images. Gemes and Adamson decode place and its mystery, reinforcing its spirit, giving it language. This work is more than a collaboration, it is a major artistic initiative that sees different artistic mediums interacting with each other. For both there is the continuum of their art. As Adamson writes in *The Language of Oysters*, and as Gemes signifies in her visual techniques, there is a continuation and reference being made to a greater art. But there is also the voice that arises from the interaction of text and image. Another, entirely sublime voice. Where Adamson is able to write with the 'spirit' of Olson, an Olson who is an oyster farmer, as much part of Hawkesbury as Adamson himself: Charles Olson sat back in his oyster-shed,/working the words, 'mostly in a great/sweat of being, seeking to bind speed'—/looked at his sheaf of pages, each word/an oyster, culled from the fattening grounds/of talk. They were nurtured from day one,/from the spat-fields to their shucking,/words, oysters plump with life. On Mooney Creek/the men stalk the tides for corruption. Gemes is able to give voice to those who inhabit her images. When Deleuze, talking of Bergson, refers to the notion of Duration, of things looked at in terms of time rather than space, he notes that change brings constantly with it new essence, new substance.

While the documentary photography of Walker Evans, in *Let Us Now Praise Famous Men*, captures in a social realist way the true grit of the American idiom, Juno Gemes' work observes place and people both in terms of their 'period' and in terms of their individual identities. So place and personality are intertwined. The scene and its players are entirely necessary to each other. Rather than a case of the captured image, it's a matter of images being organic. And as this is art and not reportage, so there is also a third element — that of the artist, or more appropriately, the spirit of the 'artist'. Things are happening beyond the frame of the picture, things are happening before and after the picture. We have a moment in time, caught, but still the pictures allow a difference according to the context in which they're seen. It's like the whole time we've been in this dump's been crammed into one day. The explosions overhead, that prick of a husband obsessing about HIS work, my novel consuming itself. I'd like to talk to the crazy woman from number one but she's walking her boyfriend round out front and there's not a chance. He's always on the nod. I've lost track of the panty sniffer. I really liked him. I popped a few clean pairs in a package and dropped them into his mailbox just after he left. I knew he'd be back to clear the mail. I'd asked him to drop the rest of his manuscript in for me to look at, some time. Maybe it'll come by mail. Taylor (1979): Even when social factors *are* recognised as antecedents of various medical and psychological conditions, it is usually considered that the problem lies in the maladaptation of the *individual* to the society in which he lives. There was a click, then he sensed light. So it *was* dark outside, someone had turned a light on. That meant there must be windows. The windows must be high up the wall because he hadn't felt any. There must be light coming in somewhere. No one had turned the light on before. Or maybe they did, maybe he just couldn't remember. He could smell something. Food. Yeah, it was Indian food. He could smell turmeric, garlic, chilli. The aromatic mixture of a curry. He could smell a wheaty smell, a glutenish smell. Maybe it was a roti bread, a nan or something. Soon it was placed in his lap. His hands were untied. Something in his hand: maybe it was a spoon. He touched the end of it — no, it was a fork. He pressed his thumb into its bowl, and wiped it clean. It kind of felt sensual. If he'd been more scared, it would have felt threatening. But he wasn't particularly scared. There was a matter-of-factness about the whole process that reminded him of the espionage books he'd read as a kid. This was what was supposed to happen. He invents the lens that can take close-ups with incredible accuracy, and here he is. But of course he hadn't invented that at all. He didn't know if they knew what they'd *really* come across. The real potential of what he'd done. Sure, they were interested in the organic-inorganic bonding. But he wasn't sure if they knew the actual value of what he'd done. No doubt he'd find out later, after he'd eaten, maybe. Anyway, they hadn't answered — revealed the key yet. So basically he wasn't afraid. And he ate comfortably. He didn't feel that good with the blindfold. It was a relief having his hands untied. The reverse, that is, that there is something drastically wrong with the society that humans are being asked to adapt to, receives scant attention. Rather, those individuals who suffer from these modern 'diseases' are labelled as 'susceptibles' ... Normal people are becoming patientised, social problems are being individualised and medicalised, and the individual is being blamed for maladaptation to society rather than the present social and economic system being held culpable for such maladaptation on a grand scale. (pp. 223–4). *Non ex hoc dicitur justum quod Deus illud vult.* Bataille is dead in the eye of the camera dead in the reminiscence of one night at Lake Toba where I'd licked every mosquito bite on M's body. With paint bought at the New Market I've painted the wall next to my bed orange. It's a colour I hate. I call it the relating colour. S is asking me whether the rickshaw man claimed the hash was Afghani or Kashmiri.

Fuck off, S., I say. It was Afghani. S.'s prime drive in life is eating. Okay. Almost understandable. Foreign embassy workers have their own brothel. S tells me that in his village there's a crazy man who fucks sheep and goats. Some guy appeared at the door this morning asking if we wanted to do The Beer Deal with him. I told him to fuck off. I burnt my chest getting up to answer the door — a lump of hash scorched its way through to my heart. Thick black smoke filled the room. Hello, Mr Anarchist, the young man had said. I watched him ride off on a late model 125 Yamaha motorcycle. S tells me his father owns a hotel and that he takes great pride in his appearance. S has got a sense of humour — he says this with a wry grin. I've been getting really scared. I eat mandrax and take morphine and still the fear doesn't go. I am sick and scared and feel pathetic. I watch air bubbles slide into my vein. The New Market. I need more books. White smocks, mouths full of gold teeth. Hash salesman. A bitch drinking filth from the gutters with full teats. Small boys trying to sell used plastic bags, rusty nuts and bolts, and corroded batteries for 1 taka apiece. Fairway's Cycle Shop, The National Science Library, and the red-haired Bengali dressed in a white suit and aloof on his rickshaw seat. I have been befriended by a rickshaw man. I realise he only wants my business, but I feel I can trust him. I feel he genuinely likes me. I need him to like me. I wanted S to like me, genuinely that is, but he is too close to The Escapee. This rickshaw man says he likes me because I am as skinny as him. Okay, I can deal with this. He sits in the street below my room refusing all other business, waiting for me to appear. He can get as much morphine as I want, cheaper than the pharmacist. I pay him the same amount. Suddenly the room is full of fleas. Thousands of them. They are eating me. The Escapee cannot see or feel them. In a sense, Gemes is a symbolist photographer as well as an honest interpreter of the real. A strange combination, but I'd argue Gemes is as much poet as photographer, and it is through the interaction of these twin poles of the creative curve that such a contradiction can work. It is not surprising that the poetry of Robert Adamson is so at home with Gemes' images, and vice versa. In fact, at times they are almost necessary to each other. *The Language of Oysters* shows this connection at its strongest. With imagery firmly embedded in the immediate, or even immediacy, of the scene, the mouth of the Hawkesbury, where Gemes and Adamson have been working together for over seven years, there is still a sense of the universal, of an artistic pursuit of grand truths. In the cameos of the river and river life, those accumulations of miniatures which add together to give an impression of the chthonic nature of the land referred to by Roslyn Poignant in *Mangrove Creek 1951* (Axel and Roslyn Poignant, Hawkesbury River Enterprises, 1993), which Gemes became aware of five years into her project, we see a language at work which can be spoken and understood anywhere. There is mystery and truth here — the two are inseparable. In her pursuits and observations of the moods of the river and its inhabitants, Gemes is constantly looking for those subtleties of change a casual observer so often misses or even ignores. The material collected by her lens is much like the inspiration that goes into a poem. The inspiration that is transferred to the page and then drafted to the point where it makes contact with its audience. Like the poet redrafting a poem, the photographer redrafts through the darkroom. Gemes does not work by subterfuge. There is an honesty and integrity in her interaction with her subjects. Be it with a local fisherman or with the texture of a surface, she allows herself to interact with her observations. In a sense it is the opposite to Baudrillard's statement, 'The sensuality of behind-the-scenes power: the art of making the other disappear. That requires an entire ritual.' Gemes does not want things to disappear. Like Adamson she is a conjurer, drawing hidden meanings out of her subjects. In both poem and photograph we find layer on layer of meaning, and potential meaning. Gemes invests in her images all the work that she has done before. Though they are not linked by A-B-C-type chronology, there is movement. These are not just stills but really frames from a discontinuous narrative. The sequence of events distils into moments that live for themselves, moments that are unique, are whole in themselves. But necessary to other moments. Gemes does not isolate these, but juxtaposes and enjambs. Her art, in this, is post-modern. Her techniques, especially in her use of light, at times impressionist. Funny bloke, that Danny. Worked with him for years but never really got to know him. But that's often the case in this business. None of us really know each other. We'd have a drink after work. He'd even go to the occasional dinner party. But we don't really want to know each other. We cooperate for the sake of research grants and things like that, but it's really our own backs we're trying to scratch. That's the truth behind it. Danny had other interests. He was always busy on some other project at home. He didn't talk about it much on the job; in fact he didn't even talk about the job much when he was here. If he talked about anything, it was painting or an opera he'd heard on the ABC or something like that. Yeah, he often played the radio when he was working, really irritated most of us. Actually, it's like he's been gone for years, not a few days. He was never really here in the first place. Right. Anything strange over the last week? the constable asked. No, that's the point I'm making: there was never really anything strange at all. And if there were we wouldn't have noticed because no one really took any notice of anything. Things just are as they are. We're more interested in what *we're* doing. The constable looked across to the sergeant. He remained motionless. Then he knitted his brows, as if he'd come across some sudden discovery. The sergeant was the sort of cop who'd gone through the whole process of suspecting the wife — foul play on that level — especially when she was *sassy*, as he put it. Then the work colleagues: jealousy motive. He was pegging away through them, and when he'd gone through all of them, he'd sit down and assess the most likely. That's the sort of cop he was. He was a bit of a sexist old pig as well. When they left, he turned around to his constable offsider as well and said, Do you reckon this guy was a handsome bloke? I mean, would you have found him appealing? Do you reckon he's been having a bit on the side? The constable looked at him and said flatly, You don't have to be attractive to be having a bit on the side. The sergeant stared at her blankly. He didn't say anything else. They got in the car and drove off. They remained silent during the entire journey. Neither of them thought about anything very much. Back at the office, the constable started writing up the day's notes. She picked up the file photo of Danny, the one they'd got from his wife. The one she'd peeled out of one of those plastic-stick photograph albums that have the yellowing lines running horizontally across the pages. A photo that was probably ten years old. He didn't seem the sort of bloke that had his photo taken regularly. And she didn't seem the sort of wife that wanted to take one regularly. Oh, he was probably a little bit handsome: you know, so what? He was of middling height, he had dark hair, and dark glasses on in this photo. They didn't look like prescription glasses. Just sunnies. The sort you pick up off a chemist's stand for twenty bucks. Not flash. Not Raybans or anything speccy. No, he was just dressed casually, just looked like any old jerk from the street. Didn't look particularly scientisty or anything. She supposed you could pick him up at the bar; or if he picked you up, it'd be all right. Who knows? She didn't really entertain the thought, it just crossed her mind to consider it. The sergeant, silly old bastard, had been trying to fuck *her* for the last two years. Couldn't stand her because she refused his advances. She didn't consider they were a hindrance to her work. But if he pushed it, she'd can him. He deserved it, he was as bent as hell. Career cop — thought everything he did was right. Everything he did that was wrong was right. You know the sort. She nipped out the back and had a cigarette, thought about what she'd have for dinner. She couldn't really give a shit what had happened to this guy. Why should she? It was a really big case, a paper job, as they said. Publicity, whatever. They would have got one of the glamour girls on the job, the sort that can appear in front of the camera. They wouldn't have a fat old sergeant who stank. Not that you could smell him on TV; but in newsprint, in photos, you'd see his pores were open and seeping. And he would be pretty unpleasant to be standing around. Nah — they'd have the young Ds on the job. Slicked-back hair, cool-looking. This case just looked like a skip-town, a change of lifestyle, or a midlife-crisis job. No big deal really. Wife didn't seem to be flustered. About that, or anything, for that matter. And her kids, they were more interested in video games. Didn't even get their names, actually — supposed to have got their bloody names. Think we just called them the boy and the girl. It was like it was just the bones of a story and that was all there was going to be. There was no filler. She couldn't even remember what the house looked like. It was in one of the wealthier parts of town, had a couple of cars. Oh, that's right, it was an old-style house. What did the wife call it? Tudor, mock-Tudor, that's right. Couple of storeys. Lots of books and stuff like that in it. Sort of place you go for burglary reports. Actually the sort of place that whodunnits are set in, she thought, as she stubbed out a cigarette beneath her polished black shoe. Gemes does not need to 'assume' another's identity as she is comfortable with her subjects, and they with her. This volume is as fresh and vital as it is because she is trusted. The camera's eye is an extension of her own. It does not intrude. She is not prying. She is not desecrating. It is not the ritual, it does not suggest the ritual, it allows, through the sensitivity of the artist, the ritual to speak its own language. The artist is there as translator. And as we know, there are good and bad translations. Gemes is a great translator! Susan Sontag writes in *On Photography*: Whatever the moral claims made on behalf of photography, its main effect is to convert the world into a department store or museum-without-walls in which every subject is depreciated into an article of consumption, promoted into an item of aesthetic appreciation. A photograph does not have to be of the place where it is taken, nor does it have to be an item that represents merely its subject. To be an item of purely aesthetic appreciation it must in a sense devalue the material of its making. This is the crime of the popular aesthetician, not the photograph as thing-in-itself. *The Language of Oysters* is not stagnant and reminiscent; does not support Sontag's statement: Photographs turn the past into an object of tender regard, scrambling moral distinctions and disarming historical judgements by the generalised pathos of looking at time past. Like the poet, the photographer of *The Language of Oysters* is interested in universal, timeless themes. Which reminded her of the preacher who'd taken her under his wing when she was a girl. Her mother used to give him tins of oysters — but that was before she hated him. Much of her childhood was hazy now, but she remembered this time clearly. Sometimes she dreamed it as if it were a story. M sat by the creek at the bottom of the valley and picked at her braces. The other kids called them 'railroad tracks'. Once, her grandfather threatened to wire them up to an electric fence. She avoided this by taking to the pine trees. All the same, she thought them ugly, and would gladly have prised them off had it not been for the potential wrath of her mother. She glanced into the baptismal waters of the creek, and cringed as the metallic reflection winked back at her. Their place in the Duration is relevant, because they are visited afresh and given added meaning. What Sontag talks of is in fact *industry*, or capitalism's exploitation of what appears to be (though is not) an instantaneous medium. When she talks of photography, such a versatile and complex art, she is in fact talking of art in general. Her argument is with capitalism and its exploitation of 'art' — photography being a convenient and available scapegoat. Gemes' photographs manage that delicate blend between the investment of time and the freshness of immediacy. I suggest this is because they live outside the concerns of Sontag's Western capitalist world, despite being conscious of this world. They are not so concerned with this, but aware enough to 'see' the effect this usage, fetishisation, has. I believe it's the consciousness of poetry that does this. Adamson himself is of the river. In it we see his people. Gemes is working from both the inside and outside. On a broader scale, her mentor Lisette Modell (of whom was said: 'I know of no photographer who has photographed people as inwardly') and the photoactivism of Tina Modotti, so admired by Gemes, have allowed her to construct an investigation of her subject quite independently of preconceived notions; as has her Europeanism, to use her eye to examine a different landscape anew, while also being invested with a direct lineage, if you like, to the place. Gemes is aware there's no definitive picture any more than there's a definitive poem. There are many. And a photograph will only be art if it is not lost to reminiscence, to the past. She is not of Sontag's sentimental recollection. There are some tough images working in this volume — 'Great Tattoo' being a fine example. Adamson's poems are also harsh and confronting when they need to be. The impact of poems like 'What's Slaughtered's Gone' counters any idea of sentimentality. The photographs, like the poems, project. They can and will do these things, but also do more. One should consider how the photographs are presented to a viewer. Arrangement, that is, *context*, is everything. When Sontag talks of scrutiny, she ignores the possibility that the photograph might 'look back' on *itself*. That it has a life of its own. The viewer in scrutinising the content is also scrutinising self. How do we decode this internal identity from what we view? Memory, in a sense, is a series of photographs that rearrange themselves. Memories are tainted and influenced by different lights, as are photographs. The content is the same but the exposition differs. Sontag would be right if she were to refer to the empowered use a society makes of its images. They must have worth. Worth can be something either of general value or of value to a particular person. Photographs have both of these. But so would ancient fingernail clippers. A general functional worth, and collector's value. But if they were archetypal images, and as such commented on their own position in the scheme of things, they'd have another worth. As does the photograph. Because it is a 'modern' art, too much is made of photography being part of commodity fetishisation. It is an artform. The camera is as the brush, the pen, the instrument upon which a composition is played. It is the composition that matters. And to compose does not mean one needs to intrude or manipulate deceptively. Somebody peeled his sleeve back. They rubbed the crook of his arm, just above the elbow. There was a cold, damp alcohol feeling on his skin. Then a syringe slipped into his vein, and suddenly he felt a little giddy. Like a slow, sick swoon. Then lulled into a narcotic stupor. This wasn't the first time that had happened. It had happened before, a lot of times before. But he couldn't quite remember when. Or where, or why. He didn't even question. He had something like a waking dream: he saw himself in his laboratory, cutting up eyes. They were looking back at him just before he sliced elliptically and took the lens out. He was being very rough with it. Usually he displayed incredible delicacy, but this time he was just popping the lenses out. He didn't know why. But he felt sleepy, and his head kept dropping to his chest. And he'd look up and see the eyes again and pop another lens out. He didn't know why. Later that night, Peter was clearing up his shearing gear. Should have done this days ago. You know what it's like, you get home from work and you just don't feel like doing anything else. It started raining and I knew I wouldn't be working the next day so I just left it. I've got to brush up these combs and cutters, wash 'em and oil 'em. Get 'em ready for tomorrow. Have to grind them later of course, go down the shearing shed and do that, the shed down the back, the new paper I put on the wheel today. It means one sees and arranges. There is a difference. The consciousness of interaction between these visual and non-visual forms is exemplified in Adamson's poem 'Meshing Bends in The Light'. This is a case where the craft of the photographer has actually become the stuff of metaphor, where the language moves not only through the way a photographer sees but also through the technicalities of the craft. The conscious link between the flesh and blood of the animal, of the river, and that of the organic growth of the photograph, is intriguing. This is where a 'third' artist is involved. The sublime artist. The creation of collaborators that exists quite independently. Conjured, it directs its own speech. It is the parallel text running with the river. The turning moon is/up-ended in the silver/gelatin and sets. The hook/stops spinning through the space. Consider the notion of the aspect of memory being not only in the subject but also in the observer. Put the pendulum on, shine 'em up, Peter said with a quick sharp laconic voice. He'd somehow perfected the art of making his drawl move as quickly as the cutters moving across the combs. Feel like a beer? he said to Mary, offering a stubbie. Yeah, why not — thanks, Pete. Kids enjoyed today. Yeah, they were in fine form. I've been thinking, Pete; he's been working on this project for years, right? Years and years and years. And I see so little of him, and yet at the same time it's not like I've lost something of him *to* that. It's just that part of him — that's where he *is*. And I've never expected to see it. Like, part of him's always been gone and I've never seen it in the first place, you know what I mean? Yeah, I know what you mean. He was always like that as a kid as well. A great brother, always a good friend, but you never knew all of him. A quarter of him was missing somewhere. Not so much *missing*, just ... hidden from view. This does not make the frame nostalgic in itself, but a medium for considering the way memory moves between experience, the seen and association. A stream of light pours/from the sky into the mouth/of Mooney Creek, the river/flows in to the memory of whoever/looks into these frames. The river flows. Memory is cumulative, it keeps flowing. With every return to the images it flows again. It has a new essence. The time of day is set but we look at it anew. We compare and contrast. It is, like language, active. Sontag says, 'To photograph is to confer importance.' Gemes would say importance is conferred on the photograph if you photograph what is important to you. And important is what is real. And what is real is what appears in the image. This does not mean we have to recognise it, or put a name to it. But the poet will attempt to. And in this process the inner self behind the portrait is doubly illuminated. There is both the tone of light, so all-important to Gemes' craft (especially her river still lifes where planes of light interact and intersect with planes of water, where surfaces are defined by the eye with which we interpret them — for each the way of viewing is different), and the tone of words — the gradations of tonalities and variations of emotion, experience, observation, perception and interpretation — melded and transformed into poetry. Though Gemes admires the resilience and courage of the river dwellers she does not attempt to idealise. She and Adamson are river dwellers themselves and see from the inside out. To communicate this culture with honesty, with a total dedication, is a matter of negotiation, of maintaining a constant dialogue with subjects and the environment, with the source of the imagery. They are active members in the field of vision, they confer meaning to place, they scape *our* appreciation, they also give rise to an aesthetic. It is interesting to consider that a fisherman as subject in a Gemes photograph is as much an embodiment of the river, in every line of his face, in the light on his skin, as he is the person. You photograph a fisherman and you get the river. And the meanings of a river are endless. Then again, I suppose we're all a bit like that. Yeah, said Mary, sipping at the stubbie. It's just that there's something ... I mean, it's staring me right in the face. I can see it but I can't put it in words. It's like you were saying about the notion of liberty — he's always known what the key is, he's always had the answer. The research is kind of like embellishment. It hasn't really been necessary, he's known it from the beginning and he's known, no matter what he did, he wouldn't improve upon his knowledge. If we're talking about the concept, rather than just the principle, then in a sense it's almost as if he wouldn't have to reveal what he knew, that he sustained his research. If all it is is an incredible principle that allows the bonding of the organic and the inorganic in a cogent, networked way, an interfacing maybe, that's fine, but that's a finite thing. You discover it, and then maybe you can improve upon it. But the discovery's finite. It seems to me that that's really not what it's about, that it exists somewhere between the two, the notion and the end result. I don't know: I'm just going to have a few beers and go to bed. I've got a long day tomorrow. The room seemed very close around him now. He didn't know if it was light or dark; he couldn't really sense it anymore. He did care — he wanted to know if it was light or dark, but he just *couldn't* know. He loathed the feeling that he was in a waking dream. He wasn't fond of dreaming anyway; that sort of cleansing of the subconscious didn't appeal to him. It wasn't the lack of clarity that he minded, although clarity was what he constantly sought. He was used to a lack of clarity. That's what research is all about, trying to find clarity; once you've got it then you've achieved your aim. It was just that he hated the feeling that he couldn't go any further, either backwards or forwards. He was just stuck, he was in a stasis. People came and brought him meals, they didn't speak to him. He didn't even ask why are we here, what's happening, what do you want? Maybe they already had what they wanted, and were doing this for their amusement. Or maybe they were waiting for a way of disposing of him; or who knows? He wondered who they really were. Were they the same people who'd come to his house, who'd taken him to the bar? He didn't know. Later it crossed his mind that the first thing he'd said to Mary when he met her was, 'You've got beautiful eyes.' He considered how gross this was, given the fact that he was obsessed with eyes, he pulled them out of the heads of dead animals. But he hadn't meant *that*. He just meant they looked great. They were like portholes into her soul or something. Gemes has described the culture of the river as being 'invisible' to most of those who live beyond its reaches. Gemes and Adamson, through being part of this culture, are able to make it visible, to give it voice. Gemes sees this mediation with place through experience and participation as a kind of activism. It is important to consider that Gemes, in identifying *this* culture does not see it as the only culture. It is simply one to which she has access, and is one which accepts her presence. Without this acceptance her constructions would not be possible. It is also important to consider that she is aware that there is also an 'unseen' culture that is some 40,000 years old acting on and with the manifestation of inhabitation as she now finds it. It is there if one looks. There are many images which directly approach this Koori presence (it is more than heritage; in its duration it maintains its past manifestations and holds a new essence for every 'new' time: ie. it is all-pervading). Images such as Ancient Koori Rock Carving, which is juxtaposed with a sweep of the river, boat cutting whitely through the water suggesting incursion and in its subtle quietness the possibility of co-existence, the juxtaposition and interaction of Buffy's Mulloway and Stingray Dreaming, the Fish Dreaming image and poem Rock Carving with Kevin Gilbert. Juxtaposition is the key here. Gemes allows us to draw the parallels. We recognise the archetypal images, the unspoken inferences of connection. The inchoate registration of the land in human life. The river isn't read but reading its inhabitants. And this is universal. The book's construction is paramount in the way we read these relationships. The attributes that elevate

Gemes into the realms of the truly great photographers — those who have retained the integrity of the observed but instilled some of themselves into the observation (from Stieglitz through to Cartier-Bresson) — are that she can observe without intervention and yet invest herself into the construction without distorting its integrity. She is there in the shadow, in the light in the eyes of her subject, and the balance of the image. But she is only there insofar as it conveys the truth in her subject. A major theme of Gemes' work has been that of social injustice, particularly in relationship to Koori culture. In a recent interview with Gemes I asked her about the relationship between her project and that of Koori identity with place, specifically the Hawkesbury: *We mentioned the* Mangrove Creek *book, and we were talking before about your work with Koori people, their culture and art, and social aspects — white domination ...* Social injustice ... Yes. *As it says in the Afterword of that book, 'The rugged terrain of the lower Hawkesbury very forcibly imprints the natural land formations on the mind. During those few days in 1951 the dominance of the enclosing bush was reinforced through all the senses, and intensified by heat. Although the Aboriginal presence had been physically obliterated, it seemed as if it had been reabsorbed into the land itself, as a deep chthonic layer, and that the spirit of place had long since claimed the more recent white arrivals and rendered them indige-*

nous.' I quote this because I notice some of your images have that Dreamtime and that deeply spiritual aspect, not only conceptually but texturally. You seem to develop even an Aboriginal art sort of feel about it. I think that's very true, because it is here in this country. That may be true — I'm reflecting what I perceive, through experience, about this country, this particular landscape. As I became familiar with the oyster-farming and fishing culture that is prevalent here, and is to a large extent an invisible culture — it simply is not visible to the rest of society or to the community — I became aware that here were seven generations. There were people who had lived in this landscape for seven generations, and whose relationship to the River was very respectful and guardianlike. This idea has been strongly with me throughout the work — it was clear then, it's still clear now. I also feel very strongly the Aboriginal presence here ... It *is* a pristine country, and as I know from a surveyors' map from the Australian Museum, and that actually dates back to 1890 ... this land is covered with over 260 Aboriginal rockcarvings. So that the Aboriginal presence for me is very strong, and the relationship between the oyster-farming community and their feeling for country, I found to have *some* similarity to Aboriginal relationship to country. But having said that, it's only now that Aboriginal people are coming back into this country. *Do you see with the multiple generations, of oyster-farmers for example, that have been here, a 'parallel' between Aboriginal land inheritance and continuity in the land (albeit of much longer standing), and this continuity within the families? Is there a cultural parallel in any way; or a spiritual parallel, maybe?* You'll have oyster-farmers who can read the River. They can know from looking at the surface what's going on underneath. And it's that kind of specific knowledge of the River that is handed on from generation to generation that has a similar resonance to 40,000 years of Aboriginal occupation and relationship, specific relationship, in a guardian/custodial sense, to country. I have to be careful here because it's not the *same*. But there are *some* similarities ... What is clear is that in Gemes' work there is a consciousness of everything else that might be going on in a picture. There is a sense of the potential and likely, a consideration of the subtexts that are operating on the primary, or seen, image. It is important to realise that the Koori spiritual continuance is of the land and not *of* the camera. Gemes is sensitive to the presence and its meaning but does not suggest that it requires 'capturing' to persevere. Rather, she acknowledges its power and invites it to work on her constructions. She knows that without this link any interaction with the place would be infertile. It is part of her collective imagination and there is no sequestering it or bending it to her purpose. It holds the energy. Gemes is merely an active conduit for its speech. It is in fact because of its *non-literalness* that a photographic image that is not directly related to a poem can illuminate the text by suggestion, juxtaposition that enhances and illuminates. *The Language of Oysters* is very much an example of photographs prompting, or to use a word of Gemes' 'provoking', the poem, while with the Mooney Sequence we have the poems provoking photographs. It is interesting to note that there is something of Adamson's 1989 volume of poetry *The Clean Dark* in this book. The idea of the image interacting and enjambing the text can be seen here. In *The Language of Oysters* there is a more conscious presentation of this process. In a review of *The Clean Dark* — 'Shadows In The Water' I alluded to the *process* of interaction between the visual and textual planes, and referred to the use of image as signifier. It is relevant to quote sections of this piece: Robert Adamson opens his latest volume of poetry, *The Clean Dark*, with a quote from Ludwig Wittgenstein's *Philosophical Investigations*: *Two pictures of a rose in the dark. One is quite black; for the rose is invisible. In the other, it is painted in full detail and surrounded by black. Is one of them right, the other wrong? Don't we talk of a white rose in the dark and of a red rose in the dark? And don't we say for all that that they can't be distinguished in the dark?* He struggled for meaning.

They were green. They *are* green, he thought. Well, he assumed they were green, still green. But that was what he'd said, though he'd never said that to anyone else, any of his previous girlfriends. He couldn't remember even thinking about their eyes. Mary's were actually stunning, though. They really stood out. He wasn't the only one that remarked on them. She even said to him, Oh, you're not the first one to say that, and laughed. They were stunning. He recalled reading, in one of those pseudo-scientific journals bad publishing houses had a habit of sending him and his colleagues, about the seventeenth-century notion of eye-beams. Of people projecting images through their eyes, and basically almost seeing what they thought. And also, by the same notion, illuminating what was there. This had puzzled him for a while. He wondered how he could best apply it to his theories of sight, how he could weld that with the *corpus magnificum* of scientific research. He considered all scientific knowledge was like a large planet floating in space, suspended; that the gravity that held it there was the hypotheses that were graduating towards proof. Or condemnation. It was a strange orreriacal analogy. He considered *his* concepts not pseudo-science but the ultimate point of science, the finest notions of science. What was it Newton said — that men of science were once also men of letters, men of ideas, in the grandest sense? The notion illuminated by Wittgenstein has been transcribed by Adamson through the silkscreen of language and article. The darkness of the page, the light of inspiration. A focal point, to be sure, but no answer, no solution. And this positive equivocation is carried throughout the collection, despite something of a refutation in the final poem. Or is this the reaction made necessary, the details anchoring the magic? The piece goes on to reference the link between image and text: The dust cover offers us death suspended, netted. Each section in turn opens with a photograph by Juno Gemes. The first, a camera mounted on a tripod aimed at a tin shed, a distillation of the art. The black and white Symbolist crossover, a tease, a tempting desire. The camera is there for a shot to be taken, the image and attainment, a result of intention. But maybe this shot will not be executed, it is as the red and the white rose, the darkness. And: The final section of the book, 'No River, No Death', is introduced by the most effective, to my eye, of the photographs. Life-shift, the wreckage of shadow and light, the plumbed depths, stilled ripples, trees, sky, shed and shack, collapsing inward, though with a poise that is almost graceful. And, somewhere, there is death. Language 'licking its flesh wounds'. 'No River, No Death', the first poem, consolidates the Styx image: Now leave from a jetty, souls going where souls go and The wharf sags with tar-drenched oyster racks/and a fisherman's punt rocks as its side for Charon. She was being called. Voices were reaching down from the hall on the hill, the hall with the glassless windows and ceilingless roof. A previously ignored daisy suddenly proved more interesting to her. Its centre beckoned. But the voices kept calling, louder and louder. She dragged herself to her feet and began to meander slowly up towards the source of the summons. Though, in spite of these reflections on death, a matter-of-fact wonderment retains a place (beyond the 'microwaved' voices of politicians /civilisation): the larrikin prawn bird starts to sing. This last line so much captures the spirit of the river dwellers. Even in death they look to the wider world, to its mysteries and wonders. There is always a dignified humour to be found in their austerity. What is fascinating in *The Clean Dark* in the context of this discussion is that the river, a place that has 'always' been Adamson's and to which he has given his signature, is the dynamic that has developed between him and Gemes. Each has enriched the other's vision. Gemes has brought another history to Adamson's. In terms of duration there's a new essence to complement those that have passed before. As with the two roses, we are talking about notions of presence. The dynamic between the concept and the observed 'thing' is at the crux of this, as it is in the collaboration between poet and photographer. The dialogue that occurs between Gemes and Adamson is very much about giving voice and illuminating the unseen. A new preacher was holding a meeting. Her mother said he was wealthy and owned a large 'surveillance' company. He was considered a good catch. She smiled to herself as she thought of the one from Kansas. He'd been too fat to travel by lift. She relished the story of his conversion, how it was that God came to him on the brink of death in a theatre toilet, holding back the trigger of his gun as his finger struggled between Temptation and Salvation. He had owned a fast-food chain, would carry a wad of credit cards, and at least a thousand dollars in his back pocket. Mangroves are a fascinating sourcing of the unseen. In Adamson's poem 'Phasing Out The Mangroves' we sense the language of the mangroves (The great hunched mangroves/ will no longer tend/ the instincts of kingfishers;) is comprehended by the swamp children but not the language of destruction, of the intruding 'modern civilisation' (the swamp children/ speaking a language of arithmetic in cracked syllables). And then there had been the dwarf who had become a preacher after God had lengthened his arms and legs. He'd spoken of tribulation with violent excitement. He'd lifted weights and asked the children to feel his muscles. He'd claimed people were after him. Ecologically, there is loss here, but the faces of the river are resilient and will build around change. In Gemes' photographs we find image after image juxtaposing the trappings of the modern world, subtly, with those of the 'old'. It's as if the spirit of the mangroves will still be struggling up into the light from beneath the 'bent glass and metal domes'. Gemes' mysterious and almost breathtakingly silent (the 'silence' is almost threatening) photographs of mangrove shoots pushing up through the mud echo these themes most profoundly because they make reference to nothing but the mystery of the mangroves themselves. It is because we subconsciously form juxtaposition ourselves through being familiar with the construction of the book and the nature of Adamson's verse, that we make such observations and feel such impressions. They are ghostly and mysterious but carry a primal power that is of the instincts of kingfishers. There is a strength there, as there is in any of the portraits of the river people. It's as if they are of the dark room, these otherworld creations. But of course they are the guts of the river itself — the art is there in nature, with all its force and wonder. He liked that notion: being a flat, unanimated research worker plodding toward a set end did not entertain him. By the same token, he recalled reading in a language book, the Bruce Andrews and Charles Bernstein book on the Language writing movement in the United States, a passage called 'Glyphs'. It was by Madeleine Burnside. He recalled it word for word. The first paragraph read, There is a contradiction between events and their description that becomes visible when an event is described without reference to the describer. Such a description does not allow for the possibility that events themselves are simultaneous, that every permutation of accident and action occurs at once, that only perception strings them into logical sequences, or that forgetting is a balance to perception. Somewhere in the south-west of Western Australia, a long way from where he was, in a very different time, his wife Mary considered that she had already forgotten much about her husband. It had only been a few days, but it was almost as if she'd never really known him. And as if it was Peter, his brother, she'd been married to all these years. That it was Peter who was her husband and Peter who was father to her children. She couldn't help feeling that her memories of Danny had been placed there, had been placed there so that she could forget them. So she could unperceive them. As if the process of this would bring her love for Peter into clarity. They could not see him. He knew if they could, his eyes would look like pinpoints, little black dots in their white orbits. That was the effect of narcotics. The opposite to amphetamines and hallucinogens, which made the eyes wide and sensitive to light, everything having a slight haze to it, or being pinpoint-sharp, almost hot to look at. Mary was kneeling by the dam, watching the ducks. The ducklings following their mother in strange patterned movements around the dam. The sun was reflecting off the water. Peter was at work. The kids had gone out to the shed with him to hang around and watch what was going on for the morning. She was going out to pick them up. She said she'd take him a lunch out; he liked that idea, he got home late and by the time he cooked the dinner and made his lunch for the next day, he was beat. She was doing that, and it felt pretty good. He said when he knocked off from the shed and was having a week off, he'd do it for her, just for a change, the way it should be. The bright light on the dam actually hurt her eyes. She squinted; her pupils were small, trying to close the light out. But inside, behind the lens, behind the aperture, deep at the back of her eyes, she felt them to be wide open. That through this small entry point a vast amount of information was pouring. That because of their sensitivity, because of the closure, she had a kind of illumination, a second sight — she could see with her eyes, and she could see *in* her eyes. It was like watching a film within a film. Or like a telescope — such a small point of entry, narrowing to an even smaller point, through which the observation is made. The distance brought closer, made larger than what's actually seen. What is seen is but the surface. Even looking down through the water of the dam. Seeing a marron move quickly backwards under a crusty shelf of clay and sticks, she realised she was really only seeing the surface. The depth was an illusion. The marron, the ducks on the surface, were all of one plane. Once they'd been driving out to interview a suspect in a robbery case, and she'd been urging for a pee, and asked the sergeant if he'd pull over. He never let her drive, even though that was the usual practice, the constable driving the sergeant. Didn't trust women drivers, he said. He pulled over begrudgingly and said, Be quick about it. They stopped outside an old toolshed or work shed in the outer suburbs. There was a fence that ran alongside it, that had one of its panels out. She went behind this. There'd been a few holes punched through by graffiti artists who'd left their logos scrawled across the corrugations of the fibro fence. She crouched down to pee, and as she was in the process of crouching, she looked up, and through one of the holes she noticed the eyes of the sergeant. She quickly grabbed a rock off the ground and threw it. It clattered against the corrugations, and she heard footsteps shuffling off, and the car door close. He'd opened it quietly, but closed it pretty loud. She enjoyed the piss. He didn't mention anything about it that day. A couple of days later, as they were knocking off, he said, You're not going to say anything about that, are you? She'd replied, That's a confession, is it? And he'd gone red in the face and said, I don't know what you're talking about. Then by way of closing the matter he said, Make sure you're on time in the morning, we've got a lot to do. We've got to sort this case out, with that scientist bloke. She shrugged her shoulders. She'd never been late in five years of being in the Force. She felt tempted to make the next morning the first. One thing that is striking in Adamson's river verse is his confluence with the river. It flows through his blood and over the page with the sleekness of a fish run. The flathead emerging from his hands in the image Adamson's Catch (52, Section V) suggests that it's difficult to separate the two. It's interesting to note that such communities are based on a cyclical understanding of survival. The predator and the predated are necessary to each other. The sense of comfort with this is not always there, and death isn't always matter of fact. There are those nagging doubts. The grandmother tells her grandson that the prawns will eat you/when you die on the Hawkesbury and the ocean is something which the river requires but is like a truth that is too awesome to face — where The colour of their skin/mingles with the blood of their predators and Our bodies are constantly drawn towards the slaughter; consider They are the flesh we feed upon come from the depths/out beyond the Continental Shelf. Gemes deals with Adamson's more sombre and darkly gestating images with care and delicacy. She synthesises them into a greater picture that can tolerate the darkness of thought. In her hands they always emerge solid and life-affirming. Though both she and Adamson deal with minutiae, the fine details of this existence, it is as part of a greater picture. Robert Adamson has spent much of his life on the mouth of the Hawkesbury. As the Bunyah of New South Wales is to Les Murray's verse, so is the Hawkesbury to Adamson's. Adamson, the great Australian lyrical poet, has developed an extensive oeuvre of songs and incantations that draw on the environment, mythology and spirit of the Hawkesbury. His metempsychotic bird poems, his codices of love and death, and evocative lyrics of place, are well known. But Adamson is also an innovator, constantly introducing new vocabularies and 'voices' into his rich and varied language, and through this the infinite languages of the river. In a recent poem like 'Creon's Dream' we find new arrivals: The river seeps through the window, the books/are opened out on the desk. When the first breeze/hits the curtains the cats scatter./It could be dawn for all I know, concentration/wanders through Creon's words to Antigone *Go/to the dead and love them* — okay so they live as/long as I do — what else can I make of it?/The bright feathers from a crimson rosella lie/in clumps on the floor with a pair of broken wings. There are new poems here as well as those taken from *Canticles on The Skin*, *The Rumour*, *Swamp Riddles*, *Cross The Border*, *Where I Come From*, *The Clean Dark*, and *Waving to Hart Crane*. It is interesting to note that these poems, regardless of where they sit in the manuscript, speak to each other. There is a sense of permanence about them. They flow between each other like the river between points on the riverbanks. In other words, the history of the place is constantly redefining the future, and vice versa. Once again, it's a juxtaposition of essences. Adamson has been distilling these essences for decades, and in many senses Gemes' images form a kind of visualisation of this process. That is how an earlier poem can interact with a later image. The poem allows entry because it is fluid, the image invites the poem because it is conscious of the total history of the place, and the poem is part of this. One is reminded of the Spanish picaresque novel with its narrative flow, collation of experience, with some destination bringing it all into focus. In a sense, the publication of this volume, with the interaction between the image and text, brings the work of both artists into a new kind of focus. Each can exist artistically without the other, but together they enrich and add commentary to the other's craft. In considering Gemes' portraiture I'd like to bring to notice two images from section IV of the book: No. 41 Lorraine Biddle (née Doyle) shows Axel Poignant's portrait of Lorraine's grandmother (Margaret Alberta Doyle — Lower Mangrove Creek, 1951) and No. 42 June (Morley) Bonser with model of Surprise II, daughters-in-law Gwen & Jan Morley, grandchildren Sandra Vassallo, Debbie Groat, great-grandchildren Kylie & Nathan Vassallo & Melinda Camera. What is emphasised in both of these images is the continuity of family and identification with the river. The classical image of thought, and the straining of mental space it effects, aspires to universality. It in effect operates with two 'universals,' the Whole as the final ground of being or all-encompassing horizon, and the Subject as the principle that converts being into being-for-us. It is a wonderful compression of time as well as emphasising of change. The grandmother is still with us — not because of the photo, but because of the spirit of the granddaughter. But what the image does, like a poem, is act as an annotation to the fact. A reminder to an outsider of what is knowledge to the insider. It is also of the spirit of Gemes as artist that she pays homage to her artistic predecessor in Axel Poignant, accepts his art as part of the river's spirit. This is like the poet recognising those poets who have rowed similar waters (with Adamson we have Shelley, Mallarmé, Olson, Duncan, Webb, Slessor, Bishop, Crane and many others). A Gemes portrait works like an Adamson poem; it allows the inner light of the subject to glow. In the poems taken from *Where I Come From* we feel this acutely. With the river as background, and using the 'child' as focus, the poet paints a complex family portrait. She had reached the hall. Silence. The congregation was assembled inside and obviously waiting. She scuffed her feet as she entered. Her sisters giggled, her mother frowned. The guest preacher was about thirty-five, dressed in a three-piece suit with a carnation in the lapel, cleanly shaven with close cropped hair. His eyes were murky but occasionally the light caught them in a way that seemed to suggest they were capable of seeing things in an unusual way. He spread his arms and at his words everybody embraced. He spoke of the river of God flowing through their bodies, of the source and the delta being the same thing — the place of God. The sisters had developed various strategies to avoid being dragged into the circle of love, such as positioning themselves in a small independent clump or standing with their backs pressed against the wall. M observed that the preacher hugged their mother particularly hard. The preacher dissolved into her father. She couldn't distinguish them, though she'd not seen her father for years. She thought of her mother as being like Mrs ... the woman who'd had her child taken away. It was because she looked so desperate. So it was her father hugging Mrs ... , saying to her: take 'My Fishing Boat': Mum and Dad are at it again/in the room/next to mine/their terrible sobbing/comes through the damp wall/they fight about something/I have done/I get out of bed/and go down the yard to the river/push my boat out into/the black and freezing bay/under the mangroves/that smell like human shit/I move along my secret channel/my hands blistering/from rowing slip with blood/around the cove I tie up on a mangrove/it rains harder/all I catch are catfish here/and have them sliding/about in the belly of the boat/they are the most ugly looking things/in the world. In image 42 the shifts and continuity between generations are palpable. Apart from genetic associations, the model of Surprise II brings out of the faces what it is that is common to each. This is their history, it makes them inseparable. This is what we feel on reading Adamson's poetry. That once it is in the blood one could never leave this place. In none of Gemes' portraits is there a sense of exclusion. Her evocations belong, as do Adamson's sensitive and passionate songs of river life and spirit, to the realm of essences. He walked across the room to a bucket. He considered that his arms, his hands, were no longer tied. He still didn't undo the blindfold, he just left it there. Didn't know what would happen if he tried. Maybe someone would step into the room and stop him. Or maybe the room would be entirely blacked out, and he wouldn't see anything anyway. He wouldn't know the difference. The blindfold had sort of welded itself to his head. He couldn't really feel it anymore. He just left it there. He walked round the room pretty comfortably now. He knew where to find food, go to the toilet, whatever. He recalled Mary telling him once of an Eluard poem that had something to do with someone standing on his eyelids. He wasn't quite sure what it meant, and he never pursued the poem. He promised himself if he ever got the chance he'd look it up. At the moment he felt like someone was standing on his eyelids. Maybe himself, standing on his own eyelids: yeah, that was it. Mary started to make her way back to the house. She was suddenly annoyed: she had a vague recollection of someone reading her diary. She could sense them going through line after line, page by page. It seemed to be Daniel reading her journal. That was very unlike Daniel. He tended to keep to himself, and he didn't look through her stuff. It had been a long-established rule between them: they minded their own business, unless the other offered. But now it was Daniel reading her private words. She could feel his gaze undressing her. Peter dragged the back flywire door open with his boot. Swaggering through the doorway, he said at the top of his voice, Saw a guy knock a lamb's eye out with his handpiece today. Belting the skull with the tension nut. The kids pulled faces. Daniel considered his fascination for *The Island of Dr Moreau*, the idea of converting animal into human, transfiguring the animal form, value-adding almost, as if being human would mean more to the creature, if you could give it the soul, or at least enrich the soul it had. In terms of his own project, this was the direct opposite: infusing human tissue with metal and plastic, he was reducing life to the inanimate. He was finding what it was that filled the gap between the two. If the tissue had a soul, or, taking it further using human tissue, the total soul, then returning it to an inorganic state or using the inorganic constituents of the organic whole, then that might bring about some understanding of what it is that constitutes the soul. One night he and Mary had gone out to see a play. It was on the phases of Einstein's life, at the Hole in the Wall Theatre in Subiaco. They went out to dinner before the play. An Italian restaurant. There was a guy with an artificial arm that had a hook at the end. He was quite effectively manipulating a fork. Daniel, as always curious, asked him what it was like having a false limb. He had judged from the guy's outward behaviour and general joviality that he wouldn't be offended, and that turned out to be right. The guy said sometimes when he disconnected his arm, unstrapped it at the shoulder, he sensed there was an arm there anyway. A ghost limb, he called it. Of course Daniel had heard about this, it was pretty common knowledge. You even find the odd *Readers' Digest* story about it. The guy said it was almost like having two limbs; and on some occasions the artificial limb, being so different from his real limb, became part of him. It was only after he'd been wearing it a while that it became uncomfortable at the joint, or it itched, or got hot. It wasn't a real problem. Whenever he woke in the morning, he would feel as if he needed to put it on, as if it made him whole. This notion that the inorganic could become organic fascinated Daniel. Once again, the reverse of what he was doing: but still the law applied. In the future he saw all things being built along these lines; that like crystals growing in solution, all technology would have to be growth-orientated. It would no longer suffice, say, to build a computer that was exactly as it had stood upon building — it must grow, and it must grow with the knowledge that was instilled in it, and it must grow with the needs that were placed on it. In the same way a building will grow with its environment, and environment will actually *be* the building. In other words, there will be a blurring between the what-is and the potential of what-might-be. He felt this as the opiate washed through his body and he sank into the illuminated darkness. In arranging the images and text into sections the authors invite us to make assumptions about how they should be read. But these are narratives, and not essays. They are taken and written from the inside and projected out. As we find Henri Cartier-Bresson saying in Paul Hill and Thomas Cooper's *Dialogue with Photography*: I have never been interested in the documentary aspect of photography except as a poetic expression. Only the photograph that springs from life is of interest to me. The joy of looking, sensitivity, sensuality, imagination, all that one takes to heart, come together in the viewfinder of a camera. That joy will exist for me forever. And Cartier-Bresson's point is as relevant to the poet as it is to the photographer. Gemes and Adamson, so defined in their own arts, are also expressing a vision that breaks free of the implied boundaries of form, that asserts itself anew and unhindered with every page — be it of text or image. In *The Language of Oysters* both artists evoke the spirit of the river and its inhabitants, and also conjure the element of art itself, so often absent from documentary observation. It is the realm of potential meanings, deep below the layers of text and image that touch us. As Henri Peyre has said of Mallarmé's '[Le Vierge, Le Vivace Et Le Bel

Aujourd'Hui]': The interested reader, who may prefer a reading different from ours, would do well to remember Robert Frost's insistence that a poet is entitled to all the meanings that can be found in his poem. I mean he doesn't *make* me as such, but almost begs me to tell him things. Make up stories. How would you fucking like to tell your husband about two naked girls licking your tits and arsehole while he's fucking you. And having to describe them, what's more, in detail. And he likes juxtaposition, he likes opposites. He fucks me and asks for contraries. A tall thin blonde, a large titted brunette. He writes fucking essay after fucking essay on commodity fetishism and fantasises about commodified sex actors that've walked straight out of the page of a porno magazine. Dear R, Could you please let me know if you are making an application to the Australia Council re my expenses for the Conference? As I said on the telephone (ie., c/- the answering machine), it ultimately makes no difference as I'm already booked and ready to go, though it would be of some help if I knew the exact situation. You can contact me by either phone or fax, if that is possible. Hilda Low was down here a couple of weeks ago which was tremendous. I sat on a 'poetics' panel with her at the Perth Writers' Festival and managed to spend some value-added time with her during her short stay (including a run into the country so Hilda could see a kangaroo!). The highlight of her stay, for me, was organising a forty-five minute reading on ABC radio, the national broadcaster. This is to be the first of three programmes I'm 'doing' on Language and Language-related poetry. The second will in fact be on the Conference — yep, I'm bringing a portable tape recorder & will be recording interviews, readings etc. from those willing to participate. Material that goes to air will be financially remunerated. Oh, here's a little something that might interest you. Not only are a number of expatriate Australian academics looking to make the journey up to Cambridge for the Conference, but some are planning to give papers on Les Murray. Actually, in a paper I've written on the evolution of 'linguistic' verse down here I note that in the 'canon' of contemporary Australian verse Murray has actually been more of an innovator than would seem obvious at first glance. Anyway, it's a long story and a particularly 'Aussie' one — I'll tell you more (if you're interested), when we catch up. Well, all the best. Looking forward to hearing from you. Yours, in this interview of conscience. This interview illustrates how direct, child-orientated problems were used to derive data from c-o-m-m-u-n-i-c-a-t-i-n-g an ad-hoc introduction to american language poetry, de-fiAntly not 'idle babbling': any queries(?)

please. Outside the manifesto. **Mountains as seen from doll position 1:** 'Pilots & meteorologists disagree about the sky.' from TJANTING, by Ron Silliman **Mountains as seen from doll position 2:** 'Seriously, these sorts of far away presentations enfold their columnar pretense.' from GRADATION, by Charles Bernstein **Mountains as seen from doll position 3:** 'In its first dumb form//language was gesture//technique of travelling over sea ice/silent//before great landscapes and glittering processions//vastness of a great white looney north//of our forebeing.' from SECRET HISTORY OF THE DIVIDING LINE, by Susan Howe. She can be heard describing the bowl of fruit by both adult parties. She is loud, exclamatory. She has the voice of Cindy-doll. The voice of Sailor-doll. The voice of Barbie. She is singing. The lyrics of her song are almost poetry. Though it is a poetry that only has meaning in itself. One of the architects of the Language movement, Ron Silliman, has said of this type of poetry, it's a 'community of concern for language as the centre of whatever activity poems might be'. And then they found themselves at the zoo with him. And when it rained they ran for shelter and were pressed close to him. M thought of the animals and their urge to move beyond the bars of the cages. The preacher touched their mother on her bottom. Later, letting them out of the car, he asked them all for kisses. Silliman would also confirm that this notion may be expounded in any style or method providing the product is not merely a 'voice poem', that is, the writer conveying to reader a 'natural' message in narrative sequence. Her song is bound to have HIM pounding on the ... roof. Charles Bernstein once said, 'there is no natural writing style.' If there is a 'natural' writing style then it is in fact based on assumed knowledge and methods or patterns of delivery, leading to, in the words of William Hartley, author of the influential volume *Textual Politics and the Language Poets*, a socially contrived basis of ... writing. Language poetry is about going beyond the boundaries 'traditional/conventional' language usage places on notions of meaning. This re-working of material through aesthetic discourse is done in a political light, or at least with a political awareness, though in a way which refutes the idea that language should only refer to that which occurs outside itself. Over the last few weeks Mary had been considering how much time she'd always spent with herself; how little she'd been with Daniel even when he was in the room. It seemed better now. Even when the police came — it was like they were talking about something that happened outside of memory. She found herself the other day barely being able to describe his daily habits. She ended up describing some of Peter's. And she had begun to consider his fascination for eyes as abject. She'd begun to consider all his habits as abject. This didn't make her angry with him. It just slightly repulsed her and made her feel nauseous. The most interesting thing she'd ever heard her husband say was that the concentric layers of sight in *Milton* held the key. He meant *Milton*, Blake's *Milton*. He was fascinated by Blake. She had an interest in Blake. It was something for them to discuss. At the moment she thought that Daniel was crossing from one circle of sight to another, moving closer to the centre. The dark, dark centre. It suddenly struck him as pretty disturbing that when his kids started doing German at school, they walked around the house saying, 'Augi, Augi, Augi' as if they were four-year-olds. It struck him as even more disturbing that once when his son was staying down with his brother Peter in the country, Peter rang him up and said that the kid had gone and shot a rabbit and then gone home with the eyes, and said, 'It's okay to kill things if you take their eyes, isn't it, Uncle Peter?' Peter wasn't too amused. He couldn't even remember if he'd actually said anything to the kid when he got home. He didn't think so. It also struck him as odd that he couldn't remember his children's names. The Language poets do not exist as an anathema. They are grounded and influenced by many earlier poets and movements, such as Emily Dickinson and Walt Whitman,

Gertrude Stein (of 'a rose is a rose is a rose' fame — a commentary on the local scene passed off as fiction, a strategy used to perfection in *The Autobiography of Alice B Toklas*, though it provided no protection from the criticism of her contemporaries, some of whom were all too keen to contest the veracity of her account of the times), Charles Olson (and The Black Mountain/Projectionist school in general), John Ashbery, Louis Zukofsky, William Carlos Williams, the Dadaists (especially Tristan Tzara), The Russian Futurists, and Surrealism. In the case of the Russian Futurists they identified with a movement that was born out of revolution in the same way as they themselves were a resistance to the Vietnam War and Watergate. Her voice oscillates as she circles the fruit bowl. Similarly, the Dadaists, with their hatred of the corrupt and war-decadent European State system sought a 'truth'. It is always different, she says. It is never the same, she sings. As Tristan Tzara had said in his 'Introduction To Dada': It seemed to us that the world THUMP was losing itself in idle babbling, that literature and art had become THUMP THUMP institutions located on the margin of life, that instead of serving man they had become the instruments of THUMP THUMP THUMP an outmoded society. It was not long before M.'s mother hated the preacher. It would seem that he made it his business to take all the women members of the congregation to the zoo. After a while he moved down to the city. In the city he didn't call himself a preacher. And he wasn't rich. But he did work in surveillance. The building's plumbing is fucked. The whole place rattles when someone turns a tap off. The toilets block and the shit flows upwards into the second-storey flats. Last week the agents came to pull the carpets out of the vacant flat next door. I'd been complaining about the stench for weeks. I talked to the workmen and they reckon it was just a sea of shit. It hasn't happened to me yet, but the toilet speaks during the night. It gurgles and belches and threatens to vomit out onto the floor. The real estate people aren't going to do anything about it. A cheapskate block of flats in a bourgeois suburb. Lots of pretension around here. The owners will knock it down and build quarter-million-dollar units on the land. We're just fillers. That's not hard to see. And that twit in number five, the one who's always complaining about the family that lives in number three, is the emperor of a decayed and insignificant empire surrounded by the opulence and hungry eyes of wealthy, successful autonomous states. We are just a fiefdom of a great land-owner, he is merely a stooge. As will be obvious to the reader by now, Language poets do not separate the political from language. And in a sense all language IS political. They'd always *been* there as far as he remembered; he'd done their homework with them, and taken them out, and read to them, and done all the things parents should do. But he couldn't remember their names. Maybe it was just that they were so well behaved, they kept out from underfoot ... but no, he remembered always telling them off for noise. They used to bring their mates around and he had to lock up his laboratory or else the kids would have been in there. No, he just couldn't remember their names. The room had gained another piece of furniture. A couch. He called it the couch of death. It was a soft, undulant couch. As he lay on it, he sank into it and it closed round him. It was made of a sort of soft leather, as if from baby calves. He found it quite disgusting. Despite his repulsion at the animal hide, he'd find himself on it, out of a need for some kind of nurturing comfort. The seasons had changed dramatically since he first arrived. It was now becoming quite hot. Maybe it was just the season within the room; it was hot and damp. He'd shed his clothes; the blindfold had remained. Yet clearly he could see something written on the wall: the wall was stark and white, and on it was written The Crystal Gate is at the outer edge of the crystalline lens in the perceptual diagram. Language poets are an extremely diverse though networked group of practitioners. There are a plethora of small magazines and presses devoted exclusively to their work, and also a communal (if somewhat defensive at times — a kind of 'us' and 'them' attitude towards more traditional and conservative schools of verse) spirit that allows extremely diverse poets to feel they share a common ground. Not until the age of about ten can the child perform the mental operations which enable her to select or draw the doll's view with confidence. Recognising association as often being random, major anthologies include: *The L=A=N=G=U=A=G=E Book*; *The American Tree*; *Language Poetries*, and *From the Other Side of the Century*. There are numerous poets and critics, and in many cases poets are also critics. Some of the most influential poets are ... The list has been pinned to the fridge with a strawberry magnet. Written in a hybrid of English and Indonesian it forms an incidental document of reconciliation that Davies (1986) [The commercial formula of *problem identification, problem ramification, problem solution and aftermath* works for both laundry liquid and drugs] might like to consider. We are not, as numerous inquiries have noted, encouraged to discover why we suffer tension, anxiety or headaches. We're simply informed that tension is bad and its symptoms must be erased. It seems we live in an age when substances can make life meaningful and prosperous ... (p. 81). The Language poet, regardless of differences of aesthetics and theory, looks to the value of the individual word. As the Russian Futurists Velimir Khlebnikov and Alexei Kruchonykh wrote in their 1913 manifesto 'the word as such': [in their poetry] 'the word developed as itself alone'. Beras, ikan, buah nanas, buah pisang, oranj, pi, paw paya ... through the combination of individual words, phrases, sentences, etc., each word is attached to another by a series of associations. The pre-Babelic notion of one universal language comes into play here. In much the same way as Marx's 'commodity fetishism' may be seen as an answer to the corruption of speech by capitalism, itself a necessary step to liberation, the confusion of Babel may be seen as a learning curve. M sat by the creek. It being summer, the mosquitoes were there in strength as usual, and ants crawled through her socks. The waters were unsettled, her skin pricked, and the smell of tea-tree made her giddy. She was to have her hair cut and visit the youth group that afternoon. The loss of mono-articulation does not deny its universal roots/associations. As in the State of Nature people used language to work together as a tool for survival, as opposed to the capitalist use of language for profit and subjugation, so the language poet tries to recapture this original 'purity' of words. In a sense the avant-garde, in general, might be perceived as being a series of rearrangements of anachronistic sensibilities.

The mould is getting worse. Almost all of my clothes have been marked, stained. It's sending me crazy. The agent says to open the windows at night, that we are causing the problem, that it's not structural. But this neighbourhood's full of perverts. There's no way I'm leaving my window open at night. She doesn't mind, she thinks it would be pretty cool if ... But I know that's bullshit really, because when I get home late and she's here on her own, asleep, the windows are all closed. These practitioners, would, of course, reject the notion of the 'romantic' poet who defines self through comparisons to the 'natural' world, looks for a specific (predictable) series of references to subvert the reader, and as a consequence makes the poet's ego central to perceptions of the outer world, regardless of persona (which is often something of a façade in any case). Steve McCaffery says: Reference in language is a strategy of promise and postponement; it's the thing that language never is, never can be, but to which language is always moving. Words, like labour and production, can so often become victims of 'commodity fetishism', assuming 'a fantastic form different from their reality' (Capital 1, Marx) — as we are 'told' *what* we 'know' we become increasingly complacent and victimised by language. Julia Kristeva, in *Revolution in Poetic Language*, examines the liberating nature of the semiotic (includes drives, their dispositions, and their divisions of the body by the ecological and social system surrounding the body, such as objects and pre-Oedipal relations with parents — Hartley), and the contrasting oppresive 'symbolic' (logical and orderly framing of language — Hartley). She says, in 'The Signifying Process': The regulation of the semiotic in the symbolic through the thetic break, which is inherent

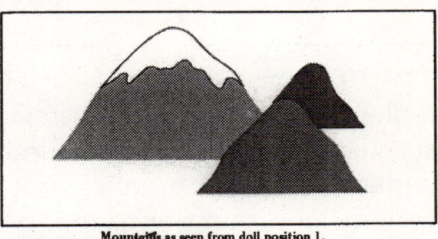
Mountains as seen from doll position 1.
Fruit in Fruit bowl

in the operation of language, is also found on the various levels of society's signifying edifice. In all known archaic societies, this founding break of the symbolic order is represented by murder — the killing of a man, a slave, a prisoner, an animal. Freud reveals this founding break and generalises from it when he emphasises that society is founded on a complicity in a common crime. In the same way, the 'romantic' poet exploits our complicities to reference his/her *self* and divert our attentions from the commonweal. I know it really pisses him off that he's a critic. He'd like to be a poet. He's got no sense of the line. His journals are full of 'poetic' ramblings, but they lack form and method. He packs us up and takes us into the country so he can feel 'inspired'. But nothing ever comes of it. He can't make things, only attach himself to other people's creations. In the course of this we become complacent and dulled to the mode of production that removes surplus labour from its producers, in Marxist parlance. It is worth noting that despite their general obsession with theory and critical practice, the Language poets tend to be anti-Academic (i.e The Academy), and in fact grew out of an antipathy towards the Academic verse of the '50s and '60s, as well as the incorporation of poets such as Creeley, Duncan and Olson into the literary canon of the era. Language poetry, above all else, should challenge the reader. Stimulation comes of disorientation. The Russian Formalists were fond of the word 'ostranenie' which may be roughly

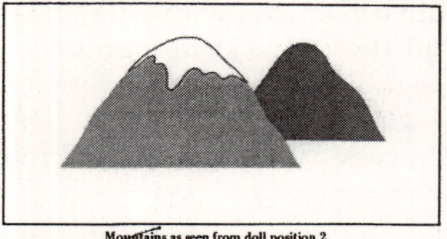

Mountains as seen from doll position 2.
Fruit in Fruit bowl

Mountains as seen from doll position 3.
Fruit in Fruit bowl

translated into 'genuine strangeness'. The lens as we have stated is an egg-shaped microcosm for the greater mundane egg, that encloses the Adam, and Satan's faces, which are, Blake writes, states created into twenty-seven churches. The purpose of the lark's flight is to redeem the twenty-seven heavens and all their hells, the twenty-seven folds of opaqueness which are enlarged into dimension and deformed into the indefinite space of the mundane shell. Blake in fact tells us that the mundane shell finishes where the lark mounts ... It stopped here. But he seemed to remember it from somewhere. He remembered it from a book at home, a book that his wife kept, that she taught from. It was a facsimile edition, that's right, *A Facsimile Edition of* Milton, *a poem by William Blake*. It was from the commentary. He was sure of that. There was more, but he couldn't remember it. But it was written quite clearly

Interviewer asks child to sit at table where model of (mountains) is seen in relationship shown here. Child is asked to select one of eight drawings of mountains as he sees them.

in front of him. He waited for more, but it didn't come. It wasn't the lens they were interested in. Of course, it was the ligaments that attached the lens to the ciliary body. It was the bonding of tissue to metal. This is what came to the constable when she was reading through a book about the eye. She didn't know why she was reading it, she just felt she should. As if in some way it pertained to the case. This was detective work. This case should have been in the hands of detectives — she wasn't sure why it was sitting with them still. It was as if it was just a regular, everyday burglary or whatever. Just being treated as

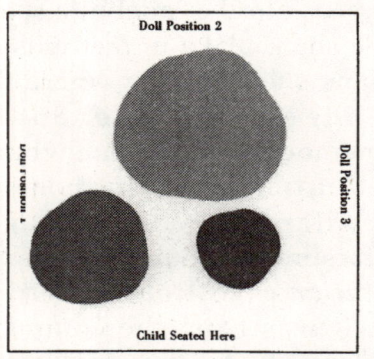

Mountains are arranged on a square board in this relationship, shown from above.
~~fruit in bowl is~~

no big deal. The department wasn't going according to the book. She pretty well did what she wanted. And since the sergeant had been caught out peeping at her, she didn't have many problems from him. She was reading an article about night sights, and was wondering if she'd ever get to use one, maybe in an all-night stakeout or something. She laughed at herself. Atropine: a drug used to cause the eye to dilate. She felt a sudden need to get hold of Atropine. She wished she had a friend in the pharmacy business, or in a hospital or something, but she didn't. That was the way it *should* work, but it didn't for her. Atropine, where would she get Atropine? Now he's thinking of *Blade Runner*. The scene of the visit to the guy who does eyes. I only do eyes, he says. He'd always been fascinated by that scene. As he prepared to spoon the eyeball out of its orbit, to cut the ocular muscles, he considered how many times he'd broken through the sclera in his enthusiasm. Sometimes, just lying there in the middle of the road, a kangaroo would overwhelm him, and just before he removed the eye, he'd become mesmerised, almost hypnotised. Much like the kangaroo itself when being hit by a car at night, dazzled by the headlights. He'd nearly been wiped out a few times himself. A couple of times he'd had cans thrown at him, and people had yelled out, 'Ghoul!' He didn't consider himself a ghoul. He wasn't really a scientific person, she found herself saying to the constable. I mean, he didn't go about things in a terribly methodical way. He operated a little on hunches. He was pretty superstitious actually: if he spilt salt, he'd throw it over his shoulders. Wouldn't put new shoes on the table or open an umbrella in the house. Funny guy. He was fascinated by the stars, he used to read his stars religiously. On a couple of occasions he even had his tarot read, at a fortune teller's. And I think in his laboratory he's got a crystal ball which, he told me, if he can't think of something, he gazes into until it comes to him. You know, pretty interested in those occultish-type things. He didn't practise it or support it, he was just interested. Funny him being a scientist; there was nothing really scientific about him. The constable tapped the table with her spoon. The cappuccino had collapsed, it looked remotely sick. It was out of working hours but she was still in uniform. She shouldn't have been in uniform, she just liked its feel. There are boundaries, but only insofar as they are constructs of a post-Babel Capitalist world (the dismantling of the 'common' language providing a complex market and consequently the ideological starting point for Capitalism). They are there to be passed through, or over, or under, or negotiated in some way. Language Poetry in Australia, at least in terms of publishing, is in its infancy, despite certain poets (such as Kris Hemensley and a circle of poets 'centred' around Melbourne's Collected Works Bookshop), having worked in a similar vein to their American models for many years. In 1991 *Meanjin* ran a special Language Poetry issue which included both American and Australian practitioners of the art. This issue prompted much dialogue among writers and theorists around the country. One of the major questions addressed was whether or not there could in fact be a school of poetry in Australia recognised as Language Poetry. It could be argued that 'Language Poetry' is purely an American phenomenon (albeit one heavily influenced by modern European — particularly French — theory and language experimentation) and that Australians have, like other nations and cultures, hybridised its theories to suit their own social, political and linguistic peculiarities. According to Sigi Curnow in her article 'Language Poetry and the Academy': The term 'Language' in this enterprise ends up exhibiting the kinds of textual dislocations with which writing itself is preoccupied; unstable, localised, 'Language' becomes a sort of shifting signifier, embracing a diverse range of practices and concerns. To conclude, I'll quote Ron Silliman quoting (a favourite Language past-time!) Marx's *The Eighteenth Brumaire of Louis Bonaparte*: The social revolution ... cannot draw its poetry from the past, but only from the future. The first poet to read in this series is Lyn Hejinian, one of the founding members of the Language movement. She is from the Bay area of San Francisco and is currently teaching at Berkeley University. She is an editor of *Poetics Journal*, a small press publisher — Tuumba Press, and has published much poetry, prose and translation. Her works include: *A Thought Is the Bride of What Thinking*, *A Mask of Motion*, *Writing As an Aid to Memory*, *The Guard*, *Individuals* and *My Life*. We will hear her break away from, to quote, 'The Gods of punctuation', however ironically, and explore the notion of narrative, and, if you like, its inflections. Through dislocation of syntax and acute use of metonymic devices she makes what at first seem mere fragments flow with fluidity and resonance. It is as if the words she enjambs *should* sit together, that the reader/audience, should expect it to be structured this way. Lyn Hejinian is very much a poet for whom language 'pre-eminently is a social medium', but one in which the political and literary are kept in perspective. McCaffery: Marx's notion of commodity fetishism ... has already been central to my own considerations of reference in language, in fact, a referentially based language, in general — and to certain 'fetishistic' notions of the relationship of audience and performer. Reference in language is a strategy of promise and postponement; it's the thing that language never is, never can be, but to which language is always moving. (Bromfield) As opposed to the reader making the 'context' through reference — like Ron Silliman — the reader approaches meaning through the poet's gesturing whereas McCaffery states that language is not up to it because of a fetishistic betrayal and must keep moving in order to approach this ideal. Charles Bernstein ('The Objects Meaning'): Learning a language is not learning the names of things outside language, as if it were simply a matter of matching up 'signifiers with signifieds', as if signifieds already existed and we were just learning new names for them ... Rather, we are initiated by language into a (the) world, and we see and understand the world through the terms and meanings that come into play in this acculturation, a coming into culture where culture is the form of a community, of a collectivity. A thought re X: driving back from Augusta I kept turning the headlights off (at night) because of the way the Renault high-beam was structured, on-coming cars would have more than noticed. Plus there was a stretch of road where I hit gravel at high speed and the car slewed. X kept falling asleep. This more than woke her. She later said I shouldn't have driven far; after the aerobatics in the Tiger Moth my (endorphins) etc would be running wild. She said 'I should have thought of that.' Maybe a little like her mis-diagnosis of the fungus on my neck as poison from withdrawal (Venus blood) — later, in London, it was diagnosed as a fungus — possibly candida-based. Funny, reminds me of Pangloss' ailments in Voltaire's *Candide*. Since that rehab business I've learnt not only the power of metaphor but the danger to the author re (an/the) audience (mis)understanding it. Shall fill out those Stat Decs though it breaks my heart to have to do this to prove that my affair with X was no delusion. Stayed at the motel in Augusta. She ate fish. Tempeh in the gourmet shop. Predation and diaphragms? The wrestle of passion that offered her constant release from her own self-destruction re her career. That I was leaving the country was her hope. I know I'm as close to *her* as one could be, but I am starting to cry. Like watching my father leave for the last time as B picks my mother up in his MG or Sprite to dash her off to the advertising agency at Boans, where she works as a copywriter. I remember an advert she wrote, the guy jumping off the jetty (Barracks) in his drip-dry clothes. The first time (the last? — no, maybe when S and I stayed with him whilst working at a market garden in Spearwood — and he told me he's sick of the story). I saw him cry and he cut himself shaving and the tears mixed with the blood and he tried to tell me he hurt. He'll hurt me. That I know. But I cried and am still full of ... Hate? I've said it often, but with the righteous indignation that comes with the belief that 'you' (one, I) are capable of infinite forgiveness. I'm on my tenth life. That's since 1963. That's what I like to say to people these days. What crap. The life. Birth corrupted me, I'm still trying to find some form of 'Heaven and Hell'. The child is breaking in with 'Fee Fi Fo Fum — I smell the blood of an Englishman — be he alive or be he dead — I'll grind his bones to make my bread'; she leaves the room with an 'I don't like you.' There is a book of Noh Drama next to me. 10 Japanese plays. Masks. Masques. Woke to memories and pain, she woke to the relief of escaping a mysterious 'paralysis' that pinned her down after watching the original 1922 *Nosferatu* and *Paris Trout* till 3am — and taking bits of conversation and saying that sounds like others she has known and then taking the comments back. I've just got scratches on my back. And on arms, legs, torso — but my body is separate from my soul. To her, they are the same. I do not see masochism in the same light as her. She's in the room now, behind me, I'm starting to write. Thus I must stop and just put 'triggers' to return to hermetically at a later date. Traps, anvils, the nightjar and gulches, racing 28s and slow dragging on the horse pulling heavily over a crop of oats — the shit and richness. The Shell signs, the Cross Roads. Station of the Cross. Like seeing Veronica Brady the other day and talking about my conversion to Catholicism — she 'regrets' my use of the word 'guilt' re Church, self etc. But believes in vocation and the ISness of God. I went to the crossroads, and headed down Station Road, just as I have any other time I've been here. I woke to Robert Frost, her and Emily Dickinson — 'annoyed' that the text was different from that she was familiar with. There's a sunbeam in the pantry and the fly and the back of the ute is failing. My Uncle and Aunt still leave notes. K's mud bricks have worked into perfect sculptures and I tell her K is being spiteful. An apology ask her in exchange for a video of *Lost in Space*. Ha! *Lost in Space* I used to recapture her childhood memories. K really knows how to hurt someone. I love you, the child (K) says. She: I love you too but not the way you are behaving. It is raining and now I'll fill my head with rain gauges and, in apposition to Descartes' (Discourse 2), In this I shall not perhaps appear to you to be too vain, if you consider that, as this is only one truth of each thing, whoever finds it knows as much about the thing as there is to be known, and that, for example, a child who has been taught arithmetic, having added up according to the rules, can be sure that he has found out, as far as the sum he was examining is concerned, all that the human mind is capable of finding out. For, after all ... The child has just asked me if I got wet riding the motorbike in the rain. I reply my clothes have dried because I am by the fire, she walks over and touches my jumper, satisfied, returns to Major West in some crisis on some unknown planet, the Jupiter 2 'crippled' DENOUEMENT ARISTOTLE: *On the Art of Poetry*: Chapter 18. Further rules for the Tragic Poet: Denouement. The complication consists of the incidents lying outside the plot, and often some of those inside it, and the rest is the No, you're you. But I'm wearing Mum's shoes. They're very nice, but you're still you. She's trying to recall her memories of *Lost in Space*. I 'tell' her to read Ken Bolton. Just friends dropping in-type thing. Cryptic? God, I'm sick of talking about *Lost in Space*. I really liked Dr Smith: Maybe because he was trying to fuck up US Cold War Imperialism using the devices of US materialism. Dr Smith 'So much to live for, but now ... but I won't die alone, they'll pay for it with their lives.' His lot worth talking about. Just watch and laugh privately. PLEASE. The preservation of (even evil) humanity against LOGIC. So what! Children to Robot: 'Where's Dr Smith?' Robot: 'He's on the planet. Dr Smith wants out.' The Mother to Judy: 'I once read that people like that are called 'Injustice Collectors' ... We'll find him' then recollections from Parry? — 'but not without finding Dr Smith ... who is presently wishing her and their (rest of the crew of the Jupiter 2) deaths. She loved Parry's 'Prayer for Earth' her favourite recollection from only ever seeing episodes of *Lost in Space* as a child once. My God, I think I saw 10 reruns. Cult-camp-up, just corporate feeding of the masses (time in which it was made taken into account) despite the parlaying. But that is the basis of US Pop Culture. WAR-holia then then war-holia then then WARHOL Good ol' Don! It wasn't really until *Barbarella* that these two grads gained their campy intellectual status, the humour is more as a relief to the SERIOUS SWISS FAMILY ROBINSON

PLOTLINE. *Lost in Space, Star Trek* etc gained their 80s/90s status by proxy. But then again, the notion of Dr Smith as a foil for US goodness/righteousness ... ? And that he seems to have no sex drive!! KGB a-sexuality? The Force Field of Logic. She has made me feel like a child. Correlation Epithet: poem by Li Po (701–762AD) trans: Arthur Cooper (note commenting also in Penguin trans 1973. reprint '74) Marble Stairs Grievance On Marble Stairs/still grows the white dew/that has all night/soaked her silk slippers./But she lets down/her crystal blind now/And sees through glaze/the moon of autumn. The Endeavour replica sails past the Roundhouse, resting place of Noongar spirits. Ah, Yagan, be a damp squint on its sails! Shallow sums too small for commercial gain — and despite the Spring the damp is rising in this convicted stone, the peeling wallpaper, lime-streaked cave drawing down skirting boards, its tribal icons of all places but the one on which it sits. These ghosts have gone — or are they merely sitting in the stone? Sulking, attempts to rein first census as a screaming cold — a dampness that leaves mildew over the marriage bed. Yeah, maybe Barbie has got 'nylon nits'. That the body is not mine to hold/that I have not known to speak/depression as have/to read/to compare with or a stick insect/wire sculpture/receptacle for an overfull spirit/that drags a luxury shadow/in its wake,/even though the dark corridors/of High Street — where light/cannot penetrate/beyond the screen. Natural Born Killers Come Out of the Hot Zone 'To Those Who Believe Anything Is Possible' Saint Bernard of Clairvaux. Biohazard level 4 — extreme risk. In the *Australian* they called it 'the next Plague' — the colonisation of humanity by viruses — filovirus — A 28 K poem. To see the virus you have to magnify it 28,000 times. Under the electron microscope it appears as slender rods or curlicues. Unbelievably lethal, it also has an eerie beauty. Its genetic code is a single strand of RNA, a molecule related to the most primitive form of life, almost as old as earth itself. An intricate braid of seven proteins, a filovirus is neither alive nor unalive but inhabits a halfworld somewhere in between. Outside the body it lies dormant, a lurking crystal cluster. But once it finds a host cell it invades, furiously commandeering the cell's biological machinery and forcing it to mass-produce virus. New viroids sprout from the cell's surface and drift off in search of new prey. The cell itself becomes clogged with blocks of viral proteins and eventually bursts. For such an enemy there is no vaccine and no cure. It spreads through the blood and body fluids and, maybe, through the air. It is rated by the scientists as Biohazard level 4 — Uniform. She shouldn't have been in uniform, she just liked its feel. Why am I sitting here with his wife? she wondered. Is it actually his wife? The papers say so. But she speaks about him as if she barely knew him. Yeah, strange. Mary had picked up the conversation again. I remember him telling me that his only interest in knowing the future was to prevent it; that nothing that could come would be good. He never validated anything he said; he just left things dangling mid-air. She felt like having something to eat, and turned to find a waiter. The waiter was staring at them both, so she motioned with her hand to come over. But he didn't. She turned back to talk to the policewoman. So, what intrigues me is why this is of interest to you — this isn't on the record, that's pretty obvious. What is it about him? I mean, he's not a particularly interesting person. Well, he *has* disappeared, she replied. Yeah, I suppose he has, but lots of people have, you said so yourself, it's no big deal. Probably had enough of work and doesn't want to pay maintenance or something — cleared out — I don't know. Doesn't really bother me, actually. Yeah, that's a problem too, you know. Because usually when wives or husbands are either overly bothered about their missing spouses — I mean, melodramatic — or they are indifferent, there's a problem there. Something we have to look at. Ah you don't think I ... ? No, no, not at all. The sergeant certainly doesn't. The D's don't: they're not even going to pick the case up. Well, there you go, said Mary. No, it's just that there's something odd about this case, something odd and intriguing, the constable continued. I don't know what it is, but it's as if there's an answer to something I've been searching for, for a long time. As if there's a *one* answer to all these little things that have been niggling away at me. I don't know what it is. I don't know either, said Mary, turning again to the waiter, who this time was whispering to another waiter and taking no notice of them whatsoever. What amazes me, Mary, is how it doesn't even bother you that he's gone. Oh, it's not that it doesn't bother me, Peter, it's just that there's no point worrying. You might think I'm a bit cold-hearted. But to be cold-hearted there has to be something to base it on. It's really not much different from when we were together. It's just that he's not physically there. I suppose so, said Peter. But *I* miss him. I'm only used to speaking to him every few weeks but it's about that time when I'd expect to hear from him. And I haven't, so that bothers me. I'm beginning to think it's not some little whim. Think I'm going to have to do something about it. So I might leave you and the kids to do as you want ... God, they've been off school for a few weeks now, it's time they got back. Yeah, yeah, I know: I was going to see to that. We'll head back up home anyway. So what are you going to do? I don't really know. I suppose try and track down those people that he'd been talking to. But the police haven't had any luck, Mary insisted. I was talking to the constable yesterday and she said there was nothing, they can't track them. His work colleagues had never heard of them. Just a big nothing. Were you really talking to the constable yesterday? Yeah, when I was up in the city for a few hours. There was a message on the answering machine, she asked if she could meet me. I rang her at work, and we met after. That's peculiar, said Peter. Off the record? Yeah, off the record. They seem not to be taking much of an interest in the case anymore, down at the station. This constable, what's her name? I don't know, an Irish name, it was McGinty or McGear or something, I'm not sure. I just call her constable. That's what the sergeant called her. That's what she calls herself. Well, I might try to track her down. How about we all head up tomorrow? I'll come up in your car and I might hire one while I'm up there because my old car's not too good in the city — belches a bit of smoke. Why not? They finished drying the dishes; then suddenly Mary said, Have you ever felt like you're part of a film, a movie, and someone's pre-scripted your movements? Yeah, most days, Peter said — I have to get up and go to work. No, that's not what I mean, Mary said. I mean that you're literally being watched, and everything you're doing is because someone else wants you to do it that way. It even goes right down to your thoughts. You think what someone else would have you think; they've set a certain stereotype for you, and you have to fit into that. Deep down, beyond what I'm thinking, in the physical reality of my being, my is-ness, I actually feel and think very different things, and it's just as if I'm rolling on from frame to frame, because that's the way the story expects me to go. Or directs me, or wants me to go. There's something to this, I just can't see it at the moment. Well, my brother always said, watch out for a hunch, Peter said. He did — don't look at me like that, Mary — he did. Gotta watch out for a hunch. If you get a shiver down your spine, watch it twice. They were a little suspicious of him, hiring the car, when he asked for a jerry-can. Got to do some country driving, he said. Don't worry, I'll bring it back safe. The guy at the desk looked at him under arched brows. Peter handed his driver's licence over and signed the papers. So that'll be ... five days, sir? Yeah, five days, that should do it. All right. Good day, then. Peter walked out to the car park and looked at his hire-car. It was stark white, a saloon of some sort. He jumped in. The road was a long black strip in front of him, disappearing into the clouds, which looked like mountains in the distance. He gunned the stark white car toward the desert. He'd spent the night before looking through his brother's stuff, reading his papers. All he could think of was *the key, the key*. He flicked on the radio, laughing to himself as the Buzzcocks' song *ESP* came on. He was thinking about some of the annotations in Danny's notes. 'If you play with that too much longer you'll go blind.' Or, 'don't read in that light, it's bad for your eyes.' These sorts of corny comments were littered throughout the manuscripts in Danny's scrawly, almost illegible hand. Peter could read it, of course, though his own hand was neater. And yet it came from the same source. See Donne: The Anniversaries, 'Yet how can I consent the world is dead ... ' Intricate manipulations bring in cans of all BRAND names — eh? Parrots stepping backwards from the ripped road's fraying edge towards the bloody hay cut — As I sense an approaching death — a requiem close behind the body's bulk, moving in tidal blood like amber made fluid long after it has frozen life is what we'd like to think that was in memoriam and eternal — I choose to spread my words more quietly. Snake Poison — the gap between nerve and muscle considered. Eight weeks ago while in Narrogin I walked down far from Garfield Street. Spotted a large (though young) wedgetail being harassed by three New Holland honeyeaters. A group of the latter seemed to be resting in a large redgum not far from the railway line. I followed this eagle and its primeness for quite

a distance around town. Occasionally the honeyeaters would break off and the eagle would ride above me. I have no doubt it was as conscious of my presence as I was of its. Eventually it broke away and headed out towards the wandering road — maybe towards the round silo, the mesa ('pink hill'), the Dryandra forest, the truncated valleys. (1) On Pope's Rewriting Donne's Satires For the Sake of Metrical Neatness [Requiem] Polistes — a native paper wasp — social wasp (i) of the class hymenoptera (membraneous — winged)
(ii) chemical
   | glandular secretions
pheromones / __ communication
     signals
      |
     | social structure
     caste system
(iii) 'population balance': - fertile queens
   unused reproductive } neutered female = worker
   organs become venom } male (infertilised) = drones
   producing/stings } for mating
no fear re collective security
*{Queen after leaving winter hibernation hunts, builds etc until the first group of workers hatches}
paper wasps = bell-shaped nest of cells
    |

      suspended from single narrow stem
(iv) attracted to individuals by:- body odours/secretions which imitate a pheromone
     — flower-scented groups
     — deodorants
     — jams/fruits etc
(adults feed on sweet/sugars — young/grubs feed off spiders and insects
* (5) A Dreary Vision
(6) Social Structure — social, creative, the lover who crashes social function
Sprung rhythm   (productive / cyclical) sporadic —
   the paper bell tolls
   when once it silently
   chimed against the summer —
   a single cell — from hibernation — expanding —

   the first tube of the season already coming as the bus squeezed into the city traffic and the smell of tea-trees was replaced by something more offensive. The issue is that the molar and the molecular are distinguished not by size, scale, or dimension but by the nature of the system of reference envisioned. Perhaps, then she ran her tongue over her braces and the city grew around her. It was not the city of her home, the small flat they'd lived in when her father came home drunk and angry in the evenings. Where the old man watched her strangely. Where the young man in number five would throw a ball for her to catch on the front lawn with the 'no parking' signs. Where the muscle-man would stamp up and down along the balcony and stare into the sky, huffing and puffing, hour on hour until his girlfriend who never spoke guided him inside. Things happen in cities, she thought. Her mother sat beside her, which M found annoying. At fourteen she considered herself well and truly old enough to make the journey alone. In fact she hadn't been to the city for months. She found herself thinking about the zoo and blushed, making sure her mother's curiosity was not aroused by pressing her face to the window. The hairdresser's upset her. It seemed so artificial. Once again, the smell was much worse than tea-tree and seemed almost death-like. She thought of Tribulation and that these were the trappings of a world on the brink of disaster. She ached to ruffle the monument that had been built on her head. She had heard the word *coiffure* in the salon, and wondered if that was what she had been given. What would people see as she and her mother made their way to the bus station? A slightly bow-legged girl dressed in grey and a neatly attired lady in her late thirties with an uplifted chin and a walk that was almost a stride. And both with strange hairdos which probably appeared wig-like. Stooks. Purple glass dreaming salt — frosted glass halo of flies the salted flesh preserves the Easterly isolating a dead dry summer — desiccation — you can walk on the salt crests, the solidified waves; the frozen sea — the decay of empire, the land realising itself out of war-waste. Salt: glacial, waiting for the tide to turn and catch you out — here you drown {Salt: like termites eating paths and leaving castings} — rend/cut the salt to let the fresh soil breathe, the water retreat. Islands of redgums, the cool if fragmented cut of gulleys that won't dry out, the requisition mosquito larvae tumbling over themselves the travesty of thirst in water then sustains life {etchings gridwork of outlines, trees} the unguent valleys below the surface, the reefs of algae and columns and shards stalagmites and stalagtites of salt the painful ore of blue sky the caves' roof cliffs of coastline/salt along gulleys sere timed flotsam and jetsam the bone-white wood worked in the flooding, sun-bleached spreads into delta anatomy of spread of fatter trees — skeletal — breaking the glassine surface crystalline ways of — below cool thick water buoyant zoo of petrified wood in all animal forms — extinct species. Salt — the first removal of history — the prelude to regeneration — white lava flows, the sand below like the Niagara of trees I helped plant as a child: sunstroke and freezing mid-summer, the farm — blocks of pasture islands in the white sea of salt, the trenches too deep in the terrain surrounding — for now only in summer or autumn — only endangered birds as companions and possession by location (island hopping) — bushes grey dried from centre to the lush green ovate leaves of the outer sphere, the outback's enemies, gall insects at forks and interstices — harsh/fragile — child's footprint (etched) cast in salt (plaster of Paris) — as distant and exotic — the way you always take some small souvenir to trigger memory — tired and trudging slowly you grasp a piece of purple glass, chunk of quartz etc. and hope the vision lost will return in another place — eater of fences — like oyster posts in a dying river — beer bottle amber trying to purple but fighting the sun with sepia, the tint of age — the dried beds exploding with each each step like — you used to make in your laboratory. Island of finches — extremities — needle sharp. Lightning-struck — blackening and drying from the centre out, silent nests and roosting platforms heaped in forks, breeze swings South and screams — who conducts this symphony? — different moisture levels whole new subterrain continues — like butter corals or in surface — language crested or scalloped funguses blackening with age. Salt disappears as the work of a multitude of insect species. Swollen shadows moving beneath glass, surface of Salt — needle bush — keep out predators — wattle bush the drone of the ultralight as it closes in to become a frenzied buzz. Dialogues and Shifting Signifiers: The potential of the avant-garde in poetry in Australia. No repetition but instigation: putting a poetics into practice. Australia as *neutral* territory for the publication and discussion of contemporary ideas in poetry. When I founded *Poetry Journal* I did so with editorial eclecticism in mind. I would publish so-called 'traditional verse', and seek also to promote experimentation — a sense of the 'new'. Rather than developing this sense of what constitutes the *new* merely from a corpus — or a body of submitted work from which one may draw comparisons and notions of what is out there, what constitutes the norm, and what is consciously playing against this — I found it necessary to supplement this material by soliciting from those whose work I was familiar with. Or maybe I should say *elicit*, because there is a kind of process of surveillance going on here. One asks in the hope of getting a certain type of poem, if not a certain kind of voice. Thus the literary journal becomes a field of data, that, regardless of its eclecticism (such as in the case of *Poetry Journal*), has been scrutinised, systemised and investigated before the public inspection. It was a clear day, and still — early spring, and the forecast was for clear days to come. There was a slight chill in the air but that didn't bother him, he was used to it. He had the feeling that wherever Danny was, it was hot. This wasn't really logical, because eyes needed to be kept cold if they were to be worked on. Very cold. But this was nothing about eyes. Nothing about technology. For some reason he started thinking about randomness. Maybe it had something to do with the landscape, the occasional hillock here, gulley there, just the randomness of it all. It struck him he should say something to his passenger. So you resigned, he said. Yeah, resigned. A lousy job. It stank. Strange having you here in the car. Yeah, well, we're both going in the same direction, it makes sense really, doesn't it? she said. Hey, did anyone ever tell you you look like your brother? All the time, said Peter. That's what I get. You do, you're his spitting image. If I didn't know better ... Well, I'm a bit stronger than him, I'll have you know. Do a bit more physical labour. That's obvious, she said. Don't worry about it. I don't mean to insult your manhood. Ha, it's not that, said Peter. It's just that I want to be acknowledged as different from him in some way. I'd say you *think* a bit different. You'd be surprised, Peter said. Maybe it just comes out slightly differently when we speak. Yeah, but you don't — I mean, laboratories and ... Yeah, there's that, but deep down we're the same, don't you worry — or pretty similar. Fuck, there's heaps of parrots on the road today. You get that a lot around where I live, especially around harvest time. The trucks spilling grain on the road — the parrots sit on the road, eat the grain and get bowled over regularly. Also the warm road in the evenings, they seem to be attracted to it. What sort of birds are they? the constable asked. They're twenty-eights, everyone knows that. Oh, I haven't spent much time in the country. But they're round the city as well. Vingt-huits, that's what they were called — some French guy called them that because that's the sound they make. Vingt-huit, vingt-huit ... Really? There was a flat silence. There was no longer the odd hillock or gulley. There was nothing: it was just flat. The low spinifex. They'd been driving for about four hours now; he'd gone out past the vast salt paddocks, the wasted landscape. They were edging on semi-desert country. Another few hours and they'd be right out in the thick of it. The earth was getting very red. Mary pushed the playback button on the answering machine. It was Danny's voice. What makes the situation of the Australian poetry editor interesting, is that an apparent neutrality — arising out of factors as diverse as the Australian ethos of individuality, of looking after your own backyard and of giving a bloke a fair go, and a general willingness of and for the culture to absorb external influences — allows for editorial eclecticism. The Australian reader, at least now, seems to enjoy diversity. Of course, the problem is, experimentation is still something that's seen as okay if the mythical 'they' (ie.

overseas writers) have done it first, but not something worth sticking your neck out for. With *Poetry Journal* I am internationalist in outlook, seeking to break down these barriers, provide a 'safe' (with all this word's attached ironies) environment in which the Australian poet may digress. Furthermore, Australian English (both *langue* and *parole*) is one which both resists and allows colonisation by other Englishes — especially the American as conveyed through cinema, music, television and other mediums of popular culture. The resistance mainly comes in defining itself against its Anglo-Irish roots. Similarly, it resists immigration — the classic idea of making English as a second language redundant, with new Australians' Australian-ness measured by their *fluency* in Australian English. This tyranny is very much the product of insecurity in self-worth. She did not ask where her mother would go for the two hours or so she'd be 'making clean, wholesome friends.' Nobody recognised her with the haircut, despite there being half-a-dozen teenagers whom she had met before. A short while after her arrival she received a surprise. The preacher made an ostentatious entry, bestowing kisses and spiritual hugs on the girls nearest him. They came face to face, and before she had time to react, he grabbed her about the shoulders, kissed her and whispered, 'God, I love you!' She froze, stricken.

He pulled back sharply and screamed, 'She has the devil in her! I felt the Devil and it forced me back!' She burst into tears and ran out. As she did not know where to look for her mother, she crossed the road and waited. There was a lot of noise coming from inside the hall. He appeared at the door once and looked out for her, though she quickly hid on seeing him, and he failed to notice. Later, her mother blamed her. For what, she was not sure. M was forced to bend over in front of the fire and 'cough the D out into the flames.' In the essay version of this paper, I explore these ideas much further, but for today's purposes I'd just like to point out that while possessing the fatal flaw of linguistic protectionism, Australian English sees itself as growing and flexible. From the point of view of the avant-garde poet, this makes it an exciting English to work with, one full of potential, less laboured by the syntactical niceties and contrariness of Port Royale English. Though I should say, regarding the latter, that playing against pure orthodoxy often produces the most definitive kind of experimentation — that is, an extension of the classical, of the linear, of the canon. Though he'd resist such labels vigorously, one could say this of the Cambridge poet Jeremy Prynne and those who consider themselves within his sphere of influence, if not school, or maybe just fellows of the notional Cambridge Leisure Centre (see Andrew Duncan's essay in the next *Poetry Journal*). It is interesting to note the split between the so called London and Cambridge schools of poetry, the former primarily formalist in nature, the latter considered avant-garde, linguistically experimental, and writing against tradition. The Cambridge School is also heavily influenced by the American Language poets, and is obsessed with theorising process. The London school does not share this obsession, and views history as a procedural linear inheritance rather than a dialectic. The conflict is, at times, bitter and loud. She *thought* it was Danny's voice. It wasn't making much sense. He was saying something like It's my voice, you can hear my voice, but I'm not here. I'm in this machine, I am part of this machine. My voice has melded with the machine. You get my point. You can hear me and sense me but you can't see me. My voice, which is a thing organic, has become part of something inorganic, the tape recorder. Like software in a computer. It's a simple analogy. Don't you get it? Can't you see the point? It's the *key*. Mary considered that she'd never really felt very enlivened by his voice anyway, and it often didn't necessarily mean that he was there. But she got the point. She concentrated — there was something else there. It was as if the background was just too quiet: there was no static, there were none of the normal sounds that came with playing a tape back. It was completely clean. Now that struck her as odd. It was as if the voice was in fact disembodied, as if it wasn't really a living voice. As if it had been manufactured in a totally clinical environment. A perfect synthesis. What's in that case you've got there, eh? Oh, nothing really. Just a change of clothes, the usual. Funny-looking case. Looks like a gun case or something. No, it's not that. Not carrying a gun, I'm not licensed to. I quit the Force, remember? And even if I hadn't quit the Force, I wouldn't be able to carry one outside of hours. I've got one in my boot, Peter said. Brought it up with me when I came up from the country. Wrapped up in a blanket. I dunno why; I always carry one. Don't use it much these days. Last thing I shot was — a ram with a broken neck ... I'm not sure. I don't like guns much. But I had the urge to bring it this time. Something seemed to tell me to. No such definitive split exists in Australian poetry at present. This is not to say there aren't splits of a kind, but they tend to be more personality-based than political, or in the cases where there's the kind of *Quadrant-Overland* dichotomy, it's more an extension of a previous generation's conflicts. Speaking purely in terms of writing poetry in Australia today, particularly as a post-Generation-of-'68 critic, I look out onto a strangely a-political and unmotivated landscape. Landscape is an interesting word here. It has been scaped by humans, and the original environment has been altered beyond recognition. I look for energy and vitality. Pockets exist, of course, as they do in any neutral zone. But these are seen by the mainstream as no more than nuisances getting away from the real task of being a non-adulterated pure practitioner who is entirely devoid of ego if not character. But of course, the human propensity to react to perceived personal slights is as strong as ever, so what we in fact end up with is a cauldron of easily offended sensibilities. She had been forbidden to visit the creek for weeks, but eventually managed to sneak down for an hour or so. She greeted the mosquitoes with joy and welcomed the ants. She ruffled her hair, which had just begun to grow back. Mosquitoes flew in under her fringe and buzzed crazily, in a frenzy to escape. She lifted her hair and thought of the animals in the zoo. Her forehead was red and itching. She thought of 'pure love, the Love of God, the shared Love of God', and all the excuses preachers used to hug and kiss and cajole their congregations. She thought of the believers and their joy. She didn't know where she belonged. Did the Devil enter her as she slept? Should she 'submit' to God, as her mother said? For me, those pockets of politicised 'verse' and experimentation represent a potential for dialogue and investigation of poetic process. Poets who are looking to create new languages, such as Lionel Fogarty, give one hope. And recent experimentalists who are utilising the techniques of the American Language school — such as Alison Georgeson or Peter Kenneally with his Bicycle poems. And feminism, in all its manifestations, has generally been a vitalising force within poetry both conceptually and textually as women writers seek to define a poetics outside the patriarchal modes of expression. Maybe it's just an image of my past I'm carrying, she said. Maybe. They pulled over for something to drink and some fuel, about the same time Mary was finishing her morning class. One of her students had asked jokingly that morning if she'd like a poke. She'd asked him what a poke was. He said, You know what a poke is. That's just your way of dismissing me. She said, If you go much further I'll be dismissing you, that's for sure. He said, That's pretty obvious. She laughed; she didn't really mind it much. He knew it, and that he'd have no chance. The little grot goes out of the room, leaving the door behind him open. She closes it, goes to the window and looks out over the campus. The rugby field is a deep emerald green. Beyond it, the river. On it a few boats are moored, bobbing in time almost sycophantically. The city has a dull grey haze over it. The phone rings but she ignores it; it clicks on to her answering machine. She's got it turned down so can't hear the voice. She considers answering the e-mail, but even that's annoying. She just stares. Would you look at that, said Peter. The constable turned across. Even though she wasn't a constable now, that was what he called her: constable. And she seemed to like it; or if she didn't like it, she said nothing about it. The constable looked across the road. On the other side was a white car. She said, So what, it's a white car. He said, That's *the* white car. What white car? she said. You know, the white car that Mary saw outside the house before Daniel disappeared. How do you know? she said. I just know. It's too intense, that white. It just has to be — it's obvious. The constable leant down to scratch her ankle. Sand fleas or something, she imagined. No, flies, flies biting her, the fuckers. Well, what are we going to do, you reckon? Go across and tap on the window, I suppose. The windows of the car were, appropriately, darkened. The sun, high in the sky and intense, glimmered off them, like radar dishes. They walked to the car and tapped at the window, one on each side. The windows opened electrically. Mary reached for her bag and pulled out a couple of Valiums. She dropped them and continued to stare out the window. She felt like having a joint, but she never smoked them in the Department. She'd been tempted a few times: on a couple of nights, late at night, she'd gone outside and lit up. But that was it — that was her policy. She smoked it at home a fair bit, the kids did as well, and of course Peter was a heavy smoker. What's-his-name, Danny, had never smoked. He didn't need to. He was more out-of-it than any of them put together. So the pockets are there, but they are isolated and often when a group of like-minded practitioners get together, they prove self-defeating through rivalry and a general lack of collective vision. The trick involves instigation and not repetition: to be conscious of an environment but seek to move in a different way through it. Language Poetry is an American phenomenon, not an Australian one. Explore its possibilities, adopt its methodologies, embrace its investigations of language post- the horror of Auschwitz, but translate it into the appropriate context. Appropriate it rather than allow it to appropriate ... In turn, local experimentation will then feed into the avant-garde *processes* going on elsewhere. However, this environment has exciting possibilities re the discussion, and hopefully, ultimately, the practice of experimentation in verse. With *Poetry Journal* I'm trying to create an international forum for dialogue between notions of poetic practice. This may occur in the form of juxtaposing poetries as diverse both contextually and politically as those of Les Murray and Wendy Jenkins, essays as different in execution and intent as Anthony Mellors' brilliant exegesis of Jeremy Prynne and the clear, concise and orderly consideration of the NZ poet Brian Turner by Dennis Haskell. What I haven't found in the Australian poet in generous supply, I have found in the Australian reader. This magazine sells, and judging from correspondence, people read, and read with interest. There is a desire to see very different things inside the one cover. A product of postmodernity is the willingness of the reader to absorb many different viewpoints in a process of reader-synthesis — and synthesising. There is a generality that hones the specific. I've always found Charles Jencks' comment on post-modernity and architecture — that modernism ended with the destruction of the Pruitt-Igoe development in St Louis at 3.32pm on 15 July 1972, rather curious in this light. But that the date and time were retrospective does fit with the idea of surveillance, analysis and deduction. And that is what I find the readers of *Poetry Journal* tend to do. As opposed to many different writers being read as entirely separate individuals, they are read against and with each other. Thus the American John Ashbery will be read against the Australian John Tranter, the English Grace Lake etc. The practitioner of end-rhyme and scannable lines will be read against the Artaud-influenced ideas of Urs Jaeggi, rendered in a bizarre Beckettian German, if such a thing is imaginable; the possibilities are endless. Of course, such a dynamic existing between reader and writer can only stimulate the willingness of Australian poets to experiment. If they KNOW they will be read contextually they, at least in theory, should be willing to step away from their normal practice. And, in a sense, this is really all experimentation is. I used the expression 'shifting signifiers' as suddenly she wondered why she felt so satisfied, not being known for anything. She'd always congratulated herself on her humility, her willingness to accept the back seat. Recently when Departmental promotions had gone round, she'd remained a lecturer. She wanted to be a senior lecturer but she didn't push a barrow. She'd thought: that's my strength, that's what makes me better than them. Things will come my way in good time. That's the way it works. Now suddenly she felt bitter: *is* that the way it works? You have to push yourself. She decided to become ambitious, and wondered what the best course of action would be. Her thoughts were interrupted by a knock at the door. Felicia opened it without waiting for an answer. Mary, have you heard? Have I heard what? said Mary in a blank voice. I got that study grant, a whole semester off next year. Off to England to research the Brontë sisters. Mary felt sick. Good for you, she said in a suitably uplifting voice. Good for you, you deserve it. She felt like spewing. Felicia was painfully thin and dressed in appropriately tight clothes. She looked like a wand. In their chapter '10,000 BC: The Geology of Morals (Who Does Earth Think It is?)' from *A Thousand Plateaus* Gilles Deleuze and Felix Guattari explore, amongst many other notions, that of the signifier and signified in a context of surface, space and territory. A complex argument evolves from the opening lines: The same Professor Challenger who made the earth scream with his pain machine, as described by Arthur Conan Doyle, gave a lecture after mixing several textbooks on geology and biology in a fashion befitting his simian disposition. He explained that the Earth — the Deterritorialised, the Glacial, the giant molecule — is a body without organs. This body without organs is permeated by unformed, unstable matters, by flows in all directions, by free intensities or nomadic singularities, by mad or transitory particles. Once again, I felt suspicious of the use of D & G in this context. Perhaps it could be replaced by a discussion of Volosinov ... meanwhile, the true object of inquiry ought to be precisely the dynamic interrelationship of these two factors: the speech doing the reporting (the 'other person's' speech) and the speech doing the reporting (the 'author's' speech) ... especially when considering that in the few weeks of going out with Mariana's mother, the preacher had held the girl's hand many times.

He had also kissed her and taken her up to the pine trees to feel 'the exhilaration of God', had told her to let the warmth enter her body. He'd not seen the Devil, or at least had not let on that he had. And they'd skipped arm in arm, singing songs that he said he'd learned as a young man ... 'G.I. soap, G.I. gravy, I wish that I had joined the Navy ... ' She was being called. Voices were reaching down from the hall on the hill. She almost hesitated, but found herself responding to the summons. She longed for the Autumn, when there would be more daisies to call her to stay with them a little longer. For the sake of brevity, I'd just like to say *Poetry Journal* hopes to be 'mapped' as a Deterritorialised zone, a body without organs. And I aim for the same in my own writings. If, in the Imperialistic way signifiers tend to work, we say that the pastoral-idyll à la Virgil or Beethoven's 6th Symphony are signifiers to the signified *farm*, I have, say in books like my most recent works of criticism, sought to deterritorialise the said signified, to have rendered it symbolic. In this sense, we might see a poet like Les Murray or the late Philip Hodgins, reterritorialising the *farm*, and, in the process, creating a series of icons. In transcribing this way of seeing into the relationship between the editor and a community of writers (within which the editor is endeavouring to prompt experimentation), the relationship between the signifier and signified becomes such that often quite contrary effects come into play — these being relative to the Imperialism with which the process is instigated. If the editor wishes to instigate change via deterritorialised or symbolic methods then the potential for the new is genuine. If she or he wishes to impose personality on the equation — ie. the signifying 'editor' to the signified *poetry* — then an Imperialism that contradicts the spirit of the avant-garde (read 'freedom') subverts the project to mere propaganda. A kind of commodity fetishisation takes place. *Poetry Journal* is as much the signified as the signifier. It seeks the symbolic in the much territorialised and reterritorialised space of contemporary poetry. As in the realm of addiction. The thumping has ceased. 'SUAMI SAYA SUDAH MENINGGAL DUNIA SAYA PIKIR' THE INDONESIAN WOMAN CRIES. L. WAS ARRESTED FOR DEALING. THE STUDENT DID NOT POST THE REST OF HIS MANUSCRIPT. *BLUE BETE NOIRE* HAS JUST BEEN AWARDED A PRIZE IT WAS NOT ELIGIBLE FOR. On the receipt of their eviction notices: For sequestration of the goods and stuff of the infection, their bedding and apparel and hangings of chambers must be well aired with fire and such perfumes as are requisite within the infected house before they be taken again to use. This to be done by the appointment of an examiner. This morning, the 'top man's' brother came with a small sample of high grade heroin. 'Is Bangalore dying?' The limbs of children litter the streets. I bought a few grams, recorded the event. The old guy is being escorted out by the cops. We are all leaving our places and make our way out on to the lawn. Bam Bam nods and I nod back. I notice the girls holding hands. I fancy they give each other a quick kiss but can't be sure. Something says this is how I'd like to see them but they're not in fact there and never were. I discover that their flat has been vacant from the day we moved in. That there are other vacant flats. The Indonesian couple stand close by. He's cradling a baby. I'd forgotten they were still there. Something seems to suggest they should have left long ago. The student is absent — but yes, he's been driven out. The junkie and his missus look almost serene. Someone says the old man has a sickness. That it's he who's been filling our heads with false dreams, with delusions. The cops are telling us to go back inside. My wife says I want you to read something. You should be interested, she says. Liking Artaud so much. I read Artaud's *Bad Dreamer*. All those who make violent or illicit love dream too much. My dreams are mostly liquid. He tells me he can taste the cum of every man I've had that day. He laps it up. Each day we wait for the sores to come but they don't. But you can be sure the germs are in there, he says and drinks deep. Sometimes blood and cum are mixed because I've been fucked so hard. I am immersed in sorts of nauseous waters where blood-red films toss and turn. He says it must be spreading fast. He hates the bastards more than me. We praise all viruses. This room we're in is like the crypt beneath a temple. The temple changes, gaining more columns, becoming more elaborate with time. But the crypt remains the same. The smell of dead irises is always out there, just beyond the stink of the flesh. I never rise up to the level of certain impressions, whether in my dreams or in real life. The flowers in our back garden are rampant. The blooms are bold. He cuts me and drinks straight from the vein. Last week they photographed us for a lifestyle magazine. *They only wear black and drink a little of each other's blood every day.* I am never settled in the continuity of my life. The old man who lets us use his place comes in and slips into bed besides us. He's too drunk and insane with guilt to detect the disease. He rubs my mate with a thick rough paw and growls. My mate gurgles and thrusts his transparent body towards the oaf. Eat, he says. The purple lips ride the long thin penis, his testicles pull up into his body and the sperm dies with the heat. We considered sticking him and drinking until we vomited it back up over the eviscerated corpse but thought it best to let him die inside his mind first. He'll sober up when he starts dribbling green from the end of his turdish prick. I say to him the temple has moved through different states. From simple Cella through Prostyle and Amphiprostyle through to the multi-columned Peripteros. Each of your erections supports a roof. A low, squat roof that doesn't amount to much. It babbles below the clouds. It is an earth-bound construction. I am never settled in the continuity of my life. He forced a candle into me the other night and I couldn't stop laughing. The hysteria's being forced out of me, I yelled and gnashed at his face. My mate licked his arse greedily. It leaks a light brown liquid, he murmured. It falls onto my leg and steams. It bruises me and stains the black sheet white. He's almost deaf and can't hear his own farts. I tell him the names for the different parts of his house: ambulatory, pronaos, naos, opisthodomus. He hits me in the side of the head. Yes, yes, the temple I say. Peripatoi, I whisper, I am your slave. Sure are, you little bitch, he says, photographing the bruises. He tells us he was once a professional photographer. A special kind of photographer. The camera is another of his cruel theatres. The place stinks of photographic chemicals. The smell should obliterate the smell of sex but I can smell through them. I size their cunts, he laughs and fumbles with his Nikon. We've never seen the photos he talks so much about. He keeps them locked up. My mate tells me that if we could rise up to the level of certain impressions we'd be able to see those photographs. But we see them as they are made and they are developed in our dreams. They are set in the gelatine that is our flesh. They are fixed with our blood. I squirm under him. Flighty little bitch! Our father taught us to fly and our mother willed us high above the clouds. If you fly high enough you won't be able to see the ground, they said. The top of the clouds were vermilion with blood. We saw the overhead light shining through the chests of our fathers. Their skeletons glowed. My dreams offered no escape, no refuge or guide. When the oaf is violent with us we see deeply. I read the cards for our friends who like to hear the details of our journeys. They shake with joy if a dark reading falls their way. They loathe respite. *The absence of emotion is worn like make-up. Robert Smith of the goth-rock band The Cure is something of an anti-hero. They weep for him.* There is no music in our life and we told the lifestylers only the trendy are interested in music. There are voices and animal utterances but no music in these dreams. Truly the rankness of severed limbs. I read of the Ebola virus in central Africa. The haemorrhaging so complete. We told him about it when he rammed his prick into my mate's arse. You're a thin little bastard, aren't you? Get some steak into you. Sell some fucking pills or something and get some food. Those fucking little tight-arsed whores in number 2 are always out of it. Do a deal with them. Make friends, travel. It makes you burst inside. Shut up bitch, I'm on the edge. Besides, I am too resigned about my thought to be interested in anything that goes on in it. It's not surprising his blood turned to water. It's almost entirely water and when you're the living dead your colour's drained out of you. We don't need to paint our faces. It's surprising how many healthy men in their prime, well-dressed with fat wallets, like to fuck a young girl who's so white you can see through her. Whose underwear is caked with the discharges of other men. Who hasn't bathed for weeks. Whose features are so fine she might still be a child. You tell them you're seventeen and they get you to pretend you're fourteen. You look nothing like their daughters. Your emotions haven't quite developed, they tell you, in case you might suspect you're in some way different from them. I ask for one thing only: to be locked away in my thought for good. You don't have periods and that's good, the oaf says one evening. There's a sore erupting on his lower lip. My mate smiles. *His* skin is perfect. She's never had one, he replies. Her entire body bleeds. She is caught in the disintegration of her cycle. He tells me that they can freeze you alive now. Like embryos. And then when things are better or they've got a cure for the disease you're being destroyed by they defrost you and it's all okay. The living dead. You see, it's even a scientifically viable option. You don't have to drink blood or let them fill you with their guilt. It costs a lot, he says. It does, I know. More than you make from your business men and I from my pills. More than all of us make put together. It's cheaper to just have your brain frozen and then they'll unfreeze it and force it into somebody else's body. Then their liquid will run through your thoughts, colour your dreams. Like tinting old films. I am never settled in the continuity of my life but travel through it like a fantastic voyage, propelled by the tides of the blood, driven by the surges of the heart. The terrain of the body is circuitous though age dictates that you'll never cross the same territory twice. The undead change the most. They cannot remain the same or their apertures will shut down and squeeze the penetrating implement until it was a severed limb. Six million died of syphilis in Europe during the Middle Ages. At least. The world was surrounded by a moat of infection that overflowed into the centre. It was like the round table and things weren't made better until the sword was pulled from the stone. The guy next door is yelling something about Cicciolina. Fucking Cicciolina! And as to the physical appearance of my dreams, I told you, a liquid. **Afterword**: *Shutting up of the House*: If any person shall have visited any man known to be infected of the plague, or entered willingly into any known infected house, being not allowed, the house wherein he inhabiteth shall be shut up for certain days by the examiner's direction.